"When a top mediation scholar and innovator turns his hand to fiction, the result is by turns trenchant, hilarious, and uplifting. Joe Folger's anti-hero makes his way into the world of mediation practice, encountering characters who treat mediation as a mere tool for institutional convenience; but under the guidance of a wise mentor he realizes that it is really a precious means of helping people find their deepest humanity in facing their toughest challenges. Read, enjoy, and grow with Folger's wit and wisdom."

Baruch Bush, Brooklyn NY

"Entertaining and engaging! Left me reflecting on my own conflicts and the challenges of maintaining compassion in the face of differences."

Christian Hartwig, Magdeburg Germany

MEMOIR OF A MISFIT MEDIATOR

A NOVEL

JOSEPH P. FOLGER

atmosphere press

To Don, the best life partner anyone could have.

CHAPTER ONE

Conference Keynote

I listened intently when Adam Maurie said he wanted to talk about a professional experience he had several years ago. "Kent, I believe that this incident might help you with your mediation practice," he said.

A good reason to listen, I thought. Adam's stories were sometimes overly embellished but always interesting and, sometimes, quite mesmerizing. In some ways he is the classic eccentric professor. Plenty of idiosyncrasies. He only drives huge junkers from the sixties or seventies like Bonnevilles or Elektras, which are sometimes held together in the interior with plenty of duct tape. This is because he feels these cars are safer than anything made today in 2010. "Built like tanks," he'd say unapologetically every time I would ride with him in one of these rattling vehicles. The suspension systems always made them seem to float like a small boat. Adam is in his early sixties and is at once very modern and yet deeply tied to anachronisms like radio talk programs, having a day of rest on Sunday, and using handkerchiefs. He only wears blue oxford shirts, no tie, but usually a cardigan sweater that has suitable references to Mr. Rogers. He was a fallen-away Catholic but clearly leads his life and professional work with a consciousness of values and spiritual influences.

The problem is that I don't always fully get the point of his

3

anecdotes—or at least not right away. Sometimes they take a while to sink in, and Adam can tell when I struggle. Adam would look at me and say with a little more formality, "Mr. Foxe, this is something to think over for a few days." I was always impressed by how Adam could encourage me to think more deeply without insulting my intelligence.

After getting a paper cup with lukewarm water and an earl gray tea bag, Adam began his narrative.

"A year after the book on mediation was published, I started getting invitations to speak at local and national conferences. The book created enough of a buzz that it attracted considerable interest and besides, I knew that good speakers were not easy to find. So, it wasn't all about the ideas. Debate experience in college and lecturing in courses gave me a head start as a speaker. Debate gave me the needed focus on substance and organization. Lecturing year after year in universities taught me that if you don't hold an audience's attention there isn't much point in being there. Talking to oneself is a great pastime for the commute to and from work and for an after-dinner walk. But it's deadly in the classroom. Attention is lost within minutes if you haven't thought about the ploy you will use to sustain your grip on the audience."

I interrupted him and said, "So it is like Stephen Sondheim's recommendation for aspiring strippers in his song from *Gypsy*, You Gotta Get a Gimmick."

"I am not sure that exactly covers it but close enough, Kent. In any event, I agreed to speak at the U.S. Association of Family Mediators' conference after a welcoming call from the incoming president of the organization. She said all the right things on the phone: the importance of new ideas for the field, the receptiveness of the group who will attend the event, the opportunity to get the word out further about the book and increase sales. She labeled her spiel as "a win for us and win for you" offer. Although I have come to detest that win-win gibberish, her proposal was nice enough. She offered a

4

generous stipend with all expenses covered to Chicago. She even said the organization would arrange the date of the conference to accommodate my schedule. A very welcoming gesture.

"As I thought about the pros and cons of the offer while on the phone, I asked how many people were likely to attend. She said, 'Probably around three hundred.'" But she couldn't be sure because attendance had fluctuated at this annual event in recent years. She did say that I would be a good draw and she would do everything she could ahead of time to get the word out. I accepted her offer. I knew the trip to Chicago from here in Philadelphia was short so I probably could limit the total time investment to two days. More than two days away wears me out. She emphasized how appreciative the membership of the organization was going to be to me for delivering the keynote at the conference.

"Little did she know.

"About one month before the event, I got a short email from her. She said several members of the board of the organization wanted to have a conference call with me. We arranged a time a week later. I asked what the call was about, and she said that they preferred to talk with me about it as a group on the phone. I immediately knew that something suspicious was up.

"The call started well enough. A spokesman for the organization thanked me for agreeing to speak and said that there was a lot of interest in the keynote address I had agreed to give at their event. Enrollment was full in the smaller break-out session I also agreed to do at the conference. As he spoke, I thought this is good news, but I sensed that the curtain was about to fall. Why did I sense this? They knew I did not need any more encouragement. I had already bought my flight tickets to Chicago through their staff, so my commitment was clear. I began thinking about the time I could spend in the Art Institute if the plug was being pulled from the gig. I also thought about how I gave sketch pads as Christmas presents to my nieces and nephews when they were preschoolers and then took them to the Chicago Art Institute to let them sketch the Picassos. Clearly my mind wanted to wander to positive memories—a reflex response to avoid the pending news."

As Adam took another sip of tea, I took advantage of the pause and asked, "Was it something to do with the ideas in the book that gave you the hunch that the curtain was about to fall?"

"Of course, my friend. Although I did wonder, as I have since I was in college, whether something bubbled up to a devout board member about my outspoken criticism of the Catholic Church. But I knew from attending prior conferences that the membership of this group is quite liberal. The proof? As my wife once noted when she attended an earlier event with me, women can be seen openly nursing their babies in the hallways of the hotel at this conference. So political resistance from the right seemed unlikely.

"Another board member—someone whose name I knew but had never met—started to speak on the phone. His voice was low and somewhat hesitant. He said that the president of the association had received a call from a well-known member of the organization. He saw the advance program description and was deeply angered by the decision to ask me to deliver the keynote address at this year's conference.

"As he spoke, I could feel the flash of emotions go through me. Even when you anticipate something like this, it still hits as a punch in the stomach, like the time I was mugged in broad daylight in Honolulu. You can see it coming but still can't believe it is actually happening as it unfolds."

I interrupted to ask Adam, "Did you immediately think the board was wavering on the invitation to speak because of the call? This was apparently only one member's protest."

Adam nodded. "Yes. Clearly, they were not dismissing this as an outlying protest. They felt they somehow had to acknowledge it, work with, or accommodate it. Otherwise, why would they make the phone call to me? And why was it that several board members and not the president alone made the call to tell me this news? It seemed obvious to me that the solitary, if it was solitary, protest had hit an organizational nerve. The disgruntled member who complained about my speaking at the conference was not being cast as a total wacko, just a partial one. And the board members were probably worried that there were others within the membership who agreed with him.

"When I asked what the basis of the member's protest was, I got a somewhat vague answer from the board member: 'He is concerned that the organization is moving in the wrong direction and is letting weird ideas about mediation practice take over,' he said. 'What concerns us is that this person was over the top with anger and resentment when he called. It was not just a substantive point he was making, it felt personalized and threatening. We were wondering whether there is a back story we don't know about here. What is your relationship with him?'"

"Slightly annoyed by the insinuation that I was in some kind of battle with this guy, I said I might be able to answer the questions if they gave me the caller's name. The board member apologized and quickly said it was Thomas Binder. He also said that Mr. Binder was fine with me knowing his name. I assured those on the call that I had heard Binder's name before but never met him and have no idea where he is coming from.

"The board member emphasized that they were concerned about the degree of threat Binder conveyed in his call to the president. They were obviously concerned about violence. But they were not saying he would be uninvited to the conference or defrocked from the organization's membership. I thought about asking for this but instead I waited to see where the conversation would head next.

"I was asked a series of questions that the board members had obviously planned before the call:

> "Did I want to back out of the commitment? I said no."
> "Did I want to meet with Binder before the conference "to make peace" since he was nearby? (I was in Philadelphia, and he was in NYC) I declined."
> "Did I want a panel of professionals to respond to what I would say in the talk? I declined again."
> "Did I want hotel security at the talk and at the conference for as long as I stayed? I thought about this for five seconds on the phone then accepted the offer. I am sure I would have drawn the line at a bulletproof vest had it been offered."

"Notice, Kent, that none of these questions went in the direction of 'Do you want us to tell Binder he cannot attend the conference?' So, he had the organization's support at some level. The board was fine with taking Binder's registration fee for the conference. And perhaps putting me at risk.

"So here I was, a peace-loving east coast professor planning to speak at a peace-loving family mediation conference in Chicago. But I needed to have a bodyguard next to me through the whole event. As my son would say, there is something wrong with this picture."

Adam smiled and added: "After the call I realized that my invitation to speak was like asking a vegan to speak at a meat-packing conference. My views about mediation were like steak on a vegetarian's dinner plate. But I also knew, Kent, that addressing the Thomas Binder response is at the heart of the issues currently surrounding mediation practice. Possibly your practice as well, Kent."

I laughed a little at his vegan comment and then got caught up in the last statement Adam made about my practice. I then commented, "Oddly enough, the Thomas Binder response to your views on mediation may have been more predictable than it seems at first glance? His views may be more widespread. Do you think that is the case?"

Without hesitation, Adam replied, "Exactly. After the call with the board, I felt I had been naive when I accepted the friendly invitation to speak at this group's conference. But from that point on, I was much more ready to deal with similar situations that followed. My naiveté had been cured, at the cost of increasing my cynicism. Now I frequently fault myself for following that precious advice: No matter how cynical you become, it's never enough to keep up. Cynicism warps your perspective on life but protects your soul. It's a bulletproof vest for the psyche."

Having been drawn into Adam's story thus far, I chuckled and then asked, "So how did this turn out? What happened at the conference with your speech? Did you feel threatened in any way while you were there?"

"Well, I really worked hard on the speech. I figured that Binder and his views were only the tip of the membership iceberg. There were probably many people who would attend this event who would feel as he did but did not call with a hysterical protest ahead of time. So I knew that it would be a serious mistake to just straightforwardly lay out the ideas in the book during my talk. Doing that would create greater resistance. I needed to come in the back door—violate the audience's expectations positively, as they say in persuasion theory. So three quarters of my speech wasn't about mediation at all. It was about change in general. Here's the kicker. I wanted to use humor. In talking about the difficulties of embracing change in our lives, I tried to be as funny and amusing as I could possibly be. Not my typical style, especially for such a formal event. This was a sure way to violate expectations. People were expecting me to hit them over the head and instead I wanted to send their heads back in laughter. I wanted to be Wanda Sykes. She makes you laugh so hard at radical ideas you don't realize you are accepting them at some level.

"I just wasn't sure I could pull it off. Even while I was speaking at the conference, I had some doubt that it would work. As I stood in front of three hundred people, I kept thinking of Dan Quayle's immortal blooper: If we don't succeed, we run the risk of failure."

"So, give me an example," I said. "What was the humor like? In the end did you indeed pull it off, Adam?"

"Okay. Here's an example. I encouraged everyone in the room to question the status quo in small ways because it encourages a mindset for change. It wakes people up and gets them out of mindless repetitive routines. I then told them about the time I was on an airplane, sitting towards the back of a crowded flight. The stewardess was going through the motions as the plane taxied on the tarmac. She robotically pointed to the exits, demonstrated the seat belts and showed how the oxygen bags worked in a way that clearly revealed she had done this routine hundreds of times before. When she finished the spiel, I got up from my seat towards the back of the plane and with a loud voice pleaded: Could you please explain the part about the seatbelt again?

"People on the plane laughed hysterically. But the stewardess needed five seconds to get it. People don't come out of trances easily. She then smiled slightly and continued with her routine. When I told this story during the speech, people loved the humor. It got a great response."

"Brilliant," I said. "You were pointing to the trances we put ourselves in, trances that prevent us from changing or seeing the need for change. It was a great way to make the point."

Adam clarified, "That was part of it. But it was more about being comfortable challenging those who are in the trances. Challenging those who think change is never needed."

I nodded and said, "I can see that. In a way you were getting them in the right mindset for hearing about the challenging ideas in your book. But what happened with Binder at the keynote?"

Adam looked into the cardboard teacup, swirled what was left a few times then started to answer my question. "Well, I need to tell you what the physical setting was like. The speech was set in one of those huge hotel ballrooms, done mostly in red hues with lots of gaudy chandeliers hanging everywhere. The kind of room, I thought as I first walked in, that hosted huge weddings with deejays playing deafeningly loud music, and bridesmaids who, when sufficiently inebriated, take off their shoes to dance unembarrassingly with each other to We Are Fam-il-y.

"But the room was now set for something more sober. There were over three hundred people sitting in those round-backed uncomfortable chairs in tight rows. No tables. The room was divided in half with an open aisle down the middle. A standing microphone was set up in this middle aisle of the over-decorated yet sterile room. It was about twenty yards from the podium which was raised about four feet above the audience. The microphone was set up so that people could walk up to it after the speech to ask questions. This was a somewhat unusual setup because, in most cases, a microphone is just passed around the room for questions. It turns out this setup suited Binder well and I wondered later whether this awkward arrangement was done on purpose by a supporter of his on the conference organizing team.

"Binder came up to this microphone soon after I started speaking. Although I never saw him before I knew as I looked down from the podium that it was him. The scowl on his face was convincing enough. Coming up to the mic at the start of the speech was clearly strategic. This way, not only could he be the first to ask a question, but he could also stare me down through most of the talk, hoping his intimidating presence would throw me off. When he walked to the mic in the middle of the room, I glanced over at the president who had

11

introduced me and who was sitting to my left. She looked a little startled but clearly was not going to say or do anything to stop him from taking his center-aisle perch. The placement of the mic allowed him to begin threatening me in full view of those who were concerned about his stability."

"That must have unnerved you," I noted.

"Not really. I was too focused on making the humor work. When you are in battle you don't think about the danger you are in. If I was successful enough his attempt to verbally attack would seem inappropriate. I did wonder for a second whether he had a weapon with him—there were no metal detectors in the hotel or conference room. But I took solace, perhaps falsely, in thinking 'who wants to hurt a likeable comedian?' If he had come to ambush me, at least the people in the room would have been sympathetic to me. They would have thought it rude and undeserved. At least I hoped so."

"But what did you eventually say about the book? Did people learn about the ideas from the speech? After all, that is why you were asked to be there in the first place," I said.

"I did not cover much about the ideas. That was the downside of taking this rhetorical approach to the speech. I lost an opportunity to clarify in depth what was being said in the book. In essence I only made two key points. That mediation is more about who you are than how you intervene. And examining your underlying beliefs about people—the parties in conflict who are in mediation—is an important place to start."

"And what did Binder ask you when he got his chance after the speech?" I inquired.

"Well, as expected, he didn't ask me anything. That would have been a move of weakness. He was all about grabbing power. He went on a rant about not asking mediation to be too many things to too many people and that my book contributed nothing to clarifying what good practice is. I think he used the phrase "new age nonsense" at some point to hit below the belt. I was only half conscious—half there—by that point and could feel the sweat down the back of my shirt. I was just relieved that the speech had gone over as intended and that he had only pulled notes out of his pocket and nothing else. When he finished, I simply thanked him for his remarks and said that people can judge for themselves whether the book is helpful in clarifying the nature and purpose of mediation."

I needed to inquire further regarding the point Adam offered about mediators needing to know who they are. I asked, "Good practice ultimately has to be based in skills, doesn't it?"

"Only in a secondary sense. The core of mediation practice is someplace else. You can't do the skills well or know what skills to use if you don't know who you are in the room and what you believe about the people who are at the mediation table."

He waited a few seconds then added reflectively: "It's about having a human soul that is comfortable being with difficult, emotional conflict."

Adam then took his tea bag out of paper cup with the cardboard handle, got up and threw the dripping tea bag in the wastepaper basket next to his office chair. He then added: "That is why Thomas Binder and others would just as soon have me dead—literally or metaphorically. The critique offered in the book was only superficially about the nitty gritty of practice. It was about who the Thomas Binders of the world are and why this shapes how they act in—and out—of mediation rooms. This is why he was threatening me. He was actually the one responding to a threat. A threat he felt when he read the book. He would die or I would die depending on who won the argument."

While standing by his desk, Adam looked at me with his intense blue eyes and asked: "Does this conference incident seem helpful to you?"

The question hung in the room like the final chord of a Beethoven sonata.

Before I could answer, Adam continued, "I am headed toward Center City past the Philadelphia Mediation Center if you need a ride."

I quickly said yes and we gathered our things and headed out of the room. I was glad we were leaving right then and could lighten the conversation because I had no idea how to answer his question. It would take some time for me to think through his provocative ideas.

His '67 Oldsmobile grudgingly turned over and we were thankfully on the road this time, in no time.

CHAPTER TWO

Mothers and Daughters

It wasn't until I arrived at the Philadelphia Mediation Center that I started thinking about the conversation with Adam. He didn't say much about the practicalities of mediation but what he did say about this kind of work was deep and insightful as usual. And I am sure his words—and the whole story he told me about Binder and the conference—were aimed at me in some important way. As he said, he had an intuitive sense of the importance of audience. I was his audience for the story he told. It is also clear that Adam has put a lot at stake personally and professionally by publishing his views about the core of mediation. His perspective sounds like a huge shift that challenges mediators' core values and shakes up the mediation field. Adam's ideas are never boring or unprovocative. Once you have challenged the Catholic Church publicly, as he has, everything else is small potatoes.

It was only six months ago that I took mediation training from Adam and one of his colleagues. It was a small group of about ten people in the training, so he got to know me and the others in the group very well. He also saw our natural instincts as mediators—our strengths and our weaknesses. Those of us who had been trained elsewhere prior to his training, like me, struggled more with the approach he was teaching. Those who had no training whatsoever seemed to do better. Unlearni is harder than learning. But I did resonate with his ideas about both the philosophy and practice of mediation. The approach seemed logical and clearly tied to what makes mediation different than other conflict intervention methods.

I remember that he did use the phrase "What do you believe about people in conflict?" several times during the mediation training but I don't recall his elaborating on it. Either that or I may have missed it. Clearly Adam sees this question as fundamental to all mediators' professional development. Our views about people shape what we think good practice is. I think that this core belief was tied somehow to Binder's threatening reaction to Adam's work. There's no doubt that Adam touches a vital nerve in the profession.

When I entered the Mediation Center, I went up to Anita, the clerk at the front desk of the mediation program, to find out whether I was still scheduled for a mediation that afternoon. People often cancel, don't show up at the last minute, or take care of their issues outside the court on their own. Anita said there was a mediation on the schedule and that my co-mediator, Karen Abrams, was unavailable today. The center tried to use two mediators for each case. I tended to mediate with Karen in most cases, but she apparently was not going to be available today. I asked Anita if there was an advance summary of the issues or topics for today's mediation. She said no, the court had not yet given her an intake sheet. All she knew was that the case was referred from the court and that it involved teens. It was scheduled to start at three p.m.

I had mediated six cases since my training with Adam. In only one of these cases, a contract dispute, did I mediate alone. Having a co-mediator helps when fatigue sets in but it does take some planned coordination and intuitive connection between the two mediators. Without it, the session gets quite chaotic, and the parties get confused. They feel they are being pulled in different conversational directions. I noticed that co-mediation with my usual partner, Karen, became more difficult after I took Adam's training. I wasn't quite sure why exactly, but it was clearly more awkward to team with her. Many of the interventions she did were inconsistent with the principles taught in Adam's training. We talked about the differences somewhat but did not go into detail. For the most part, I just let her take the lead. I held my instincts back. That seemed only fair. I felt she would have needed to take the training I took to really understand what was different and why my responses would be at odds with hers. I mentioned this once, but she seemed uninterested in taking another training. A few times she asked me why I was so quiet during a session we did together. I usually hedged and said that she was really "on", and I didn't want to disturb the flow. It would have been too challenging to her to say more.

All my prior cases involved only adults, so I was a little apprehensive as well about working with teens, although I assumed there would be adults with them in the session. The dynamic would surely be different, especially if the teens' relationships with the adults were strained. I cautioned myself that I am not a family counselor. Nor should counseling be the goal of the mediation.

The Mediation Center is on the second floor of an old social services office building about two blocks from the Philadelphia family courthouse. Anita's large oak desk is in the small reception area which also has several chairs and a few mission-style end tables with the usual variety of worn and outdated magazines on them. Behind the reception area are five mediation rooms of various sizes. On the floor outside each room is a noise absorption contraption that looks like some kind of insect or rodent catcher. It was supposed to lessen the chance that people outside the room could hear the conversations inside. As far as I could tell, these contraptions did not work. I often heard conversations from a mediation in an adjoining room, especially when things got heated. During my last mediation, I heard a man yell "You bitch" several times as he slammed the door and left the mediation room next door. I could not tell whether he was yelling at the mediator or the person with whom he was in conflict. I never complained about these little machines because they were Anita's idea and she had received substantial praise for finding them. In organizations and marriages, some criticisms are better left unsaid, at least that is what I often told myself.

I asked Anita which room she reserved for my mediation. She said the mid-size room with the round table. She assumed that there would be adults with the teens so having the larger room probably made the most sense. I liked this room because it had several table lamps. I could keep the harsh over-head lights off which made the space softer, more mellow. The round table was conducive to open conversation. The mediator was not sitting at the head of a table because there was no head. Many people assume the mediator is some sort of judge as they enter the mediation room, so the circular setting is helpful in dispelling a power-based perception of the mediator's role. On the other hand, a round table implies that a cooperative conversation is going to happen. But in most of the cases I mediated, the parties were facing off and, I felt, they would have been more comfortable sitting across from each other with considerable space between them. The roundness of the table seemed forced on the parties, like sitting two relatives apart at a family dinner table. Everyone knows it will not make a difference by the time dessert is served.

It is sometimes unclear which cases the court will take off its dockets and decide to refer to mediation. From my limited experience, I could not see a clear set of criteria supporting these referral decisions. Some cases seemed better handled in court. But if the parties were underage in this instance, it would make sense to avoid the courts if the issues were not easily prosecutable. There were no youth programs annexed to the court other than for drug abuse. I wondered whether I needed special training to work with youth, whether there were developmental issues involved in a way that I was unprepared to address. Nothing about working with youth was raised in either of the five-day trainings I attended.

I decided to write down the two key questions Adam raised with me so I would have them in front of me—a way to keep them in mind throughout the mediation session: Who am I when I am mediating? What do I believe about these people? I sensed these were important questions, although they did seem heavily philosophical and far from practical. I hadn't thought about heady questions like these since I was in an undergraduate philosophy class at Northwestern University years ago. My first mediation training was mostly about the phases and techniques of the process so these much broader and probing questions were interesting and challenging. I appreciated the way Adam focused on the core of practice, not the superficial methods.

The questions did get me thinking about why I wanted to mediate in the first place. I have quickly learned that mediation does not offer a lucrative career unless you are mediating something like big money contract disputes in the entertainment industry in L.A. My motives were only partially clear to me. These motives included giving back to the community, honing my skills so I could deal better with my own conflicts and, as one seasoned mediator said to me, "help to relieve the pain people are in." I must admit there was also a voyeuristic motive as well. Stepping into conflicts in other people's lives was often intensely fascinating. It made me see what people say and do to each other over tough—or sometimes trivial—issues. And it made me think about my own responses to conflict when tough or trivial issues arose in my own life.

Some people I knew personally went to mediation for a business dispute and hated the experience. They vowed they never would go back or recommend the process to anyone else. When asked why they said they were disappointed with the process because they didn't get to talk about what was important to them. The mediator chose what could be discussed. So I knew there were pitfalls in this process and maybe Adam's questions would help me to avoid some of the traps. I would hate to be a mediator who turned people away from mediation for good.

Anita came to the doorway of the room I was in and said that the parties were now at the reception area. I asked her who was there. She said, "Two teen girls and two older women, their mothers. One of the mothers came to talk with me. She said that she and her family have had only bad experiences with the courts. She mentioned that she was unfairly treated by a biased judge in a custody fight. She also wanted to know whether you were African American. I told her you were not, but you were a good mediator who was always fair to everyone. She still seemed uncomfortable. She said she was suspicious that she was not told to bring a lawyer with her. It makes her feel vulnerable. I just don't think anyone before me had really explained what mediation was to her. It is probably the same for the other woman."

"Thanks for letting me know about her concerns. I don't doubt that she has had unfair treatment by the courts. Family court has an especially bad reputation with some communities in the city. Judges here are quick to take children from their homes or forego support. I hope she knows I am not acting as a judge. I need to emphasize that. Maybe I can build their confidence in this alternative court service." I then asked Anita to bring the women and teens back to the mediation room when they were ready.

Two minutes later the four African American females came to the door of the mediation room. I invited them in. Anita had not told me that one of the young girls—both were around 15 or 16 years old—had a very young infant with her. Seeing the pink hat and blanket, I assumed the infant was a girl, probably about three or four months old. One of the adult women was hefty and wore a black shiny coat with a huge pink collar. She had dark-rimmed glasses and a gold-plated necklace that said Jesus Saves in script. The other woman was slender and wore a white top with a red and black flowered silk scarf around her neck and tan dress pants. The two girls were in jeans and sweatshirts. One had a dark green backpack with her, out of which she took a pint-size baby bottle and set it on the table.

As they took their seats, the mothers instinctively pulled their chairs closer to their daughters and away from the table. The seating was more angular, more confrontive than the round table encouraged. They had squared the circle. The lines in the room had been drawn by them before anything was said.

I introduced myself emphasizing that I was a mediator, not a judge. I said this meant that they could make their own decisions about how to handle whatever brought them to court. I was there to help them find agreements and create a signed settlement that would be sent to the court. They could end the mediation and go back to court to have a judge address their issues at any point if they chose to do that. I said, "I will not talk with the judge about any of the issues discussed here today. Nor would I reveal anything anyone says. This is confidential. But you should all know that I do have to give a broad overview of the outcomes of your discussion to the court." I then asked if there were any questions or concerns.

One of the women asked, "How long will this last? I have my own business and it has got to stay closed until I get back there today."

"The session can last up to two hours but how long it actually goes is up to the four of you. You can end it at any time if it is not helpful," I responded.

The other woman inquired, "Can I get advice from my lawyer if I have questions?"

I assured her that she was free to contact her lawyer at any time or if she wanted him or her here, she could do that as well. She said, "Thank you, let's see how this goes for a while."

I then asked if they knew each other. One of the mothers spoke first and said that the two teens knew each other but she did not know the other woman or her daughter.

I said, "Well maybe it's best if we go 'round the table and each of you give your name. I will then know you and you will all know each other." This comment received no immediate response. It felt too formal. So, I looked at the woman who just spoke and asked, "Would you please go first?"

The lady with the large pink collar said with almost no expression, "I am Adele Johnson. This is my daughter Tanya." She sounded cautious—somewhat suspect—as she spoke. I sensed she was concerned about how her words might be used by me. Still worried that perhaps I could pass judgment of some sort.

The other woman followed, "I am Belinda Charles and my daughter's name is Latisha."

It was clear that the two mothers were ready to do the talking for their daughters. It felt like they were worried about what their daughters might say, as lawyers worry about what their clients might say in a hearing. They ignored my request that each person introduce herself. I sensed that any formalities would be ignored, so I hesitated to talk about ground rules for the session. I felt that discussion would be out of place—too process-focused—for the climate in the room. I noted to myself that I could always bring this up later.

Latisha had not stopped looking at her infant since she entered the room. Tanya stared repeatedly at Latisha, did not look at the baby, and did not react when her mother introduced her. Neither teen looked at me. They kept a disdainful focus on each other.

I was afraid that a pattern was getting set—that the mothers would continue to speak for their daughters. I wanted to break that tendency, so I said, "The court has asked you to come here to resolve whatever issues you have. I would like to hear from Tanya and Latisha about what is going on and what you want to say to me or to each other." There were about five seconds of silence then Tanya, still looking at Latisha, spoke in an angry, defensive tone.

"She and her nasty friends came at us two weeks ago after a basketball game at school. My best friend was slugged, went to the patient care center on Alleghany for stitches. She had no insurance so needed to pay hundred fifty at Instant Care and her mother yelled at her when she got home for getting into a fight and paying the money. Now my other friends and me need to get back. We will get back at you. We'll do it."

I looked at Latisha and hoped for a response. There was none for a few seconds. She then blurted out, "If she touch any of us, we will fight them wherever we friggin' need to. A day will not go by before we respond to these bitches. They better know that."

Belinda looked sternly at her daughter and said, "I told you before we got here to watch your language. This is court and you can create more problems for us by how you speak here. I told you we are vulnerable as soon as we walk into this building. You are not on some street corner. Court officials easily come against us for almost any reason."

The girl's language was rough, and I wrestled with whether I should squelch it. Shouldn't they be talking respectfully to each other in this setting as my early training insisted? But this is the way the girls expressed themselves, so who was I to alter their voices? Vulgarity is in the eye of the beholder. Changing their speech might mean shutting their voices down. Besides, I thought there were much bigger issues to tackle. It was coming clear to me that this was more than just the two teens. The "we" language and the immediate mention of friends getting hurt, suggested that there were groups, maybe well-formed gangs, behind each of them. This was more than a one-on-one fight. I could feel myself becoming tense and anxious as the reality of what was at stake here began to sink in.

Both mothers became increasingly concerned as they realized how big the conflict had gotten. The two girls continued their war of words.

"You bring your mother here to protect you today, but she won't help you out there," Tanya said, raising her voice and pointing toward the window. "Your mother be as dumb ass as you. She raised you. Could be no different."

Belinda looked at Adele and pointedly questioned her, "Are you going to let your daughter get away with that kind of talk here?"

Adele immediately turned to her daughter Tanya and raised her voice. "You don't talk with anyone about adults that way, do you hear? Nobody. It ain't right for any of my children. And I won't have it here." Clearly, both mothers were trying to shape the tone of the conversation by admonishing the way their daughters were speaking.

Latisha responded as if she did not hear Adele's chastisement of Tanya. "Don't you say nothing about my mother. She be here because she was told to. She's not here to help me. We don't need no help from anyone you hear, bitch? We will get you and your kind when and where we need to."

Tanya quickly reacted. "You better shut your mouth because we have the street tools to end this better if we need to. You don't need just your pissin mother. You need all your whore sisters and pimp brothers out there to protect you."

"I always have all I need to protect me. You the one who'll get it. Your ass is out there."

I was thrown by their ritualized insults. Their talk had its own rhythm and direction that made it tough to interrupt. I felt I needed to try. I looked back and forth at each girl and asked, "Who else is involved in your conflict?"

Both girls ignored my question. It was as if I was not there, that I was an observer sitting in the room—only a witness to a round of dangerous escalation.

Tanya continued her rant. "You get what you deserve. Just stay away from any man I am with, or you will get what you got coming. You don't know what we can do, just like you don't know your daddy."

Belinda looked at Adele and said, "If they both keep talking this way, we should end this. They will only lead us into more trouble here." Adele nodded her head, as if to say I understand. Tanya looked away and said nothing.

I reminded them that "Mediation is voluntary so you can end it at any point. It is up to you."

Belinda then looked at both girls and asked, "How many times will these attacks go back and forth? One of you has to be smart enough to walk away. Otherwise, where will this end up?" There were a few seconds of silence. Neither girl responded to Belinda's plea.

I could see that Adele looked drained as she started to speak. Looking directly at me she said: "I am afraid, like Belinda, where this is heading for these two. They are talking about street tools. That's weapons. There is too much of this out there on the streets." She paused, her voice wilted, and she put her hand softly on Tanya's arm. "I can't lose a child to this crazy gang stuff. Tanya knows this. She should know the pain." She looked away, holding back tears. "I'm hoping her father will be able to help me get through to her when he gets back from Afghanistan in a few weeks."

I had missed the street tool comment. Or if I heard it I didn't get that it meant street weapons. I wondered what else I had missed. My mind didn't know where to land as the room became filled with pain, insults, anger and the clear promise of more violence.

Belinda listened but did not speak. She looked overwhelmed and determined to keep her composure whatever transpired in the session. Even if it meant saying little or nothing.

The girls gave no hint about how this street warfare started, what its source was. I looked at Latisha and decided to ask about it. "How did this fight get going?" Even as I spoke the words, I sensed their futility. I was desperate to be relevant to what was going on in front of me. But digging for the origin of this battle seemed irrelevant to where things stood between them. What difference did I think it might make?

Without hesitation, Latisha said, "Bitch gave me that mean look at the basketball game. My friends saw it and I was pissed. I was put down in front of the friends who respect me. She deserves what she gets. If she comes at us with her gang of thugs, we'll get back. That's the way it is. Got to be. She won't listen to nothing else."

I wrestled with the violence that was in both of these girls' immediate futures. I felt enormous pressure. Pressure that slowed my brain. I felt I needed to do or say something that would block the progression—that would turn the dangerous cycle away from where it was headed. But that seemed impossible. A look at a basketball game is not a bounced check, not damage to a car, not a decision about who would have a child on the holidays. No, it was not about negotiable issues that I had dealt with before in mediation role plays and in real cases. This was about who these girls are and what threatens how they see themselves. It was about the need to protect their *selves* at a very vulnerable age when self-image is all that matters. It was about living or dying over what counted most to them in life.

My thoughts wandered back to my initial mediation training—the one before Adam's. All the prescriptions raced across my mind. Control the negative interaction and help the girls think rationally so they can problem solve and construct creative options or solutions. What are their underlying interests? What is practical? How can their issues be negotiated? This conflict did not seem to fit the standard mediation thinking. It did not feel like there was a concrete problem to solve or a tangible issue to negotiate. But I thought I had to try something.

I started making feeble suggestions. Looking at both Adele and Belinda, I asked, "Could one of your daughters attend a different school? Physical separation might cool things down and stop contact with each other. This could be a way to avoid future violence. They would be less likely to run into each other."

In response, Adele said, "The last fight happened at the mall parking lot so changing schools is no help. I am sure Belinda agrees. I have told my daughter that violence is unacceptable anywhere out there. That really is the point we are making to our daughters. If something happens between them out there, the police will be brutal toward them. I can't even think about it."

I saw immediately that my suggestion was foolish—that it came from the wrong side of my brain. The girls could always find a fighting venue wherever they went to school. Social distancing might prevent the spread of a virus, but it would not stop the spread of violence between two determined teen gangs in one city. There was no de-militarized zone in the city.

I tried again. I looked at the two mothers and said, "Are there any punishments you, as parents, could give to deter your daughters from further fights? What could change their motivations?"

There was no answer from either mother, just incredulous looks that said you've-got-to-be-kidding. It was at that point that I heard my own naiveté. I saw how out of touch I was by pushing for impractical solutions to an elusive and treacherous situation. I began to think that this is one of those cases that are not mediate-able. Like conflicts involving racism, homo-phobia, white supremacy. These are the soft underbelly of conflicts that most mediators steer clear of. My early training was all focused on having people negotiate settlements to tangible issues. Phrases like, log-rolling, splitting the difference, negotiation zones, reality testing, and best alternative to a negotiated agreement crossed my mind. These were all standard mediation practices, but they seemed irrelevant to what was unfolding across the table in front of me.

I also looked down at the two questions that I had put on the table. I hoped that they might be helpful. They were of no relief in the moment. The pressure was too great for me to have time to think through their implications as the session unfolded. I was about to quit—stop the session and resign myself to the inappropriateness of the case for mediation. At least that would be a somewhat satisfying face saving move for me. I could think of nothing else.

But then, without any prompting from me or their mothers, Latisha slowly raised her eyes from her baby girl and looked directly at Tanya. She spoke softly but firmly, with a clear sense of insistence. "We shouldn't attack each other when we have our baby girls with us," she said.

I looked over at Tanya. Without saying a word, Tanya's face softened as she thought about what Latisha said. She did not say a word. She simply looked at the ceiling and nodded in agreement.

Latisha handed her baby to her own mother sitting next to her. With her lap empty, she looked younger and more vulnerable, as if she had lost the protection that her child provided for her. Belinda held the baby close and lovingly, as if to protect her from the danger nearby. She clearly had bonded with the infant through its short life, almost as if she were the primary caretaker.

Silence then fell on the room. There was no more to say. I had no idea what prompted this dramatic change in tone, but it felt like the mediation had just ended on its own. That short exchange was sincere and powerful. It felt like the one truly hopeful moment of the whole conversation. This felt like a human connection made on their own, drawn not from walking through phases of a mediation process or by my misguided attempts to find a grand solution to their escalating violence. I knew that the possibility of violence was still there—it would always be there—but they had taken the one willing step they could take on that afternoon in Philadelphia. It felt like they created a small bond that might deter their worst instincts on a dangerous street in this city.

Although this was a clear point of agreement between them, I felt it was inappropriate to ask if they wanted it written down. That would be out of touch with who they are and what they expect. Instead, I just thanked them for coming and said that if they wanted to return, I would be available to them. I heard my own perfunctory farewell comments. My words seemed unnatural given what had transpired in the room. It felt as if I was reading a script.

The girls' eyes never met again. They left the mediation room without saying a further word to each other or me. Both Adele and Belinda thanked me politely, although I could tell they felt little help had been given. I wondered whether they thought that things would have gone better if they had an African American mediator. I wondered the same thing. I could hear Latisha's baby crying as they walked through the reception area and left the Center.

I was in a blinding fog. My memory of any specifics from the session had already eluded me. I stood up at the mediation table and tried for a moment to clear my head. I wasn't sure whether anything of significance had happened or whether I had anything to do with what transpired. I wasn't even sure I had said anything for the last hour.

I realized that I forgot to ask them to fill out the feedback forms for the mediation session. Or maybe this didn't cross my mind because it would have been out of touch with what had just happened. I sat back down and had an overwhelming feeling of failure come over me. I read over Adam's two questions as I gathered my things. I could hear Adam saying to me, "Mr. Foxe there is a lot to think about." Perhaps there was more here than I could manage on my own.

CHAPTER THREE

Language and Actions

Soon after the women left, Anita came back to the mediation room and asked, "How did your session go?"

"I am not sure. It was an unusual and difficult case," I said. "The girls seemed to be leaders of two street gangs that are at war with each other. Did either of the two mothers say anything as they left?"

Anita replied, "Not a word. They didn't seem in a hurry, but they were not talking to the girls or each other. They just looked a little frustrated. I am afraid to ask you this, Kent, but did you have the parties complete the mediation feedback forms?"

"Actually, I didn't," I said without giving Anita a reason. I reassured myself about my oversight. I felt like it would have been inappropriate to ask them to comply with such bureaucratic details. Questions such as "Did you reach a problem-solving solution?" or "Did the mediator keep the session moving?" just seemed out of place. I could not imagine either the mothers or daughters answering these questions.

"Well, I shouldn't need to remind you that this is important," Anita admonished. "The court requests these post mediation forms on a monthly basis. Without them, we can't document the great work we do here. I know I mentioned this to you before. Your cooperation would be appreciated because

I am accountable for this."

"I'm sorry. Maybe there is some way to reach out to them at home?" I said somewhat insincerely. "Do we have their addresses?"

"The court has them. I will see what I can do," Anita said in her usual icy tone. She wanted to make sure her reprimand was heard.

I knew I was making more work for her and that she was irked. I once suggested to Anita that she give the parties the forms when they exited through the reception area. My suggestion was met with a response that fell someplace between disdain and outrage. Anita seemed overly dedicated to her clerk job for a smart young woman in her early thirties. She was hard to get to know personally because she restricted her comments mostly to work-related topics. At least with me. One day she was listening to a female singer in the office, and I asked her about her favorite artists. She mentioned a few local talents that she heard live at Outlayers, a popular music venue in West Philly that is known for great concerts and somewhat questionable clientele. She had a boyfriend who I had seen in the office a couple of times when he met her for lunch. That was about all I got to know about her. She seemed bright and talented. I wondered why she was not pursuing a more fulfilling career. It just seemed she was there to get the job done efficiently and be ready to leave each day at exactly four-thirty.

After Anita left the mediation room, I felt I was not yet ready to leave the Center. The details of the girls' mediation were starting to return to me, and I could tell I was about to review them obsessively. I knew my mind would not let go easily. I needed to think right then about the questions Adam had given me and how they related to the difficult mediation I had just done. I was afraid I would lose touch with what happened and how I was feeling if I waited or became distracted by the ride home. I also knew that writing down my

...oughts and reactions would help to clarify my thinking.

I walked across the room to a small table that had a desktop computer on it. This computer was used to write up mediation agreements for the court. I logged in and began to write my thoughts about the case, hoping the fog in my head would lift and that I would get some insights about what had occurred.

Who was I in this mediation? I realized that this is a deeply challenging question. To start with I did not know whether I was able to define myself to the women or whether they had defined me. I tried to be someone with a helpful process and a set of questions that might shed light on the girls' conflict and its evolution. But I felt I was being overly analytical with every question I asked. I was acting as an expert on conflict rather than a supporter of their conversation. Taking the expert role did not get me or, more importantly them, very far. In fact, it may have been an obstruction.

Finding the source of the conflict seemed important to me but it didn't seem important to them. What was important for them was the need for revenge—regardless of whether it started with a look at a basketball game or a snub at a party, or a planned assault. Finding out about how long the girls knew each other, where the attacks occurred, how many girls were involved—all topics I pursued—really were more for me than them. The questions filled my need to know, not theirs. They were irrelevant to what was actually transpiring in the room.

Looking back, I must have sounded more like Dr. Phil than a skillful, neutral mediator. Dr. Phil is the self-proclaimed expert in the room, giving advice based on minimum knowledge of the people and repelling any resistance to the

32

solutions he forcefully recommends. I don't think I went quite that far but I was headed down that big-ego road through the information seeking approach I took. Or was the expert role the role I was supposed to be taking in a case like this? When youth are involved and violence do the parties inevitably need an expert to steer their values and actions? And would taking that role turn the mediation into a masked counseling session?

Deep down, I knew I was analytical because that is what I know how to do. It was at least a way to attempt to stop temporarily the vitriolic interaction between the girls. This approach and the choices I made got me thinking about my study of philosophy in college. I remember that the eccentric language philosopher, Wittgenstein, made an important point that seemed relevant here to me. One of his major insights was that spoken language always serves functions. We don't just say things, we do things with our words. Language is used to describe, to deceive, to declare, to insult, to insinuate, to investigate, etc. I was, of necessity, doing things to the parties and their conversation with little conscious awareness of the effects I was having.

This point got me thinking about what function my questions had served during the mediation. Why did I use my language so often to search for information? What did I think I was I going to do with the information after I had collected it? More importantly, what did they think I was going to do with it? The information seeking contributed to defining myself as a judge or an inquisitorial lawyer. While it is easy to tell the parties at the outset of the mediation that I was not acting as a judge, the language I used erased my own declaration of my role. What I did with my language during the session over-rode who I said I was. A troublesome realization!

We hope by asking question people will see their own answers

My language also defined myself as someone who was responsible for the grand solution to the problem. I was thinking hard about what might be realistically helpful, what might stop the escalating cycle of violence. I felt responsible for what might develop on the streets of North Philadelphia after the session. I felt obligated to stop the next attack. Was that a responsibility I was supposed to take on? What good am I as a mediator if I exclude stopping violence from my set of goals? But trying to end it seemed out of reach.

My motives were to protect, not control. There seems to be a fine line here. One person's protective move is seen by the protected as unwanted control. Not to mention that my ideas and solutions—my protective moves—were rooted in naiveté and, to some extent, arrogance. If anything, my efforts got in the way of their own constructive steps, their ability to say what they wanted to say to each other and what they might find that worked for them. However small, any steps needed to be their steps.

In a way, I am sorry I had not asked them if they wanted to commit to a second mediation session. Their work may have been just starting because my interventions had gotten in their way. They may have wanted to check in with each other a few weeks later to see if they had kept the agreement about the babies, a possible trust-building turning point. But I could not see this option because I wanted to fix it all. I wished I had thought of Sondheim's lyric from an early Broadway show of his about how little ripples can create big waves. But that's the thing about mediation, you rarely get to find out what happens to the clients after the session is over. You see the horrible car crash but never find out whether anyone survived the accident.

34

More important than how I was defining myself was how the women and girls were defining me. Was I inescapably seen as a paternal figure just by being a middle-aged male in the room? Was I seen as another authority figure in the teens' lives who was untrustworthy and undependable— someone who would easily walk out of their lives as maybe other men had? Was I going to be defined this way no matter what I did or said? Or did I appear to the girls or their mothers at least to have an honest intention to help? One thing was for sure, they knew intuitively that I would not be able to find the workable solutions to their dangerous problems.

As I finished that last sentence, Anita came to the mediation room door and saw me typing at the computer in the corner. "We need this room for the next mediation that starts in fifteen minutes," she said matter-of-factly.

"Is it mine?" I asked absentmindedly.

She responded in a familiar condescending voice, "No, Kent, you are scheduled to mediate with Karen Abrams the middle of next week. Check with me on your way out for details. And please write up the mediation report for the judge who sent your teen case here."

She then turned and left hurriedly leaving the door open.

I thought that fifteen minutes would give me a little time to think about Adam's second question. I started to type again.

What did I actually believe about the women and girls? I believed these people were different from me. I could see what sociologists call "gaps" that existed between us—a gender gap, a cultural gap, an economic gap, an education gap. I wasn't sure how these gaps were influencing the session, but I am sure they were impactful in important ways. These differences paralyzed me in the room, made me feel unsure of my footing. I felt very old, very male, and very white in the mediation room. And I knew that these feelings were influencing what was understood or misunderstood by me and by them. All the training on cultural and gender differences in mediation would not have filled the deep gaps that were there in the room. Sensitivity is not an effective bridge to lifetimes of difference.

My questions felt out of touch with their world. When I asked if the mothers could punish their daughters to curtail the fights or when I heard that a look at a basketball game launched the retaliatory cycle, they knew that I did not get it. What I think I did get was that the teens were caught up in defending themselves from degradation. Their fight was meaningful to them because it was about their sense of self, their teen dignity. Being a fighter is better than showing weakness even if it means injury or worse. Haven't I heard that many times on a much larger scale in ethnic disputes and persistent warfare? I knew that at base, most intense conflict is or eventually becomes identity conflict. How people see themselves always matters more than the material issues they say they are fighting over.

I stopped writing. My thoughts wandered to my father and how he would respond to a road rage incident. "That SOB can't cut me off like that. I'll show him," he would say as he sped off toward the perpetrator. It was all about defending his ego even if it meant endangering his family on the road. He was blind to that possibility. His behavior was rationally irrational. There was a defensible reason for it but it was dangerously counter-productive. I thought about how I would always be terrified when he did this. Anything could have happened if he caught up with the driver who offended him. I thought about how easily people go to the mat over threats to how they want to see themselves. These girls were no exception.

I also must have believed, until the very end of the session, that the teens were unable to address their own issues in any constructive way, although I may not have been fully conscious of this belief during the session. But it had to exist in me somewhere, otherwise, why was I foolishly supplying the solutions that I thought would work for them? It wasn't until they pledged not to attack when they had their babies with them that I saw some capability on their part. And yet this step towards finding connection seemed so meager—so insignificant—given what might happen when these girls went back on the streets again. It seemed to do nothing to prevent the worst damage they might do to each other. Yet it truly came from them. It was theirs alone.

expect the best

This mediation had taught me a valuable lesson. A mediator has to truly believe that the people have what it takes to make their own best decisions. Otherwise, we just get in their way. Or we become pseudo-judges or counselors.

I stopped writing and thought that this underlying optimism is probably needed for all professionals who work with people—counselors, therapists, leadership coaches, life coaches, social workers. Despite any advice a professional may give, people have to find their own way. And you have to believe they can. A tough commitment for the helping professionals.

I realized it was past time for the next mediation to start although I was surprised that Anita had not returned to snatch me out of the room. I sent what I wrote about the case to Adam via email. It would be good for him to see what his questions had triggered. Although the analysis resolved little about what I would do differently, it did provoke some practical cautions. It also settled my mind some as well. It helped to shut off the annoying obsessive review switch in my head.

Anita had reminded me that I was required to complete a short form about the number of parties involved, the issues discussed and whether an agreement was reached. This task was easy in some ways but difficult in others. I would have to wrestle with whether a sufficient agreement was reached to prevent the case from returning to court. I could see an argument being made in either direction given what transpired in this mediation. It was a troublesome decision. One I would just as well avoid making. I decided to err on the more cautious side and say that not everything was resolved and that some form of violence was still possible. I worried, though, that this statement could create risk for the girls and their mothers.

I printed what I had written, got up from the computer and gathered my materials. As I walked past Anita's desk, she said, without looking up from her computer, "The mediation scheduled for your room was cancelled. One party opted out at the last minute."

I made a point of asking Anita for the exact time and date of my next mediation. She said it was scheduled for next Wednesday afternoon at four. I said thank you and wished her a good day. She did not respond.

As I walked down the stairs and headed out of the building, I felt befuddled and a little depressed. Was this an un-mediate-able case as I had convinced myself earlier or was I just an inept beginner? I had little confidence in my instincts after what unfolded in the mediation room today. The stakes were too high for someone who lacked confidence. I was not sure I should mediate next week—or ever.

CHAPTER FOUR

High Flying Conflicts

I drove out of the Center's parking lot in my Subaru Forester and arrived home around seven p.m. My spouse, Gianni (he goes by Gio for short) greeted me with his usual "Is that you?" as I entered the side door near the garage. Gio and I have been together for 15 years. We are a traditional gay professional couple, careful who we come out to, discreet in public with displays of affection, and no children or tattoos of our own. We have had plenty of involvement, though, with a wide range of nieces and nephews who rely on us from time to time for money, advice on dealing with their parents, and summer vacations at the Jersey Shore. On the more challenging side, they also have turned to us for advice about drugs, anorexia, unwanted pregnancies, and coming out. It's great to be sought after and it's even better to be able to hang up the phone without further responsibility for their lives.

Gio is an accountant by day and a ballroom dance instructor by night. He worked his way through college teaching the hustle during the seventies and eighties. Gio has been a supportive spouse. He takes an interest in the consulting and mediation work I do and has become a curbstone mediator based on the long conversations that I and some colleagues have had about our cases when he was with us. He is better than me in our personal lives at sustaining relationships in the face of differences. He can tolerate strong expressions of emotions and anger and not hold grudges. That, he says, is due to his pure Italian heritage. Both sets of grandparents were Italian immigrants. His conflict advice is always get it all out in the open and deal with it. He is not afraid of conflict and doesn't believe in grudges. That is a positive, well mostly a positive. At times, my more staid Northern European background doesn't prepare me to deal with an openly confrontive style. I have a tougher time recovering after it all is put out in the open.

Gio grew up in South Jersey, so he still has many extended family members in the area. His closest living sibling, his older sister Mia, lives in Southern California. I grew up in the Midwest and came to the Philadelphia region for consulting employment. I have no immediate family in the area—my three sisters and their offspring live mostly in the Midwest. We count on Gio's relatives and our friends for most of our social activities.

One year for my birthday Gio surprised me with new New Jersey license plates that read: MEE D 8. Somehow, he always finds gifts that are appropriate and amusing. And he likes being a booster for endeavors that either one of us support, including his antique muscle car collection. I often tease him about having a picture of his 1968 GTO on his desk at work rather than a picture of me. I guess I have to be officially declared an antique before I am publicly displayed.

We live in a large two-story country Tudor home not far from Philadelphia. Our township is mostly middle class, and very gay friendly. Our house was built by a wealthy German engineer, Joseph Eisenberg, in 1929, at the height of the depression. It is a lavish home for that period, with three bedrooms, an upstairs office and a maid's quarters over a two-car garage. We learned from a friend of the original owner that the Eisenbergs' live-in maid's name was Abby. It was indeed "the help" era. There is still a working foot buzzer under the dining room table placed where the original wife sat. She used it to call Abby when she was needed for service at the dining table.

The house is built like a red brick fortress. It has a remarkable steeply gabled slate roof and flagstone walkways to the front and back entrances. So, we feel lucky to live in it and, maybe because of its size, we entertain overnight guests—mostly family—quite often. We have had many parties and receptions with up to 60 people. The Eisenbergs, we have heard from a friend of their family, loved to entertain. And the house suits social functions beautifully.

We have decorated the interior with a twenties look. We have original deco lamps and chairs from the period and several prized Nichols floor rugs we found in the New York City carpet district. These are rare rugs that are brightly colored with stylized flower prints from the deco era. They set the pre-modern tone for each room on the first floor of this much-loved home.

Over a lasagna dinner in our dining area, Gio reminded me that his nephew Bill's ex-wife, Brigid, and their two teenage children, Linus and Sarah, were coming in from Denmark on Sunday. They planned to stay with us for the better part of a week. Bill is one of Gio's nephews who lives nearby. Now in his late thirties, I have known Bill as long as I have known Gio. Bill had a somewhat troubled childhood. He ran away from home at 18, joined the army and was stationed for a while in Scandinavia. For most of that time, the family did not know where he was. In Denmark he met and married Brigid. The marriage only lasted until their two children were toddlers. Bill moved back to the U.S. and was barely in touch with the children as they grew up. He would only make an occasional phone call on their birthdays and holidays. There was no animosity, he just drifted away from a family that was so far away.

"Are we going to have Bill, his girlfriend and the Danes for dinner on Sunday?" I asked.

Gio replied, "Maybe, let's see how it goes. You know how unpredictable things can get when Bill and his lady friend are involved. They are not that dependable. I will start planning things tomorrow and keep you posted."

Gio always tried to support his three nephews, including Bill, because his sister died young from a rare form of cancer. Giving support to his nephews was sometimes tricky, as we both found out, especially with Bill who we knew had undiagnosed mental challenges. We often discussed what Gio's sister would have done to keep all three of her boys in line if she had lived. We both agreed that things would have been different. She was a strong matriarchal figure for the family. Her death left a vacuum that only chaos filled.

Changing the topic away from the family visit, Gio asked, "How was your mediation today? You look a little tired."

"Terrifying," I replied.

"What? You never used that word before to describe a mediation," Gio said wide-eyed. "Why terrifying? Did someone have a weapon or something? Were you in danger in that unsafe municipal building that I keep worrying about?"

"Maybe terrifying is too strong. It wasn't a personal safety issue for me. It just was a case that challenged me deeply and was upsetting. But I'm too tired to get into it now, and I have to get up early to get that flight to Denver for the consulting work. I will tell you more when I get back on Saturday."

Gio looked disappointed and a little irritated. "These consulting trips are becoming more frequent, and they cut into our time together," he pointed out. "We hardly have time to talk with each other some weeks. If you keep depending on this kind of work, I can see you will be gone a lot."

"I know, Gio, but it is the best way for me to make a living. These consulting gigs pay well and there just is not enough mediation work here—or maybe anywhere—to earn a living. Very few mediators can make a career of it. I want to do meaningful work but also make sure I am earning enough."

Gio looked unconvinced. "Well, we need to find trips we can take together. Maybe some of them can be work-related. We can turn them into a mini vacation. I have never been to Denver."

As I headed to our upstairs bedroom, I reassured myself that my work travel was necessary. I also felt that some time away from each other was good for both of us. I knew Gio saw it differently and I wondered how much I was rationalizing. I sensed the threat Gio felt by distance. It made me wonder what was behind his concerns. Did he not trust me? Was there a problem in a past relationship? Was he jealous of my opportunities for travel? I tried not to get too involved with these thoughts at the moment because they might block a peaceful night's sleep. Or they might block my sleep because I hadn't thought about them enough. I wasn't sure. But I went to bed and hoped for the best, falsely promising myself that I would think about this sensitive issue more.

The next morning I got up at six a.m. and headed to the airport. The assignment in Denver is with a large investment firm. The goal, as the manager said, is to help his IT group work more effectively together. I've come to understand that phrases like "work more effectively" are usually euphemisms for deeper issues. In this case, I knew from the advance interviews I conducted with the employees that the IT group was steeped in workplace conflict. Most of the issues were concerns that the team members had with the manager himself and how he ran the group. The manager told me there was no reason for him to attend the team building session— "The issues," he said, "stem from their inability to work well together."

This tendency for managers to point a finger at their work groups was quite common in my consulting experience. When a manager asked for team building for his workgroup, nine times out of ten it was needed because of unaddressed conflicts that festered and undercut communication, relationships, and productivity. The team building session usually became a type of group mediation, often with the manager on one side and the team on the other. The manager's decision not to attend was typical when the conflicts were actually with the manager. It is just easier to point a finger toward "them" rather than admit your own role in the turmoil.

But conflict was about to arise long before I reached Denver for the corporate team building session. Overcrowded planes are a breeding ground for intense conflict and psychological damage. My flight to Denver was no exception.

I had taken my usual aisle seat in row eight on the flight. Booking aisle seats close to the front of the plane is the only proactive step, short of taking drugs, I've found to counter the claustrophobic hit that walking on a plane delivers to me. Taking an aisle seat is all you can really do to get a little more head room. Short flights are the worst—the shorter the flight, the smaller the plane and the greater the claustrophobic attack. It usually takes at least 30 minutes for me to adjust to the feeling that I am in a narrow tunnel with no way out.

Not to be outdone by the pharmaceutical industry, the airlines know that this mental condition can be turned into profits. They can get more money for an aisle seat by preying on the claustrophobic good souls who must fly. What worries me is that there is probably no end to the airline industry's exploitation of the weak when they put their mind to it. Next it will be additional charges for multiple visits to the restroom. Perfect for capitalizing on irritable bowel or weak bladder maladies.

As I buckled my seatbelt, I was thinking of Adam's comic take on the stewardess's safety routine before take-off. I was also thinking that corporate meetings with self-absorbed IT employees can sometimes be as mind-confining as the fuselage of a 737. The only difference is that you can't book your seat by the exit door ahead of time. And you can't get up fast and leave, even if there is a convenient exit. These team-building sessions always are somewhat nerve-wracking and unpredictable. I never sleep well the night before I am going to facilitate a group that may or may not want to be there. There is always the chance that the group will symbolically kill the team-building facilitator rather than address their own issues. It is easier to blame an outsider who tried to help rather than admit that the turmoil is within the group. I have been the victim of it a couple of times and, because it is a psychodynamic twist, there is almost no defense against it. You just try to remain professional and survive with non-defensive reactions.

Just when most people seated themselves on the overly crowded plane, I heard the stewardess raising her voice to the passengers sitting one row behind me.

"Miss, the cat is as welcome as anyone else on this plane. Please calm down," she insisted.

The passenger she was talking to, a 50-ish woman who was overweight and had jet-black hair with gray roots, quickly retorted, "The cat cannot stay this close to me. Put it in the overhead bin if you have to. I don't care. Just get rid of it. I don't care, I am not moving from this seat."

"We are just trying to meet everyone's needs," the stewardess explained. "We need to work at this constructively, problem solve." The stewardess's stilted vocabulary revealed that she was obviously trained in beginner conflict management techniques.

"Damn it, I didn't have this need until she sat down there with that cat," the passenger quickly responded. "Get her to move someplace. I've paid the full amount for this ticket. I didn't intend to buy a seat in a flying pet store. That animal smells funny and is making strange sounds."

The woman with the cat—a 40-ish redhead with a light green turtleneck—remained quiet and did not look at either the stewardess or the complaining lady next to her. She seemed only to be protecting her cat while trying to stay under the verbal fray.

The stewardess stood in the aisle for a few seconds, then said, "Well, there are other ways to handle this. But we can't shut the airplane door and we can't start moving until one of you changes seats with someone and gets situated comfortably. I realize that there are no empty seats on the flight but maybe someone will be willing to change with one of you."

As heads around me began turning to see what the raucous was about, I tuned out the distraction by fantasizing that the stewardess was on the intercom asking, "If there is a mediator on the plane, please identify yourself." I knew I would have had to respond to her request. I had mediated several difficult neighbor disputes over pets that turned terribly ugly, so my confidence level would be high.

In my mediation fantasy I saw myself calmly walking up to the distressed stewardess and offering my services saying, "You called for a professional mediator? I am fully insured." Quickly getting myself into what is known in professional circles as "a pure state of mediator mindfulness," I would turn to the two disgruntled women and say, "I am a professional mediator and my first question for you is a simple one, "What ground rules do you need in order to have this conversation productively?" I could see in my mind's eye that the stewardess would be overjoyed by the immediate positive impact of this first intervention.

Just as my mediator ego was beginning to alleviate my claustrophobia, my tarmac fantasy ended abruptly as the stewardess brushed my elbow rushing up the narrow aisle. She looked irritated as she headed to the front of the plane, apparently unsure of whether the silence she had imposed in row nine was going to last. She had failed to arrange a seat switch for either woman. Instead, she arbitrated the cat conflict, like a judge demanding child support from a delinquent father. She simply told them to deal quietly with their situation. But she knew intuitively, like most judges in family court, that her imposed settlement—insisting that they both retain their current seats and be satisfied about it—was probably not likely to last until Pittsburgh.

I turned around and looked at the woman who was outraged by the cat. She was reaching for the magazine in the seat pocket in front of her and ended up staring blankly at the first random page that she opened. I thought about why she might have been so indignant about having the animal next to her. Maybe she was allergic to cats and would soon brake out in hives or begin gasping for air, the way a woman did who was apparently allergic to her seatmate's perfume on a flight I had taken from Chicago. Maybe the cat hater had a similar allergic problem.

Or maybe she was HIV positive and susceptible to toxoplasmosis, the infectious parasitic disease cats carry that can be life threatening to those who are immune depressed. But I knew intuitively—maybe from my mediation experiences—that she would not have been this nasty and obstinate if something serious like this was imminent. Serious needs prompt accommodation, cooperative action or escape. If she could have died or passed out from the cat, she would have just moved—fast—and been relieved that she had escaped the danger. There would have been no huffing, no dagger looks, and no verbal assaults on the stewardess. She would have protected herself.

No, I knew it was more likely that she had some type of irrational feline repulsion. The kind that twists the mind into believing that it has no rational recourse when the source of the fear is in eyeshot. She had no choice but to retaliate. After all, admitting that her fear is irrational is admitting, to some extent, that she is losing her grip on reality. Who can readily admit that they are neurotic to anyone, no less strangers on a plane? The mind has a remarkable way of protecting itself from itself.

I conjectured about what was going on with the women behind me, I could see that my analytically prone mind couldn't help but dive into the range of possible motives and reactions that were advancing this conflict. It was similar to what I had done in trying to respond to the girls' gang dispute yesterday. For better or worse, my tendency—my core disposition—is to over-think conflict situations. I thought this might be something to explore with Adam perhaps. Is this who I am? Do I do this in my own personal conflicts to my peril? Or is analytical thinking about conflicts a good thing in some circumstances, especially in mediation? Maybe being analytical helps mediators be with difficult emotional conflicts.

I also thought about the young woman who had carefully tucked the cat into a blue vinyl carrying case with mesh windows and placed it under the seat in front of her. I am definitely not a cat lover—there is something unsettling about the way they move, so furtively and unpredictably. But I could feel for the poor animal all cramped up in that little pup tent of a carrying case. Was she taking this cat with her because she had no friends left in Philadelphia to watch it while she was away? Was the cat promised to her ex-husband in the spoils of a messy divorce? Was she taking it to her 70-year-old mother who had recently moved someplace west of Denver for drier climate? All I could tell from her face was that she was somewhat dumb founded by the indignant reaction her seating partner threw at her, and she was definitely not about to move.

Although there were endless possibilities laying beneath the surface of this fuselage skirmish, one thing was certain, neither woman was thinking about the other at all as the events escalated. There was no recognition of, let alone sympathy or concern for, possible human weakness or back stories. Instead, each woman pulled inward, wallowed in her victimization, and remained assured that the other woman was out to make her miserable. The real irony, of course, is that by assuming the worst of each other they did make each other miserable. There they sat, inches from each other, adamantly avoiding eye contact. Acknowledging each other's presence by acting as if they were not acknowledging each other's presence. A draining task for a four-hour flight.

As the airplane door shut and the stewardess started her series of mundane announcements, she felt compelled to say something about the delay that was off her introductory service script. Indirectly admonishing the cat combatants, she improvised, saying, "I apologize for our slight delay. I hope the rest of the flight goes smoothly." It was clear that the cat incident had thrown her off-kilter. Her departure routine was disrupted. And she wanted every last person on the plane to know it. With her language, I could tell that she was warning people on the plane, not apologizing to them. A big difference that I am sure most passengers felt.

As the plane sped down the runway, I drifted back to the memory of another more treacherous flight cabin conflict. It is etched in the part of my brain that believes I will die on an overcrowded plane someday.

I was on a very crowded flight from Seattle to Philadelphia in the late nineties. One hour into the flight I could hear the loud voice of a man about four rows behind me. At first all I could make out was garbled noises and short shrieks. I soon realized that these sounds were from someone who was in a full-blown panic attack. He was terrified and pleading to get off the plane. As he grew louder, he quickly drew two startled stewardesses to his seat. At first, they tried to quiet him, asking him what was wrong and whether they could bring him something. When nothing seemed to help after ten minutes one of the young stewardesses lost it and started yelling back at him. This only provoked the man further. She seemed to be mad at him, as if he were personally insulting her—maybe by setting her back with other chores she was supposed to be doing at that point in the flight.

All of this was in earshot of a dozen passengers who were sitting in nearby rows. The usual silence on the plane was broken as passengers started nervously talking with each other, as tends to happen in the very earliest stages of mob hysteria. They were reaching out to see if others were developing the same fear about what this man in his early twenties might do.

The woman sitting next to me said out loud, "Can this guy open any of these exit doors from the inside?" I wasn't sure whether the question was intended for me, but I answered it, trying to assure her that this was not possible. She looked unconvinced. I felt unconvinced.

Her fear immediately triggered my own doubts about what the man could do. I felt the contagion of fear destroying any rational defenses I could muster. I began to sweat. I then got mad at the stewardess who was now yelling at the man. Wasn't she trained to handle these kinds of situations? Couldn't she see that trying to calm this guy down by yelling at him was like trying to escape from telemarketers by continuing to answer their questions? The stewardess's emotional and loud reactions were fueling his panic. He needed calming reassurance, a gentle touch, someone to speak softly and hold his hand lightly.

I was then somewhat startled to look back and see the copilot walking down the aisle toward the man. This was getting serious. When the panicked passenger realized that the tall, tan man in the white shirt was the copilot, he lost control completely. He started screaming. "Who's flying this plane?" he screeched and pointed decidedly to the cockpit. "You have to get back up there. How is this plane flying while you're back here? Get back in the cockpit now! Please!" He was overwrought with fear at this point, thinking that no one was in the cockpit controlling the plane.

If the fear hadn't taken me over, I might have laughed at the unfolding situation but in the moment, all I could think of

was, how is this pilot going to deal with this guy? Could he
anything that the stewardesses could not do? We were headed
for a likely landing in Salt Lake City and the poor guy would
be arrested there by Utah police.

The pilot's first move was a bust. "I will bring this plane
down at the nearest airport, if you do not settle down," he
warned in a harsh, authoritative voice. This was counterproductive. The man became flushed, threw his head back, and
kept yelling. He was outmaneuvering the pilot at this point. If
he kept screaming, he realized that he had some hope of
getting off the plane soon. The pilot seemed to sense his bad
move, so he tried again.

The pilot's next move was brilliant—crisp, with a hint of
therapeutic paradox. In a less authoritative tone, he said, "I
will go back to the cockpit and fly this plane only if you calm
down right here and now." Basically, the pilot offered an
appealing deal based in the deeper fears he himself had
instilled in the panic-stricken passenger by walking up to his
seat. It was a deceptive but effective maneuver.

This ploy immediately registered with this afflicted young
man. He accepted the pilot's deal without protest or much
hesitancy. The man quickly put his head down and said
nothing. The stewardess walked up to him a few minutes later
with a stack of magazines and a set of Bose headphones.
Amazingly, the man never spoke again as we flew through the
remaining four hours back to Philadelphia.

As I thought about this incident, I noted that this afflicted
passenger had it in him someplace to maintain control and
overcome the panic. All he needed was the right motivation
and some helpful support. How the airlines staff viewed him
was crucial in discovering his own capability. I told myself to
think more about what this meant for a mediator's efforts to
deal with people in debilitating conflicts.

I also warned myself that it is a dangerous time for a
frequent flyer like myself to have a psychological weakness of

any kind. And I wondered for a few minutes whether claustrophobia gets worse with age, like far-sightedness, prostate growth, and intolerance of unruly three-year-olds. I needed to keep claustrophobic tendencies in check in these times of tight security and passenger posses taking responsibility for maintaining decorum on their own flights.

At the gate in the Denver airport, the stewardess who squelched the cat dispute was standing next to me in the aisle as we waited for the plane doors to open. There was some kind of delay at the gate. I rekindled my mediator fantasy and decided to say something to her. I said lightheartedly, "I am a mediator and thought about offering you my assistance earlier with the cat fight."

She rolled her overly mascaraed eyes, gave me a friendly smile and said, "I needed all the help I could get. Mediators are wonderful. We had a mediator for a contract dispute that the stewardesses' union had with the airline company. The mediator made a very fair decision in the case. He clearly took our points into account, and we got most of what we wanted. Our greedy company had to live with the outcome because the mediator's decision was binding."

I smiled back and said, "I see." She clearly was talking about binding arbitration, not mediation. A very common and irritating misunderstanding in the public's mind. For many people, it is all the same thing. I resolutely vowed right then in that plane that I would somehow find a way to correct the public's perception of what mediation is and isn't. It would take some help from the media. Maybe there were student filmmakers who would like to make a documentary on mediation. Or maybe a reporter could do an effective TV news series that one of the networks would run. Adam had many connections at the university that might make this happen. I did give myself one caution. I told myself that I need to understand what mediators actually do or don't do before anything is fed to the public. According to Adam, there are some pretty important differences—differences that some mediators fight over.

As I exited the plane, I saw the lady with the cat. She looked tired and disheveled. The stress of sitting next to a spiteful passenger who hated her, and her cat had taken its toll.

CHAPTER FIVE

International Crisis

I finished the six-hour team building session and made a quick getaway from the corporate venue to the Denver airport with its circus tent silhouette. During the limo ride I was thinking how I would respond to Gio when he asked me, as he always does, whether he is interested or not, "How did it go?" The answer in this case had to be that it was tough but in a way that was different from prior team sessions I conducted.

From the first discussions in the morning the prevailing sentiment was that the day would be a waste of time because there was consensus that the issues were with the manager and the manager chose not to attend the session. Because I had a sense of this before going in, I began to feel guilty. Were these people seeing me as just another fleecing consultant who would waste their time on a Friday afternoon? I desperately wanted to avoid that perception. So, I immediately turned the agenda in a multi-pronged direction that I hoped they would find useful. I put these questions on flip charts in the room: What are the issues with Elliot Susskind, our manager? Are the issues addressable? What are the risks? How best could the group—or separate individuals—raise and address the concerns? What is the strategic approach needed to be successful?

As it turns out, these questions worked well, and they took

five hours of discussion for the group to answer. The session was seen as productive and, by the end of the day, the employees thought it was good that their manager, Elliot Susskind, did not attend because it gave them a chance to clarify what the issues were and how best to address them. According to the group, he oversold their IT services to internal clients, misrepresented budgets, pointed fingers at undeserved employees in corporate forums, and played favorites repeatedly.

One of the participants suggested that I offer to act as Susskind's executive coach, a role I have taken on with other senior leaders in various organizations. In this case, I could use a condensed summary of the comments I heard in the team session as a basis for providing feedback in the coaching assignment. The feedback could be compiled anonymously as a protective move. The group all agreed with this possible coaching endeavor and encouraged me to contact the HR representative, Bridgette Foy, to see what was possible. The group doubted whether Susskind would be willing to participate in the coaching process. He would see it as a sign of weakness.

In retrospect the fact that Susskind had told me he did not want to participate in the team session at all was a sign that he was part of the problem. But he was sponsoring the event, so I had no choice. Or did I? In a way the decision to take on the assignment was an ethical dilemma. I could have pulled out of the gig—turned down the money—but then the employees would not have been able to prepare for the confrontation they wanted to have with him. So at least there was an upside to the consulting engagement.

On the flight home I was able to upgrade to first class with frequent flyer mileage. The trip was thankfully conflict free. Although I was tired and just wanted to rest, I ended up talking with the passenger next to me for a while. He was a thin, good-looking man somewhere in his forties with dark hair that was just starting to turn gray. He had deep-set, gray-black eyes and was somewhat tan. He wore an attractive white shirt that had navy blue lining inside the cuffs and neck. His clothing and carriage created the impression of being a sophisticated, well-educated European gentleman. I was somewhat glad that he started a conversation. His looks alone could hold my attention and keep me awake.

"What brought you to Denver?" he asked me as we taxied to the runway.

His voice was low and quite soft. Given his demeanor and style, I wondered whether he was, as we used to say in the seventies, a "friend of Dorothy's"—a not-so-subtle reference to not being in Kansas anymore.

"I was here on business, organizational consulting. And you?" I asked.

"I gave a lecture at the University of Colorado."

"What was your topic, if you don't mind me asking?"

"I am a professor of dentistry at U. Penn, endodontics. I came to excite an audience of dental students about the ins and outs of root canal complications," he said sardonically.

Based on his answer, I immediately understood why he was sitting in first class even though he seemed overly humble. He was probably world-renowned for some innovative dental preservation technique he created. As he spoke—without any recognizable accent—I looked down and noticed that he had no ring on his wedding finger. After several seconds of silence, I decided to pry a little, even though it meant furthering the conversation and delaying my needed rest. My curiosity about his sexual orientation had gotten the best of me.

"Does your spouse ever go on your trips with you? I asked flatly.

His face changed and he looked away slightly. "She used to travel with me. She passed away twenty months ago. Breast cancer."

"I am so sorry to hear that," I said. I was also sorry I pried. Specifying that it had been twenty months since his wife died, suggested that he was still grieving, counting time since losing her.

"Thank you. She was special. I loved her very much. It has been difficult to meet someone else, even though I know she can't ever be replaced. And you? Are you coupled?"

"Yes, for fifteen years. I can't imagine being out there looking for someone. I have a lot of friends who are single and looking. I know it is tough." I managed to successfully avoid coming out with my response—a rhetorical skill I have mastered over the many years. I can introduce myself to strangers and talk about my life, while not talking about my life openly. It takes skillful omissions of gender pronouns and other subtle linguistic choices. The danger is if you say too little, that is a dead giveaway as well. I was not afraid of coming out, but it always seems like an imposition on someone else when you are just starting a conversation.

"I can't take the bar scene or the dating websites," he said. "Too impersonal and awkward. First meetings with someone feel confrontive, not comforting. If you meet on a website the person never looks as good in person as they do in their posted photo. You have to get over the shock of seeing them as they are before you open your mouth to greet them. A tough task! But I am hoping to meet someone at the new production of *Les Mis* at the Academy of Music tomorrow night. I have my single seat ticket in the center box on the first balcony. I love theater, especially musicals."

I wasn't quite sure what to make of his plan to meet someone at the show. So, I said, "*Les Mis* is wonderful, and I hear this is an innovative production. Do you have a blind date at the Academy?"

"Possibly. I am never sure whether I have a date until I get to the theater," he said.

I became even more befuddled, so I inquired further. "Isn't

it difficult to meet someone at the theater?" I felt I was prying again but now he had sparked my curiosity. There was no stopping me at this point.

"Well, you have to narrow your chances down statistically. You can't take a seat just anywhere in the theater."

The confused but interested look on my face encouraged him to continue.

"You see, I check ticket sales and seat arrangements and I only purchase a single ticket next to a single seat that has already been sold. Sometimes I ask the ticket agent at the box office to check for the single seat purchases. Most of the agents are accommodating and none have ever asked why I was looking for this type of location in the theater. They probably surmise though."

"But how do you know it will be a woman who bought the single seat next to yours?" I asked.

"I don't know that until I arrive at the theater and take my seat. If it is a show I have seen many times before, I arrive late and stay until just after the intermission. If it is a man, I just watch the production and keep to myself. But it has been mostly women who buy the single seats and I have had a couple of follow-up dates that were wonderful, although the relationships did not last. I have to be careful, though, because I tend to fall in love way too fast and women sense that I still might be on the rebound. Or when I tell them my wife has passed away, they think I will never get over her. Sometimes I think I won't."

Although this dating approach had a tinge of stalking to it, I admired his creativity, and I was sure he could afford the ticket purchases. I just wondered how effective it could be. He seemed confident that it would lead to success. From what I have seen with friends who are on the mid-life dating scene, it is all about keeping hope alive no matter what the method they use or what the cost of the search is in time or money. If it is a needle in a haystack search, you've got to keep believing that the needle is there someplace. I could tell he was looking for encouragement.

"Well, I wish you the best of luck—if it is luck. You probably remember what Anna sang to the young lovers in *The King and I*. You hope that you meet someone by chance but in the end, destiny intervenes, and it isn't chance at all."

"I've always loved that romantic song. And the lyric is right. I believe destiny will take care of it. It seems like a long shot, but it actually isn't. There is an inevitability to it if you put yourself out there. I just want to be in a creative and beautiful place when it happens." He paused and then reached for his wallet in his back pants pocket. "It's been nice talking with you. Can I have your business card? It would be good to have it on hand. Organizational consulting is really needed at the research lab where I work."

Since we were both over forty, we still had business cards to exchange. Mine said:

Kent Foxe Ph.D.
Organizational Consulting, Executive Coaching,
and Mediation

His card read:

Daniel Simel D.M.D. Ph.D.
Professor of Dentistry, University of Pennsylvania

I put Daniel's card in my wallet. I waited a few minutes and then shut my overhead light off and leaned my chair back—classic "leave-taking" behaviors, as the nonverbal communication specialists would say. I fell asleep fast for the rest of the flight, lulled into dreamland by the comforting thought that I was lucky to have Gio in my life all these years.

I arrived home in the late afternoon. That night, over a dinner of pasta fagioli, Italian sausage and broccoli rabe, I filled in Gio about the girls' gang mediation and the dilemmas it posed for me. Gio always provided a grounded perspective on the mediations I conducted. After hearing about most of the case he focused on the violence and asked why the court was not taking this case on. He wondered why it had been referred to mediation. I said that the court was so over-loaded with cases like this—and violence was so common on the streets of Philadelphia—that the judges were desperate to have these cases off their dockets, especially those involving youth. Some hoped that mediation would teach the youth a lesson without inflicting overly tough or unenforceable punishments. Of course, this is built on misguided notion of mediation.

Gio felt I did the right thing by trying to find solutions that kept the girls separated even though these ideas may have been impractical. Sending a message to stay away from each other could not be a bad thing, he pointed out. He was somewhat unimpressed with the girls' commitment not to attack when their infants were with them. He felt I could have achieved more, especially with their mothers being there with the girls. "Why couldn't the mothers have come up with more solutions? It seemed like they did not try to work together very much to improve the situation," he observed. We soon left this discussion and moved on to more immediate topics of concern in our own life.

Gio had made the plans for Sunday. Bill and his partner Rosa were driving up to JFK airport to pick up Bill's ex-wife Brigid and his two children. Brigid never remarried and was in her late thirties. Linus was sixteen and Sarah was fourteen. Bill had not kept in close touch with any of them since he returned to the States. They had not seen their father in person since they were starting grade school. Even the Skype calls were few and far between. Perhaps because Bill did not have money to help support them. Gio knew they were feeling neglected by their father and that this trip, in their eyes, was one that would build closer ties with their American father and some of his relatives, especially Gio and me. We knew that these European in-laws felt ignored by most of their American relatives ever since Bill's mother passed away. Gio said he invited all five of them to our house for dinner after they return from the airport. He would make his Italian specialty, spaghetti with red gravy and crab legs. Getting everyone together seemed like a good idea. It would show that we cared about our Danish relatives and wanted to give them a warm family welcome.

Gio and I discussed what the teens needed to know about Bill. Given their ages and high expectations for the visit, this was a tough call. When I first met Bill, he had just returned from the army and his service tour in Europe. It was never clear whether he left the army early, completed his tour of duty, or was released dishonorably. I never asked Gio or other family members about this. I am not sure they knew. Anytime Bill saw me at his mother's home he would corner me to tell me about his research project. He knew I was an academic type so he assumed his historical investigations would interest me. They did—at first. He was intent upon finding secret bunkers in Germany that he said were used in the Second World War by the Nazis. These bunkers, he claimed, stored a line of German planes that few people had ever seen. He would go into great detail about the size and place of the bunkers and planes, including why they were not used in the Second World War, and why they would be so valuable to find now. He was convinced that he would receive a windfall if he found them. And he often talked about the money he needed to head back to Germany to further his quest.

For the first two or three conversations I took his interests seriously. I asked a lot of questions. Although his answers were not totally illogical, the overall picture he created made little sense. The whole thing seemed increasingly odd to me. But when I talked with Gio or other family members about it all they would say was something like, "That is just quirky

Bill."

Over time, the conversations with Bill became stranger, more far-fetched. He told me about his worries of being followed by the CIA. He said that the government somehow found out that he was hot on the trail of the valuable bunkers and wanted to put a stop to it. In one of these conversations, he told me that a large black limo was often outside his house monitoring his movements. It was then that I knew for sure that his research project stemmed from a deeper, unstable place in his psyche. This was a fabrication his mind needed to create.

Although undiagnosed, the evolution of his schizophrenia became more and more evident as he aged. As the years went by, he reported seeing characters coming out of the TV and having imaginary friends who helped him get through the day. He also became increasingly concerned about being followed by government officials because of what he knew about the buried airplanes. His paranoia grew and he seemed more and more withdrawn at times. Gio and I worried that his condition might eventually lead to worse behavior or total incapacity. But there were no clear signs of either, at least from the little we knew of his life.

Gio openly confronted Bill several times about his issues but he refused to seek help. Like many people with mental challenges, he did not think he was ill. His experiences were normal for him, and he was functioning daily, although at a minimum. He usually held menial jobs in the food industry like delivery man or dishwasher. Despite his innate intelligence, his issues kept him away from a more stable and supportive career. And he had a partner, Rosa.

Rosa was barely together herself. She was a recovering addict living on disability. She always looked disheveled and wore heavy, sweet-smelling cologne, probably to hide her body scent. She wore clothes that were much larger than needed to cover a disturbing bulge at her center. Strangers might assume she was pregnant. Both she and Bill constantly looked like they were in bad health and were struggling to keep their lives together. There was little question that they were losing their struggle. But realistically they were a tragic match for each other. Gio and I kept our distance for the most part. We knew we could not provide the kind of sustained help that each of them needed. We also knew that people who really want help will ask for it.

Although it would be difficult, Gio and I felt that we had to somehow explain Bill's condition to Linus and Sarah without sounding judgmental. It would help them understand why Bill was so distant over the years and how he might act while they were here visiting with him. Gio decided he would find a time to have this conversation with them soon after they arrived from Denmark. But for this visit, the problem centered on Rosa as much as Bill. And we had not prepared them for Rosa.

At our Sunday dinner with the Danish relatives, Rosa made a point—out of nowhere—of commenting about how great it was to live in America and that other countries could not measure up to us. She also declared her many grievances against "mooching" immigrants and open-door immigration policies. She said that people should stay where they were born and stop "diluting" the American population. She made these comments without looking at any of the European visitors sitting at the table. Instead, she focused on Gio and me. I think she somehow expected that we would support her views. As Rosa spoke, I could hear the upbeat voice of the character Anita in *West Side Story* singing the praises of Amer-ic-a as she fought with those who wanted to return to Puerto Rico. It was defiant pride with an exclusionary point.

It was obvious to the Danes that Rosa intended to slight them. Although they clearly heard her, they did not respond to her comments. Everyone just let the comments pass without a noticeable reaction but with considerable discomfort and embarrassment for Gio and me. All we could do was to keep changing the topic. The two teens were incredibly restrained throughout the dinner. We learned later that they had a foreshadowing of the dinner conversation on the way back from the airport. On the drive she had made similar insulting remarks about "foreigners who want to live among us." They sensed that there would be more trouble with her during their visit. After the dinner, the two teens did not attack Rosa but said that it was important that they have quality time alone with their father. They wanted to avoid her as much as possible. We agreed.

After Bill and Rosa left that evening, Gio and I had a conversation with Linus and Sarah about Bill's unstable mental state. They listened intently and said it confirmed their perceptions, although they felt it did not excuse his failure to stay in contact with them over the years. They wanted a father to love and to love them, regardless of his issues. Linus was concerned that this form of mental illness might be genetic and that he might be vulnerable as he aged. Gio said he did not know whether schizophrenia was genetically transmissible. I said it was doubtful because most cases start early in life, trying to offer him some reassurance even though I had a few doubts about my own claim. Linus was an exceptionally bright kid who seemed stable but somewhat introverted. It was hard to tell whether he might be predisposed toward Bill's issues. It was something I thought we should look into further at some point.

When he left our house after dinner, Bill said he would pick up his two children at ten a.m. tomorrow. Gio told him that it was important to Linus and Sarah that they had time just with him. Bill nodded but looked concerned and made no promise. It was hard to tell what he was thinking or feeling about the teens' request.

Bill drove up to our house right at ten a.m. Monday morning. Rosa was in the front seat of the car with him. The Danes could see her from our sunroom window. They both were upset. They did not walk out of the house and said they would not get in the car with her again. Gio and I walked out to the car and told Bill that the teens expected their father to be alone. Rosa immediately became defensive and indignant. We were the object of her anger.

"I have a dentist appointment this morning, so I had to come along," she insisted.

Gio thought quickly. He immediately offered to drive Rosa to her appointment in his car and wait for her outside the dentist's office. She adamantly refused Gio's offer, saying, "I want Bill with me. He's not just my driver. He's my boyfriend. He needs to be there with me."

"You are being unreasonable, Rosa," Gio responded. "Sarah and Linus only have today and tomorrow to have time to get together with Bill. Then they head to Washington and the Jersey Shore for sightseeing. Bill wants to drive them around the neighborhood where he grew up. That would be good for the teens to see. Please show some consideration for them."

It was clear to both Gio and me that the teens' wishes were of no concern to Rosa. She was incorrigible. She sat defiantly in the car shaking her head and complaining to Bill. Bill looked uncomfortable but remained quiet. Gio and I were at a loss. We went into the house and told Linus and Sarah that Rosa wanted to go with them. Sarah held back tears and Linus quietly looked away.

"I am not getting in the car again with her. She is vicious. You see that, Uncle Gio. Can we just try again later with him alone?" Sarah asked.

"Let me see what I can get Bill to do, I'll try again," Gio said.

Bill and Rosa had already driven away when Gio went back outside. Gio called Bill on the phone and told him again how important it was to his children that they had some time alone with him. Bill suggested that we meet on South Street—a funky area of the city with interesting shops, coffee bars, and restaurants. He wanted to show them around. "Let's meet this afternoon around two o'clock at the corner of Fifth Street and South," Bill said. Bill sounded sincere and we thought that Rosa would surely be done with her appointment by then.

Gio and I drove the two teens to Philadelphia and parked near the planned corner just before two o'clock. Brigid offered to stay home so that her son and daughter could have time with their father. The four of us waited near the corner as the scheduled meeting time went by. Finally, about two-thirty Bill showed up. He wasn't alone. Rosa was walking behind him pushing a baby stroller. She had her daughter's toddler—her granddaughter—with her. When Sarah saw Rosa with her father, Sarah lost it. She started screaming and waving her hands frantically in a release of violent energy that easily could have attracted local police. Rosa screamed back at Sarah. Both started swearing at each other. It looked like a fight was about to break out until Gio stepped in between them. People were gawking as they walked past the explosive scene. I worried that someone we knew would come by and see the violent debacle that was unfolding around us.

Rosa stepped around Gio and Sarah. She headed toward me as she continued her walk down the street. As she approached me, I said to her softly, "Just let the kids have time..."

Before I could finish, Rosa stepped forward and said, "Fuck you, you fag. Stay out of this—you're not part of this family. You have no right to question us."

I was stunned. The last time I was called fag was when I walked toward the entrance of a gay bar in Cleveland in my twenties. Hearing her say the word had a sobering, fearful effect on me immediately. The word was not just said but thrown at me with an intent to injure and repel. My response was totally self-protective. The shock only allowed me to avert my gaze and move out of the way. I could say nothing.

I wasn't sure whether Gio or Bill heard Rosa. Bill just stepped away from the whole scene without saying anything. He called Rosa to come with him. She scurried toward him, and they both left without saying anything to either Linus or Sarah. Bill was pushing the baby stroller as Rosa continued to swear loudly. Looking back at us she screamed, "Keep those fucking foreigners away from us, Gio. Do you hear me?"

I stood at the corner and suddenly realized what was going on. It was so clear that I wondered why I hadn't seen it earlier. Rosa was desperately clinging to Bill and lashing out at us because she feared she would lose him. She was afraid that Bill would rekindle his interest in Brigid by spending time with his Danish kids. She could not let that happen because, in a real sense, her life depended on him. And Bill could not defy Rosa by spending time with the kids alone because his life depended on her. It was an enveloped, collusive relationship that froze each of them in their place. The Danes were like the friends Nick and Honey in Albee's play, *Who's Afraid of Virginia Woolf?* Bill and Rosa's symbiotic relationship was being upended by the Danish intruders who were unveiling the weakness, the vulnerability, and the explosiveness of this tragic couple. They believed their precarious relationship might not survive the intrusion. And that terrified both of them.

When we got back in the car and left South Street, Sarah cried steadily in the backseat. She knew that there would be no chance to spend quality time with her father. She and Linus would have to come to terms with the reality of Bill as a man, and not just their own wishful image of him as their father. This was a cruel but inevitable realization for them. They could blame Rosa—as we all might—but deep down they and we knew it was their flesh and blood who walked away on that street corner in Philadelphia.

All Gio and I could say was that we were sorry and that they should remember that Bill has problems, as we headed to a nearby Thai restaurant for lunch. While we ate, we talked about what they might do for the next few days and avoided any mention of Bill or Rosa. Gio lightened the mood by talking about some positive highlights of the family history.

Later I told Gio what Rosa had called me, and I said that we may have to vow never to let Rosa in our house again. A tough line had been crossed. It would take a lot to move beyond her revealing behavior today. She showed a side of her that was tragically weak and dangerous.

"You are probably right," Gio said. "I feel badly for Bill. He seems trapped. He is going to miss out on the love of his family in order to hold on to Rosa. I think he feels the loss but does not know what to do about it. Rosa is here for him. The Danes are not. He has to survive day to day. But what is your professional opinion about this as a family conflict situation? Could this be mediated? Would someone like you even try to intervene in a situation like this?"

Gio's question sent me back to the girls' gang conflict and the questions with which I was wrestling. I reluctantly responded, "It feels unlikely because I can't see Rosa being willing to sit down to have an honest conversation with those two teens. She would just offend them further. It seems highly unlikely that she would talk about her underlying fears and jealousy. She is too weak. And I don't think Bill's kids would want to be anywhere near her, at least for now."

Another troubling doubt about mediation had now crossed my mind. Is mediation only for people who already want to cooperate? People who would deal with things successfully on their own anyway. Can people who are hurting, fearful, intolerant, hateful, or jealous even consider sitting down with the source of their disturbing emotions and speak to each other constructively? Would they only repeat the hurts in mediation that they each had inflicted on each other previously?

These questions then hit even closer to home. I became

uncomfortable when I thought about what I would do if someone asked me to sit across from Rosa in a mediation. What would have to happen for me to be willing to have a conversation with her? And if I wouldn't be willing, what does that say about my belief in mediation? Was I a doctor who wouldn't heed the advice of his own physician? I did know that if I was in a mediation with her, I would want the distinction between mediation and arbitration to be clear. The last thing I would want is a mediator to make judgments about what I needed to do to save the relationship. I would want to be able to decide whether I wanted to save the relationship or not.

In thinking about the conflict with Rosa, I realized, in a way I hadn't before, that we are asking a lot from people when we ask them to mediate their serious conflicts. Just walking into a mediation room is a huge step for most people to take.

CHAPTER SIX

The Observation

I woke up early the next morning, still somewhat shaken by the events of the prior day. Mostly I felt sadness for the two Danish teens. The stark reality of who their father now was had hit them like a debilitating illness. Gio was still sleeping but would be getting up soon to take the Danes for a tour of the family's history of houses. I poured a cup of Constant Comment tea and opened my email. There was a message from Adam. He offered a few reactions to my reflections on the teen mediation. Just in time, I thought. I was scheduled for a mediation with Karen, my co-mediator, Wednesday afternoon. I wondered whether he would reply directly to my confusion and questions or whether he would be more indirect by telling me another rich anecdote from his noteworthy professional life. To my surprise, he did neither.

Kent,

I read with interest your thoughts about the teen dispute you mediated last week.

A very challenging case! I was impressed with your thinking about the questions we had discussed. You wrestled with what the girls were able to do on their own and what your role was as mediator. I thought you were quite tough on yourself. You probably had a larger hand in helping the girls do what they could do than you realize. The girls found a way to go where they wanted to go. You did not block their path completely. You laid some groundwork for them to raise a key trust-building issue on their own. Although it seems small, it is highly significant. Small steps count in mediation. We can't expect people to turn away from months or years of deep-seated conflict in one short meeting. We need to have reasonable expectations.

I have a couple suggestions for you—tasks of sorts. When you have time, make a visit to the Manhattan Mediation Center. Tell the director, Thelma Wight, that you have been sent by me and would like to observe a mediation by one of their most relied-upon mediators. Then also ask Thelma to set up a meeting with Judge Edmund Boroughs, a family court judge who sends divorce and family cases to the Manhattan Center. See if you can find out from the Judge what his expectations and goals are for mediation.

I think you will find both of these tasks worthwhile. I will send an email to Thelma today to mention you will be contacting her soon. I know she will be more than happy to arrange your visit. I know this means a day trip to New York but I think it will be worthwhile for you. It will give you a sense of how things work outside of the Philadelphia program.

BTW, you don't have to stop mediating just because you are still working on your skill. In this human endeavor of conflict intervention, it is all about self-reflection and personal growth. Experience counts.

Let's talk soon.

My best to you and Gio,
Adam

I was curious why Adam wanted me to visit the mediation program in New York. He had mentioned that some of his students did internships there and that he has other ties with the director. Maybe he thinks this is an exemplary program, one he wanted me to study and model in Philadelphia. But he clearly did not say that to me in person or in his email. I am sure it will be a useful experience even though it is somewhat inconvenient. Getting around New York is never much fun, but fall is the best time to be there. The air is clear, you can feel the pending holiday mood, but the seasonal rush hasn't started yet. Maybe I could catch a Broadway musical while I am there. There have been rave reviews of the revival of Sondheim's *A Little Night Music*.

Later that day I called the Philadelphia Mediation Center and asked Anita to confirm the mediation on Wednesday at four p.m. Anita checked on it. "It was cancelled yesterday. One of the parties withdrew his participation," she said. She also said she would try to reschedule it and promised to get back to me. I wondered why she hadn't called me to let me know of the cancellation. It always feels like I am not a top priority of hers. She still may not be over my failure to reliably use the mediation feedback forms. Or perhaps I did not adequately apologize to her for the oversight after the teen mediation. Anita is a tough one to gauge. Her vision is narrow, and she can be naive, although her informal influence on the program is often larger than it should be. I keep telling myself that she is just doing her job as she sees it.

I then googled the Manhattan Mediation Center to get the phone number. I called and asked for Thelma Wight. Adam had already alerted her that I would be calling so she was quite receptive on the phone. She said that Wednesdays are the best days to observe mediations because all the judges are in session, and they refer many cases in the middle of the week. She wanted to know whether tomorrow was feasible. I hesitated for a moment, then said yes, that would work. When I asked about a possible meeting with Judge Boroughs, Thelma said she would try to set something up in the afternoon but couldn't promise at this point. She emphasized that the judges' schedules change constantly, and Boroughs was one of the busiest judges at the court. She asked how late I could stay. I said any slot up to six p.m. would work for me.

I was surprised at how accommodating Thelma was. It was almost as if she owed Adam something. She must have assumed that I am a student of his. And, in a way, I am. A trainee and mentee but not a university student of his.

I knew that Gio would want me to go sightseeing in D.C. on Wednesday when he heard that my mediation was cancelled. He would be upset that I chose not to be with him and the Danes but since Thelma was being so receptive, I decided to take her up on her offer. I hoped that Gio and the Danes would understand. Gio knows my commitment to mediation, and this was an important opportunity Adam had opened for me. Better to grab the opportunity when it was available than to possibly miss out altogether down the road. Bureaucracies are notoriously fickle and can shut their doors to outsiders suddenly, especially when there is a change of program administrators. But from Gio's perspective, family commitments are always more important than work. It would be a tough sell.

When I told Gio about the meetings in New York he was clearly irritated. "You know how important it is for us to spend time with the Danes, especially after what happened with Bill and Rosa. They are only here for a few more days."

"I know, Gio, but this is something that Adam really wants me to do and the administrator was willing to get me in right away, I didn't want to lose the opportunity. Who knows when I would have the chance again?"

"Not a good excuse," Gio retorted. He walked away, clearly with attitude. It made me feel somewhat guilty, but I was resigned to stick with my plan.

On Wednesday morning I took the 8:10 a.m. Amtrak train to New York, then the southbound express subway to lower Manhattan. The Amtrak train was full but there is always much greater space and leg room than any airplane provides. People rush to take seats near the windows so they can plug their devices in the sockets along the wall. This is great for me because it means many aisle seats are available—a claustrophobe's prized location. The subway was another story entirely. The subway car was a shoulder-to-shoulder, standing room only squeeze, like being in a packed elevator that is moving horizontally instead of vertically. While standing there I realized that if I sneezed, I would have sprayed at least five people around me. My claustrophobia almost got the best of me after three subway stops. I started to sweat, hyperventilate and look up at the ceiling to see beyond the shoulder of the man in front of me. In such situations, I've learned to distract myself. I closed my eyes and imagined that I was looking at the ocean on a white sand beach in Cape May—our favorite vacation shore point in south Jersey. This self-deception sort of works, at least for as long as I can keep my eyes closed without getting dizzy and nauseous. The proponents of visualization as a remedy for claustrophobia don't say much about the side-effects of their prescriptions. I was relieved to ascend the well-worn subway stairs and feel the cool fall breeze that was blowing steadily across Manhattan.

The Manhattan Mediation Center was on the third floor of the borough courthouse. The building had metal detectors and a substantial number of security guards who watched a steady flow of people enter and exit at the entrance on the first floor. The steady buzz of the passersby was distinctly New York. No other crowded city seems to feel the same. It has something to do with the pace of hustle I thought, standing just inside the revolving doors. People are more determined and quicker than they are in Philadelphia or Chicago. It made me think that Sondheim had captured the unique bustle of New York wonderfully in a song he titled Another Hundred People. In this city, people move in rushing, amorphous crowds through the wide sidewalks. It is impossible not to get swept along with the throngs. You know where you are going but the crowd around you seems to have control of how you get there. It is exhilarating.

When I got to the third floor of the courthouse, I could see that the mediation program occupied about half of the space on this level. The wide room was fairly open but the dark paneling on the walls and the heavy tan curtains (or maybe dingy white) on the three windows gave the place an outdated and somewhat stodgy feel. I almost expected it to smell stale. Not a place you would want to spend a lot of time in, I thought. In addition to a large waiting and reception area, there were several offices with name plates on them and six small rooms that were designated by the signs on the doors as "Meeting Room #1" through "Meeting Room #6." I wondered why these meeting rooms were not labeled as mediation rooms. I concluded that this was probably a converted administrative space that was never fully converted. It was clear that the accommodations for mediations were not a top priority of the court. Mediation can easily be the poor stepsister of the judicial system. Adam had told me about court mediation programs in Florida where all of the mediations are conducted in the hallways outside the judge's chambers. At least there were private rooms for the mediators in this program.

I walked up to the reception desk and asked for Ms. Wight. The receptionist asked for my name and photo ID then directed me to a corner office. As I got to the office door, I saw a well-dressed, light-skinned African American woman in a black sweater with matching silver necklace, bracelet and rings. She was busy typing on a very outdated computer with a small screen that sat close to the middle of her stodgy dark walnut desk. At the doorway I interrupted her at her computer and said,

"Ms. Wight, Hello. I am Kent Foxe, I talked with you yesterday on the phone."

"Welcome, come in. Glad you could make it so soon. May I call you Kent?" she asked politely.

"Absolutely," I replied.

"You are a little older than you sounded on the phone," Thelma observed.

"How do you know Professor Adam Maurie?" she asked.

"I took his mediation training about a year ago and he has become sort of a mentor of mine. He thought it would be good for me to see how mediation works here. I mediate at the Philadelphia mediation program. We do mostly court-referred cases."

"How many cases have you mediated?" she asked.

"Only about twenty or so, most were co-mediated. We use a co-mediation model in the Philadelphia program."

"How well does that work?" she inquired.

"Well, it works fine when both mediators are on the same page. It takes some coordination though. It's also helpful when a mediation runs long, and fatigue sets in for the lead mediator. There's always someone then who can step in and take the lead. It can also help to provide gender balance when clients are men and women. Both feel supported."

"We use single mediators here. Frankly, it's cheaper. All our mediators are strong-willed so I am not sure that co-mediation would work anyway. Most want to be on center stage. I don't think our mediators would want to share the credit for their successful cases. They tend to see themselves as mini judges with less power than the real ones here.

"So, to get down to business," she continued, "there is a

family mediation that is scheduled to begin at eleven-thirty this morning. That would mean only a short wait for you. It would be a good case for you to observe. I need to ask both parties for their permission, but it should not be a problem. Most people are surprisingly unselfconscious when they get to mediation. We will tell them that you are a new mediator who is learning. This case has been assigned to one of our most experienced and successful mediators. He is very good. The judges count on him a lot to deal with their most difficult cases. I am certain it will be instructive for you."

"Thank you, that sounds great. I was wondering whether mediators who work at your Center are paid for their services, or do you count on volunteers?"

"For family cases, yes. They get paid. Seventy-five dollars a case but only if a settlement is reached and the case therefore does not go back to the judge. The parties split the fee. Trained volunteers do the small claims cases. This saves the judges a lot of time. They hate dealing with small claims disputes. One judge refers to them as "small potatoes" cases because they cannot involve amounts over five hundred dollars. These cases give the volunteers a lot of practice. Some go on to do the more difficult family cases—usually divorces—once they are trained properly and have the experience," she explained.

"Do you think it will be possible for me to talk with Judge Boroughs at some point today as well? I know you said that this can be tricky."

"You are in luck. I have set a meeting with Judge Boroughs at three p.m., if he doesn't have to cancel that is. Judges' schedules are chaotic. Boroughs is a big supporter of mediation, so he tries to accommodate my requests. And he always enjoys acting as a mentor. We'll just have to see how things are working out later this afternoon. I can talk to you about it after you finish the observation of the mediation."

"That's perfect. How long have you worked with the judge?" I inquired.

"We've been developing and managing the mediation program together for about fifteen years."

"Wow, I didn't think mediation had been attached to the courts for that long."

"It seems like a lifetime, actually," Thelma said somewhat sarcastically.

"It's a lot of work, I am sure. Do you also mediate for the program, Thelma?" I asked.

"I have taken the training, so I understand the five-step process and I help to evaluate our mediators, but I do not mediate. I don't think I am cut out for it either. People irritate me too much, especially when they are embroiled in a nasty fight with each other and won't budge. I just want to tell them to shut up and figure it out. My job is enough out here—I put the frying pan on the stove and let others jump into it." Thelma seemed amused at her own figure of speech; one I could tell she had used before in describing her role.

I waited in Thelma's office and at 11:20 a tall slender man, probably in his late fifties, came to the office door. He had on a blue and white plaid bow tie, a white shirt and a well-worn gray herringbone suit. He took off a small black beret as he stepped through the doorway and greeted Thelma.

"Hello Thelma, how are you today? You're looking lovely as usual," he said.

"I'm fine and you look your usual dapper self as well. Looks like you have a jaunty new cap." Thelma replied.

"Yes, it is a gift from an admirer of mine who recently went to Paris."

"Is this someone significant I should know about?" Thelma asked playfully.

He raised his eyebrows and replied, "Not quite yet."

They seemed to enjoy the mutual compliments and light banter with each other, even if it clearly was perfunctory and a little overdone. Compliments often work even when they are not entirely sincere.

"I hope you are well rested. We have two family cases for you today. Hope they are not too tough for you," she said with a knowing smile. "And Thomas, we have a guest visiting today. This gentleman is Kent Foxe," she said as she nodded toward me. "He is a mediator from Philadelphia. He will be observing your first mediation this morning. He is looking forward to it."

Looking at me, Thelma continued the introductions. "Kent, this is Thomas Binder, the mediator you will get to observe today. He has done a lot of good work here for us at the Center. You're lucky he has been assigned a case today. I am sure you will enjoy the experience."

I stood up to reach for the outstretched hand before me. As soon as our palms met, the name struck me like a blinding bright light in a pitch-black room. This had to be *the* Thomas Binder—the man Adam had to deal with when he spoke at the conference. The mediator the Conference Board had warned Adam about. The man whose hand was in mine was the reason he needed security with him at the event.

As I shook Binder's hand and looked at him, I felt stymied. How did this happen? Was it a set up by Adam or Thelma, or even Binder himself? I had no way of knowing how this got arranged or whether it was just coincidence. I was immediately grateful that Thelma did not tell Binder that I was connected to Adam Maurie. Perhaps Thelma held up the Adam relationship on purpose or she might have told him beforehand. I was left wondering whether Binder knew of my connection to Adam. It was a lot of uncertainty to deal with in the moment. Part of me wanted to end the event right there and part of me was desperately curious about how Binder would do his work. There really was no choice but to go through with the plan. I was just relieved that the handshake was over.

I decided that if the topic of Adam somehow came up with Binder, I would say that I did not know Adam well or at all. I would not want him to think I was a fervent disciple of Adam or anyone else for that matter. I was also not ready for the kind of confrontation Binder had with Adam at the conference. I was not confident that I could hold my own in a full-fledged argument with him. He already had formed his ideas about Adam's views on mediation and would use that to his advantage in any discussion with me.

Binder stepped backed into the office doorway and said we need to get to the mediation room before the two parties arrived. He then listed several instructions for me as we walked to Meeting Room 3. "I will show you where to sit in the room. I want you to catch everything that happens but not be intrusive in any way. Please do not take any notes. It may send the wrong message to the parties. They might think you are from the court. And we don't use co-mediation here so please do not comment or intervene during the process. I will handle the session throughout."

His bow tie was well suited to his condescending tone of voice. He was unnecessarily emphatic about what he wanted me to do and not do. His personal aura would assure anyone that he was self-consciously over-confident, if not the very personification of arrogance. There was an imperviousness about him that would have made me feel distinctly uncomfortable, even if I hadn't known about him through Adam's conference story. He seemed to have no awareness of how his comments made me feel. I decided to remain quiet and feign agreeableness. I tried to take him as offensively avuncular.

Meeting Room 3 was quite small. It had enough space for a six-foot diameter round table with four chairs around it and two additional chairs on one side of the room. There were no windows, just harsh overhead fluorescent lights. I took a seat away from the table but directly on the diameter so I could see the faces of the disputants and Binder during the session. I wanted to be unobtrusive but still able to pick up anything that transpired around the table. Binder did not comment on my choice of seat. Nor did I look at him for approval.

Right at eleven-thirty the clerk at the front desk escorted a man and a woman to the mediation room. Binder said hello to both of them and, without shaking hands with either of them, pointed to the chairs at the table. His tone was clearly one of polite indifference. He gave them his name and then, looking across the table at me, said that there would be an observer who was here in a learning capacity. "I believe you both gave your permission to have him here. Is that right?" he inquired. The man and woman both nodded in silent agreement.

Binder chose not to introduce me by name or give me the opportunity to introduce myself. I took this as a way of making sure I was invisible and would have no impact on the parties. Binder knew intuitively how to keep someone in their place. Looking mostly at the man he then started the mediation saying, "I know nothing about your case except that it was referred from family court and that it involves your divorce. I don't know whether either of you are familiar with mediation so let me say a few words about it before we begin." I noticed that he did not wait to find out whether they were familiar with mediation. If they had said yes, it probably would not have mattered. He knew where he wanted to go, regardless of what the parties felt they needed to know.

Binder proceeded to tell them that as the mediator he was here to help them reach a settlement and that he would do whatever he could to get them there. He added that "The judge who referred the case will be quite unhappy if you do not reach an agreement here in mediation this afternoon. I have done this work long enough that I have a good sense of how your judge handles divorce cases and the issues that need to be settled. So, you need to work things out here for your own good. I am neutral when it comes to any differences you may have but I will be looking out for anything that might make an agreement unfeasible or difficult to enact."

81

After this introduction, Binder laid down the ground rules for the process. These were handed to the parties—and me—on a half sheet of paper entitled: Thomas Binder's Ground Rules for Mediation:

I will decide who gets to speak, including who gets to speak first.

No interruptions. Speak one at a time.

While you are listening to the other person, take notes so you don't forget what you want to say.

Any foul or insulting language is prohibited at any point during the session.

I will ask many relevant questions to obtain the facts of the case. You are expected to give honest and complete answers to all questions.

You are required to keep your comments limited to those that advance the negotiation of a settlement. Mediation is always future focused.

If I see that the negotiations are not moving or the tone is getting too emotional, I will ask you to go to separate rooms and I will shuttle between the two of you to carry messages and proposals.

At the end of the session, I will write up the points of agreement reached and both of you will get to review them, as will your lawyers if you choose to do so.

I wondered if these were standard process rules for all mediations at this court. If they were standard, why would they be labeled as Binder's? I also noticed the use of "I" rather than the more generic "the mediator" in the wording of most of these ground rules. This sounded odd to me. It came across as over-personalized and autocratic. One thing was for sure. The overall message of these guidelines was totally consistent with Binder's persona. He wanted to emphasize that he was in control and that the only acceptable outcome was an agreement. I thought about what Thelma said about mediator payments. The mediator does not get paid unless a settlement is reached. Thomas had as much—or more—investment in producing an agreement as the parties themselves. The ground rules maximized an efficient path to an agreement so he would save time and not have to walk away from the session unpaid.

"Any questions?" Binder asked. Neither the woman nor the man raised any questions. I wondered whether they had paid any attention to all the rules that Binder had just read to them. I had the feeling they were overwhelmed by too many prescriptions that did not seem immediately relevant.

"I would like you to start, sir. Please give me your name and tell me what issues are outstanding between the two of you, issues that have not been settled or addressed completely at this point. Please try to be succinct."

The man was in mid-life, about forty or so. He had on a maroon cotton shirt and loose-fitting jeans. He had a somewhat concerned expression on his face that looked like a cross between confusion and fear. He spoke slowly with a slight quiver in his voice and only looked at Binder at the end of each of his sentences. He was clearly more comfortable looking away than at his wife. There was no hostility, just a sense that he was struggling to be comfortable with the process or maybe the divorce itself.

"I am James D'Antes. Diane and I were married for nine years. She wanted the divorce and I would like to know why she really wants it. I don't think she has been honest with me, mediator." He then turned to his wife and said pointedly, "What is going on with you? Can I get an honest explanation? Or are you going to play the same games here that you play at home? Don't I deserve better?"

Before the woman could respond, Binder deliberately interrupted. "You need to know that this is not going to be a therapy session, Mr. D'Antes. We cannot focus on what issues produced the divorce or who initiated it, only what you and your wife need to address to complete the divorcing process. To be specific, I am talking about topics that need to be addressed in the divorce settlement itself. This is what the judge expects you to do in this session under my supervision. As I said in my introduction a few minutes ago, mediation is future oriented. It is not about how you both got to this point in your relationship. I am not here to referee your fights about what has happened between the two of you. That is irrelevant."

With this forceful comment, Binder made clear he would set the agenda and approve the topics for discussion. Conversations about difficult emotional topics or past factors that might influence their decisions about the terms of settlement would be squelched. As I listened to the husband from the sidelines, it occurred to me that Mr. D'Antes might shape his views about the divorce agreement based on what he found out about his wife's desire for the divorce. Why she wanted the divorce mattered to him and might guide what he wanted out of the divorce. But clearly these types of topics were labeled out of bounds in Binder's mediations.

After Binder completed his stern admonishment, he waited for D'Antes to continue.

Mr. D'Antes looked confused. He had to regain his voice. "I guess we have to discuss what to do with the business—our business," D'Antes said apprehensively.

"What kind of business is it?" Binder asked.

"A small printing company," D'Antes replied.

"You own this business jointly with your wife?" Binder inquired.

"Yes, for over ten years." D'Antes answered.

"Okay, anything else that needs to be settled? Any children—custody issues?"

"No kids. We have already agreed to just sell the house and split the money."

"Thank you. That's helpful. You can say more in a while." Binder turned to the woman and said, "Now it's important to hear from you. What is your name?"

"Diane D'Antes. Please call me by my first name." Mrs. D'Antes, a woman in her forties, was well dressed in a navy-blue suit with a flowered silk scarf tied loosely around her neck. She came across as confident and careful but perhaps a little skeptical. I wondered whether she was concerned about the controlling mediation style that Binder was enacting. There was only one mediator, I thought, and the mediator is male. At the Philadelphia program, gender balance was one of the reasons for using co-mediation, especially in divorce cases. It is easy for a woman to feel underrepresented with only one male mediator, no less a domineering male like Binder. I thought about what Ms. Wight said about their mediators wanting to be on stage alone. Binder was definitely the main character of this divorce production.

"Sure, I am happy to call you by your first name, Diane. Please tell me what you think needs to be settled here today. Are the issues the ones that James just identified? Or are there others?" Binder asked.

"James is right. We've written up all of the issues around the house sale and savings accounts—we have no differences there." She took two sheets of paper out of her case and handed them to Binder. "There are no issues with any of this as you will see. We do need to address the family business. What are we going to do with it? Do we sell it? Do we let it continue and I buy James out? How would profits be divided if we move in that direction? This is where we hit a roadblock and it is obviously important for many reasons. We have not gotten through this issue."

"I noticed that you did not say that another option for the business is that James might buy you out of the company," Binder pointed out.

"That's right. It's not a realistic option for us. You can ask

James to confirm this but I'm sure he would agree. You see, I started the business and I run the business. James is limited. He can only work in a service capacity, repairing machines and making deliveries. He has very little education and could not handle the management of the business. It would not work."

"Is that right, James? Do you agree with what Diane is saying?" Binder asked rather pointedly.

"Yes, it is going to be tough for me to find other work if we sell the business. I am worried about that. Jobs are hard to find especially for me. Diane knows my limitations." James replied.

"So, you are saying the business should not be sold?" Binder clarified.

"I am not sure. It is a tough call," James said.

"It is important that each of you know your best interests. Diane, what do you think should be done with the business? Surely you must have a preference that meets your underlying interests."

"Well, I know that he is going to have trouble finding work given his lack of education and limited work experience. It would be best if I bought him out but let him continue to work for me on a salaried basis. Our marriage difficulties have not stemmed from work, and they have not impeded our performance in the separate roles and responsibilities we have taken on in the business. We stay out of each other's way and keep issues from home out of the company."

Diane's comments were delivered formally and objectively, almost as if she was a consultant stating the results of an organizational assessment of their business.

"I think that might work best. I have no concerns about working for her after the divorce. And it would help me out a lot," James said. There was no force or enthusiasm behind James's statement, just resignation to the reality he was facing at this critical juncture in his life.

Binder paused and then chose his words carefully. "So, I think you are heading down a dangerous path right now. This is a divorce we are negotiating. I am concerned that if James continues to work for you, Diane, it will be too risky. Several negative results are likely to happen. First, there is going to be what might be called a lingering psychological marriage between the two of you. It will prompt too many difficult conversations that could go on for years as part of the emotional after-shocks of the divorce. The entanglements will remain for both of you. Second, I believe that Mr. D'Antes needs to get on his own two feet. Working for you, Diane, will make him more dependent on you. From a reality testing point of view, this seems unworkable, not to mention highly destructive for James's own professional development. Few could imagine that any self-assured man could continue to work for his wife after a difficult divorce. I also could not let such an agreement go forward to the court because I doubt the judge will sign it. It is important that you rethink this."

After this harsh rebuke, Diane looked down at the table and fidgeted in her chair. James looked disconcerted. It was a hard message to hear, and I wondered (and worried) about how they would respond to Binder's flat rejection of their own favored proposal for what to do with the business. After about ten seconds of uncomfortable silence, James spoke.

"You must do a lot of cases like ours. I guess you have a point there. I can see that I will continue to be dependent on my ex-wife if I stay working for her. It could be difficult for me to find work, but maybe it will be easier than I think. This would mean that she will give me money for my fair share of the business, right?"

"Right, we would have to figure that out to both your satisfactions." Binder said.

Diane then reacted to Binder's assessment. "I really don't see us having problems at work and I think that James is underestimating the challenges he will face when he is unemployed." Turning to James, Diane said "Few managers would tolerate your absenteeism the way I have James. I understand your issues and know you are working on them. Most competent employers would take this sketchy record under consideration when they decide whether to hire you. But I can't stop you if you don't want to continue with your job. That's your choice. I just need to say that I have trouble seeing you standing on your own two feet. And I mean that sympathetically. The decision we make on this could set your path for life."

Binder responded. "I see that you still care about James and his livelihood, Diane, but you do not know what may be best for him. Maybe the reality of the divorce has not set in for you either. That may take some time."

James became somewhat defensive as he thought more about Binder's comments. "I know that I want self-respect as I walk away from this marriage. I don't want to be the weak one. Let's talk about the details of buying me out," James insisted.

And with James's comment, Binder ignored Diane's concerns and launched the discussion of how much the business was worth and how much James would get from the sale to Diane. Binder had his way with these clients. Diane indicated that it was a relatively small business with profits of 60 to 70 thousand per year.

I was amazed at how smoothly and easily Binder had controlled the outcome of this decision. And I worried about it. I kept thinking about the dangers he ignored or was willing to overlook. I had difficulty focusing on their discussions when the financial details were being settled. I kept wanting to rewind the conversation to the legitimate concerns the couple raised, and Binder ignored. But Binder's protective problem-solving approach to the issues would not allow for a reconsideration.

I thought that the 'what-ifs' in this agreement were significant and under-discussed throughout the session. What if James did not find work? What if he did find work and couldn't hold down the job? What if, without employment, he turned to drugs or alcohol? Something Diane might have been implying when she commented on his "issues." Would Binder be held responsible if this agreement didn't work out for James? I knew that the answer to that—Binder would not be held responsible at all. He could always say that the parties could have rejected his advice if they wanted to. Or that he was using the standard mediation technique of "reality testing" where the mediator tests the suggestions parties make against the reality of their possible success. It seemed to me that Diane was doing a better job of reality testing than Binder. Binder's reality testing was just an effective persuasion technique to align the parties' perceptions with his own protective prescriptions. There is power in the mediator role and using it to achieve agreements that you think will work, despite the parties' views, seemed highly dangerous to me.

Adam's two questions came back to me—Who are you when you mediate? What do you believe about the parties? — as Binder orchestrated the final details of the agreement between James and Diane. As the session came to a close after 30 quick minutes, Binder suggested that both people have their lawyers review the agreement before it was sent forward to the court for official approval. Neither James nor Diane said they wanted to do this because of the additional costs involved. James also said he didn't want his lawyer to question what he agreed to.

I hoped that Adam did not want to talk with me after the mediation. What would I say? Should I speak honestly about my concerns? Would Binder feel threatened by a view that smacks of Adam's critical perspective on mainstream media- tion? If I wasn't steeped in that alternative view, I would be applauding Binder for the good work he had done. I would be complimenting him on the efficient negotiation of the issues, negotiation that protected the parties from making a bad choice in Binder's view. Saying anything seemed difficult.

89

After Diane and James left, Binder and I stood up and glanced at each other. "I hope you enjoyed watching this case and that you learned a great deal from it."

"Yes," I said unenthusiastically. He paused for a few seconds expecting flattery then, when none was offered, he quickly continued, "Sorry, but I have no time right now. I need to talk with Thelma about the next case and grab a bite. Take care and hope to see you again." I could stop worrying about what to say to him about the mediation. He clearly did not want my feedback if it was going to be critical. A simple thank you was all he wanted and all I gave.

I followed Binder to Thelma's office to see if the meeting with the judge was still on. She said as far as she knew Judge Boroughs was available at three p.m. She instructed me to go to his office on the fifth floor about ten minutes before the appointment and it should work out fine. I left the building to get some air and lunch. I hoped that my path would not cross Binder's as I headed down the elevator and walked into the welcome buzz of the crowded New York street. I quickly became part of the next hundred people hurriedly wandering by.

What we do to protect our best interests

CHAPTER SEVEN

The Interview

After lunch I took the elevator to the judges' chambers on the fifth floor and gave my name to the receptionist at the front desk. She said, "Please have a seat here. You are a little early. Judge Boroughs should be with you in about ten minutes." I spent the time thinking about a range of questions I wanted to ask the judge. I also thought about Binder's mediation and his revolt against Adam's concerns about practice. The gulf between the two of them could not be larger. I wondered where Judge Boroughs stood on Binder's methods. Perhaps another area to explore with him in this interview, I thought.

After about 15 minutes the judge's clerk came over to me and asked if I was Mr. Foxe. He then showed me through the door to Boroughs' chambers and left me standing in the doorway. Before taking two steps inside and before anything else was said, the gray-bearded man behind a large cherry wood desk said to me: "Oh so you are the one who is making me stay late tonight." There was a lightheartedness to the way he made the comment—with a knowing twinkle in his eye—but it was enough to throw me off a little. I immediately realized that I would have to be somewhat on guard. He was one of those people who is comfortable teasing others they have never met before because their position of power allows it. Even though you feel invited to joke back, it is not always welcome. It's a risk to respond in kind.

I decided to play it safe. I just gave him my name and extended my hand. He didn't stand but did shake my hand and casually pointed to a small overstuffed gray love seat in front of his desk. His desk had almost no papers on it, just a large collection of shiny paper weights. There must have been 20 or 25 glass weights all of which were eye-catchingly beautiful. Some had brilliantly colored fish inside while others had various leaf, corral and jewel formations on or in them. It is the kind of collection that friends and relatives probably contributed to as gifts over the years. Even though they could not be missed, they seemed like an all too obvious topic to start talking about, so I chose not to comment on them. I felt it was a slight risk on my part not to compliment him on something he so proudly displayed. Was this a secret test he engineered to evaluate people he was meeting for the first time? Clearly, I was self-conscious about how to interact with his honor on his home turf. Probably best just to get on with the point of being there, I thought.

Hoping not to sound nervous, I immediately stated my purpose for the visit. "I am a fairly new mediator from Philadelphia and thought it would be helpful to get a judge's perspective on the goals and accomplishments of mediation in your courthouse." I felt like my throat needed to be cleared—a definite sign of inner tension. I managed to get to the end of the comment without interrupting myself.

"Are you planning on writing a paper or article on our program?" he asked.

"No, I'm not even planning on taking notes. This is only for my own development and curiosity." The judge seemed satisfied with my brief statement of purpose, so I continued. "I understand from Ms. Wight that you have been a supporter of mediation for almost fifteen years. That's quite an accomplishment for the courts."

"Yes, Thelma and I have been going at it for a long time. I was on the first alternative dispute resolution task force whose members established mediation programs in courthouses throughout the state. Only Florida got moving before New York. We designed our programs based on their work but with adjustments to fit our own needs and context. We had some legal restrictions that Florida did not have and with its huge retiree population they had access to a much larger professional volunteer pool. There are a lot of highly educated people with a lot of time on their hands in the Sunshine State."

"It sounds like you were a mediation pioneer way back when," I said.

"That's a good description actually. I had a lot of bruises from the covered wagon rides. It took a while to get other judges and the local Bar Association on board with the idea. Lots of resistance from the townspeople, so to speak. Lawyers were afraid that it might mean a huge loss of business for them. They believed that mediators would be handling cases that they would normally have negotiated on their own. This created a lot of animosity. When I went to any social function that the Bar sponsored, many of the prominent lawyers in New York would not even talk to me. There was a lot of initial hostility. I had to make some compromises at first. For instance, only having lawyers as mediators in our program. That was risky in retrospect but necessary at the time. We've gotten beyond that now although, to tell the truth, most of the family court mediators are still lawyers and that gives me a sense of comfort. And some lawyers in the area still think they are losing money because of mediation. So be it. You can't please everyone."

The judge then took out a brown paper sack which held a plastic zip lock bag with carrot and celery sticks in it. He handed me the plastic bag, but I declined the peculiar offer. His teasing continued. "You should really make these raw veggies part of your daily diet. Good for needed roughage in your system," he said as he put the bag down on his desk. I hadn't heard the word "roughage" since my mother was alive. He was clearly of a different generation.

I wanted to be sure he knew I did not want to waste his time, so I jumped in again with a focused question: "I'm interested in knowing what you see mediation contributing to the courts and its clients? Why do you work so hard to keep it up and running?"

"Because Thelma needs a job," he joked. "God knows what she would do if I dumped the program. It is as much her baby as mine. But beyond that I can answer you best by showing you what I have in the top drawer of my desk," he said. The judge then opened the drawer and pulled out a legal pad with about 15 names and slash counts next to each name. "These are what I call my mediators' batting averages. This page displays the number of cases given to each mediator along with his or her success rate. This is the way I can keep track of who is reliable and who isn't. It is a simple guide for deciding who gets assigned the mediation cases. No guess work or favoritism on my part this way."

I was tempted to say, "what a clever decision-making method" but chose instead to ask him the slightly less condescending question, "What constitutes success for you?"

He looked surprised that I asked him to define success. The furl in his brow and his open palm gesture said it should be obvious. "The rate at which agreements are reached of course. I don't refer cases to a mediator unless he or she maintains a ninety percent or higher average over the first five or six cases. The would-be mediators are not given a second chance either if they don't meet the standard the first time around."

"That's pretty steep, most baseball players hit under three hundred. You're expecting three times that—a nine hundred mediating average," I pointed out.

"Mediators who know what they are doing have no problem reaching the standard. Maybe because they know

94

how to hit the ninety mile an hour pitches thrown at them during heated mediation sessions. So, let me ask you, what would be the point in giving cases to mediators who can't reliably take the clients off my docket for good? It would be a double waste of time if the cases went to mediation and then came back to the courts. Getting an agreement ninety per cent of the time is fair and most mediators accept this as a reasonable criterion. Although they really don't have a choice. I set the standard and strongly recommend it to the other family court judges. I believe all five of us are using it now. You can check with Thelma about that."

"Do a high percentage of the mediators reach the standard? Is it more than half?" I asked.

"Oh no, relatively few make it. It is about twenty per cent of mediators who end up mediating over the long haul. Those who make it appreciate the policy because the case load is not spread too thin. They get more work this way."

"Do you know how the twenty per cent of the mediators who achieve this rate get there?" I asked.

"I'm not sure I know what you mean," he said. He seemed confused but not irritated by the question.

"I mean what process do the successful mediators use to reach their agreements? Their methods of achieving the high rate of success that you require," I clarified.

"It's not magic or based on some tricky methodology. I have only seen a few mediators mediate and I have not taken the full training myself, but I know one thing from being on the bench all these years. If you don't tell people what to do, nothing changes. Most people cannot make a good decision for themselves especially when they are in conflict with someone else. The emotion and fear blinds their judgment. You must be the sane one in the room that pushes for what is needed in each case. Otherwise, you end up with nothing."

He offered his prescriptive comments with slow, careful emphasis. He had clear views of what people in conflict are pable of and what mediators must do as a result. It was apparent by his tone of voice that he had offered this assessment of what works in mediation many times before, probably to the mediators themselves. The practice in this court was coming from the top.

"The authority and influence of the mediator is key to reaching settlements," he continued. "Some of the best mediators tell me they never allow a divorcing couple to sit in the same room. Too much emotional stuff going on to be face to face. This makes sense to me whatever the settlement issues are. People can't think clearly if they are looking someone in the eye who they believe is trying to take their kid away from them. Divorce is a battlefield on fire."

Boroughs then looked down at his collection of paper weights and carefully picked one of them up. He passed it over to me to look at closely. It had in it two miniature lime green dragons spewing bright orange and yellow flames from their mouths. "This was given to me by a senior mediator in our program. He found it on a trip to Croatia. He said this is what people become in conflict. He was right of course. And this says everything about how controlling mediators must be. You can't let a mediation session devolve into a fiery dragon match.

"Some of the mediators who are familiar with my thinking on family issues tell the parties that they know how I will handle the case if it comes back to court. And that I will not be happy if they do return to court. So, they say to the clients why not just agree to those terms here and now? At least that's an honest revelation on the mediator's part and it does make the parties stop and think about the sensible thing to do. And by the way, I am very irritated when the case heads back to me after the parties' failed attempt at mediation. Especially if they were sent to one of our experienced successful mediators—one of the strong ones. I know then when the case comes back to me that these people are trouble."

I thought the judge's comments about his reaction when a

case doesn't settle in mediation was telling. It brought back Binder's use of the 'here's-what-the-judge-will-do' strategy in the mediation I had observed earlier that day. I also thought about the advice Binder imposed on the divorcing couple who wanted to go in a different direction than the one he pushed them toward. It certainly was a 'tell-them-what-to-do' move. Clearly, this judge supports these strong-arm tactics and sees no risk in them for the parties. He also cares little about whether mediation is not that different from arbitration—something that is already confused in many people's minds like the stewardess on my flight to Denver. This was a reminder of the vow I made to correct that public's perception.

"What if a mediator does not know how you deal with cases or particular settlement issues?" I asked, hoping the question wasn't too confrontive.

"Then they are not likely to make a prediction to the clients of course. At least I don't think that they make that leap. Some of the issues around joint custody of children, for example, are quite obvious anyway. There are guidelines which all mediators have and that are easily applied to the case at hand. Parties need to accept the mediator's interpretation of how the guidelines fit their situation."

I was tempted to say "This sounds like arbitration or the work of a judge" but I managed to hold back. Instead, I asked, hopefully without a hint of indignation in my voice, "Is there anything a mediator should *not* do to get an agreement in your view? Are there any limits?"

The judge answered quickly and confidently, apparently not being in the least affronted by the question. "The one thing I don't approve of is when the mediator swears at the parties to calm them down or get them to a better place. As mad as I have gotten on the bench, I draw the line at vulgarity. We've had several complaints about this from mediation clients so Thelma has had a conversation with those mediators she suspects might go overboard. I understand that parties get wild in these cases, but decorum is important for the mediators as well as the parties. I sometimes look the other way on this one too if it is one of our strongest mediators who happens to lose self-control at some point. Chances are the fiery dragons took him or her over the edge."

"So, if I am hearing you right, mediation in this family court is about the efficiency of case management. Mediators are primarily a relief squad for judges," I said.

"As you can see from the raggy state of our physical accommodations, mediation has to be all about the court savings. We cannot hire enough judges to keep reasonable caseloads on our dockets. Mediations save the courts hundreds of hours each year. That to me is of enormous value to our citizenry. If it makes the parties feel good about themselves or each other, then all the better. But you can't really expect that, although it's usually economical for the parties as well. The parties know they save on lawyer fees if they work things out in mediation. I don't think I mentioned yet that I don't approve of having lawyers in the mediation rooms. They can be right outside the door or can be called any time if the parties need advice. But they usually get all the advice they need from the mediator. My best mediators know the issues as well as most lawyers, but they also understand the human element in conflict and don't become intransigent like most lawyers. After all, prolonging a divorce negotiation is in a lawyer's financial interest. Money, my friend, it's about the money."

The judge then stopped and took the light-hearted tone he began with. "I have a friend who recently got divorced from his wife after twenty-seven years of marriage. He said to me, judge, do you know why divorce is so expensive?" The judge paused for three seconds then said, "Because it's worth every penny!"

I chuckled a little, not so much at the joke but his presentation of it. It was easy to see he loved delivering the punch line of that quip and had done so many times. He enjoyed entertaining. And he had an ear for comic timing.

The judge's characterization of mediation made me think of the song Joel Grey sang in Cabaret "Money makes the world go around." Money certainly has spun mediation into prominence in this courthouse. I also wondered whether this judge would have concerns that lawyer mediators can face charges of dual representation if they give legal advice that is directed at both clients. I remembered Adam emphasizing that lawyers can only represent one side of a case. I chose not to ask the honorable judge about this—or to hum the Cabaret song to him, even though I was tempted to do both.

The Judge then asked me, "Have you observed any of our mediators?"

"Yes. Just one, today actually. Thomas Binder."

"Great. What did you think?" the judge asked enthusiastically as he leaned over the desk toward me.

The judge seemed uninterested in getting a sincere response to his question.

But I still felt that I had to be careful and assume that the expectation was to be only positive about what I saw in the mediation room today. I didn't want to miss the mark. "Well, he certainly kept control of the parties. And he didn't swear at them," I said with as neutral a tone of voice I could produce. It was clear that the judge heard no irony in my response.

"I bet he reached an agreement too. He is a strong mediator who often handles our toughest cases. We can count on him. No problem with his batting average. He often tells me there is no one way to do mediation, you just do what is needed as things unfold. He sets no limits on himself. I sense that he wants to be a leader in the mediation field. I can see that happening."

I decided to take a measured risk. I asked, "Do you know Adam Maurie?"

"Never met him. I know he's written a book about mediation, but I haven't read it. Binder told me it should be burned, so I haven't jumped at reading it."

"I guess that's better than not stirring any reaction at all," I responded, trying hard not to sound defensive.

"Maybe, but some things are not worth wasting paper or time over."

Probably because of his ingrained judges' role, it is clear he would have the last word on any topic under discussion with anyone, whether he was knowledgeable on the topic or was relying on hearsay evidence. I decided to go no further into the discussion of Adam or the book.

At this point, I felt restless, almost agitated. I stood up slowly and said that I didn't want to take any more of his time. I thanked him for his helpful insights, shook his hand and began moving toward the door. As if to prove my point about getting the last word, he said, "Let me know if you want to mediate any cases for us. We are short-handed one mediator." He laughed a little and added, "That is, if you think you can meet our high standards."

As I kept walking slowly toward the door, I thought about saying, "Who says I would *want* to meet your standards?" But thankfully I realized I was already beyond ear shot and did not respond to his question at all. He probably assumed that I did not hear his invitation.

On the way out of the mediation center I stopped to thank Thelma. She said she was glad that both the mediation and the meeting with the judge worked out today. She then added, "I hear it was an impressive mediation and that you learned a lot from observing it." Binder had obviously talked with her about the case, and he presumed I could see how great he was. The judge's selection method for mediators leaves plenty of room for mediator hubris in his pool of mediators. He fit the judge's bill perfectly.

"It certainly did have a lot of opportunities to learn," I said avoiding an ironic tone that could easily have slipped out.

"Great. Then it was worth the trip from Philadelphia," she

asserted.

Thelma then asked what time my train headed back to Philly, and she offered a meeting room if I wanted to use it until I had to leave. I thanked her for the offer and said that I needed to head to the train station. I might be able to exchange the ticket for an earlier train. Or, I thought, get a last-minute ticket to see Sondheim's *A Little Night Music*.

I felt a real sense of relief as I left the courthouse and walked several blocks to the express train subway stop headed to Penn Station. It was the relief that comes from not having to act as if I was someone other than myself, like stepping out of a character's role in a long play. I now realized how much I was holding back. I had fretted over the lines I was expected to say as I observed the mediation and talked with Binder and Boroughs. I started to question whether I had held back too much, edited out too many of my thoughts about what I saw and heard. I decided it was necessary and appropriate because, in the end, I was a guest visiting their mediation home. They were the hosts, and they were very proud of their work. Speaking up more could easily have been perceived as impertinent or ungrateful. But I had a lingering sense that I was being deceptive by what I said and what I didn't say during the day. This doubt stayed with me, as I waited for the subway. Was I just reaching for a rationalization for my own cowardice?

I decided I was too tired to spend a small fortune on a Broadway show ticket, even though it meant missing Angela Lansbury playing the wise and cynical Madame Armfeldt. On the train home, between short naps, I had time to think about what the experiences of the day had taught me. There was no question that both the mediation and the information from the judge were highly instructive. Adam was right that the trip would be worthwhile, but I was not sure whether he wanted me to learn what I actually did learn. And the experiences surely raised a lot more questions about the value and uniqueness of mediation. Adam was up against a whole court system, not just single practitioners like Binder.

When I got home, Gio and the Danes had just returned from their trip to Washington. The teens said they had a great time with Uncle Gio and were impressed by all the huge white monuments on the national mall. They all looked tired but seemed quite happy and up-beat. Gio is the social animal in our relationship, so I was certain he kept them entertained all day. He loves having guests around and family always receive special treatment. It was enjoyable enough for him that I could tell he had forgiven me for opting out. At least that is what I wanted to think.

I asked Linus what he thought of D.C. "Impressive. But I must say, Denmark is much more modest in congratulating itself and its historical leaders," Linus said with a twinge of Scandinavian sarcasm.

"Linus, you are right," I said. "Modesty is never seen as an American virtue, especially by most Europeans. Americans always overstate their successes and minimize their historical failures. Confederate soldiers are still seen and revered by many as heroes so that we can say no side lost the Civil War."

I sat and talked with Gio and the Danes for two hours to make up for the time I lost with them that day. I enjoyed their company and thought about how things might be different if they lived here, rather than in Denmark. They needed the connection with their father's side of the family, and we could easily offer that to them. But leaving Denmark was not an option, especially with their father's state in life. This is why Gio and I knew that their infrequent visits were so important.

CHAPTER EIGHT

Everything is Beautiful in the Ballroom

I woke up early the next morning. When I entered the kitchen to make tea, I was surprised to see that Sarah was already awake and sitting in the breakfast nook. I asked how well she slept. She responded with an unenthusiastic, "Okay." She looked sad. I could tell that the debacle with her father was still hitting her hard.

"I know how disappointed you are with your father," I said. "Maybe you could call him at some point today. Uncle Gio or I could make the call to be sure that he answered and not Rosa. Does that sound like a good idea, or do you want to leave it alone?"

Sarah hesitated for a few seconds and then seemed to perk up. "Yes, that might help. I want to express my feelings and disappointment to him. He's should hear me out. Although this trip has been tough, it is great to know that you and Uncle Gio are here for us. You are our only caring and sane American relatives. My father may just have too many issues going on in his life. I'm starting to get that now. I am so grateful that you and my uncle are here to help me through this."

"We love you and your family very much, Sarah, and we need to find ways to get together more often," I said warmly. "Gio and I want to make a trip to Aalborg to visit. It would be wonderful to have you show us around Denmark. I've been to Copenhagen once and loved it, although I almost got run over by bikes several times. Once in front of Tivoli Gardens."

Sarah laughed. "That would be fantastic. Let's plan your trip soon. There are a lot of wonderful places in Denmark both of you would enjoy. We are not far from the northernmost tip of the country and the beautiful seaside town of Skagen. The view of the North Sea is spectacular there. You would love it."

"It sounds fantastic. Let's get Gio pinned down on some dates before you head back," I said. "Gio sometimes complains that I travel too much alone for work. This would be a great trip for us together. It would combine sightseeing with a family visit, what could be better?"

"I was thinking about you and Uncle Gio this morning and was wondering how you met. I heard it was tied to Gio's ballroom dance teaching, but I don't know the details. It would be nice to hear about it. Would you talk about it?"

"Sure. I am happy to tell you some of the story. I knew from an early age that I could dance. Both of my parents were good partner dancers and my mother danced with her brother in movie theaters when she was a child, as my grandmother played the piano for them. Like most artistic talent, the ability to dance is simply a gift, sometimes a genetic disposition.

"But while I was growing up, dance was not seen as a male sport by any stretch of the imagination. And taking lessons was just not an option for a working-class boy. Too sissified. Athletic boys did not dance, they played baseball. I tried that sport because my father played it but was afraid of the hard ball. I found myself wishing it was never hit to me. And I hated coming up to bat—so much pressure and the chance to be hit in the head."

"So what made you finally start dancing?" Sarah asked.

"This is where Gio comes in. Entering the bizarre world of ballroom dancing came from dealing with deep grief. Before Gio, I was dating someone for a couple of years who died of

AIDS. It was devastating to watch a talented thirty-year-old wither away from the dreaded cancer, Kaposi's Sarcoma. He was a concert pianist who started taking lessons when he was eighteen and played in the Tchaikovsky competition when he was twenty-three. We traveled a lot together during his final two years but the scars on his face were a dead giveaway that he had the "gay cancer." When we traveled internationally, we were always worried that we would be stopped at a country's border. Not much was known in those early years about how the disease spread, so the fears were somewhat understandable. But we were never stopped—even on a trip to Saint Petersburg before the Soviet Union fell. I felt very lucky to know him, but his death has never left me. I guess that's a good thing.

"When he died, I needed something to reverse the downward slide I was on. I was new to Philadelphia without many friends of my own and his friends pulled quickly away after his death. For many their pain was too great to stay connected with me. That took me a while to understand and accept but I got it eventually."

"Did you try going for therapy?" Sarah asked.

"I thought a lot about doing talk therapy, but I knew myself too well. Deeper self-reflection would just paralyze me. There were too many days when I watched myself tie my shoes rather than just tie them. More introspection was not what I needed. There was plenty of painful reflection during the two years of watching my friend's body disintegrate in front of me."

"How sad. That must have been really tough. I guess therapy is not for everyone," Sarah said. She paused for a few seconds, and I could see she may have made the observation for herself.

"More than anything, I needed to get out of my head. I knew things were getting bad when I started standing in front of a mirror for long periods of time in a somewhat desperate effort to get out of my own thoughts—to see myself from the outside. It was odd, but strangely helpful on the bleakest days."

"I decided that it was time to start taking ballroom dance lessons. I immediately liked the left-brain challenge of it, the music, and the push it gave me to be around new people. It helped me overcome my introverted, melancholic side which came from my father's Eastern European ancestry. When I walked in the dance studio, there was Gio. He was my instructor in a beginning group class. I started learning the foxtrot."

"Did each of you know immediately that you both were gay? How does that work? I've always wondered about how gay people hook up after meeting someone," Sarah inquired.

"We both sensed it and soon went out for dinner where we came out to each other. This was a hard time for Gio because his sister, your grandmother, had been diagnosed with stage four cancer. We talked a lot about her illness and what it was doing to the family. It was an emotional time. Very tough on the whole family."

"I must have been about three at that time. I barely remember my grandmother," Sarah said. "So how much dancing did you do?"

"So, true to my more introverted side, I was drawn to the classic standard dances. These are the tuxedo and ball gown dances: waltz, fox trot, Viennese waltz, tango, and quick step. These dances were appealing to me and difficult to do well. They require two people to move smoothly as one, sharing a common balance point and trying to achieve the elusive sense of flight that the best teachers try to elicit from their students. When these dances are done effortlessly, it makes anyone watching believe they are at Cinderella's ball."

"Right, that is what I have seen on the TV dance shows from England. It's beautiful," Sarah said.

"It looks effortless but is very difficult. The studio I was in had a history of entering its students in competitions and I soon succumbed to the temptation. The achiever in me wanted to take dancesport, as it came to be called in the nineties, more seriously. This meant facing the well-known and feared challenge of partnering."

"Partnering must be difficult when you are gay," Sarah said. "I'm sure you couldn't dance with Gio in these competitions and women dancers probably have fewer partner options."

"Right. Partnering is more challenging than dancing sometimes. I have seen ballroom dancers stomp off the floor, brutally swearing at their partner because they missed a step. Fights during lessons are common and many successful partnerships dissolve at a moment's notice after a volatile clash while taking a lesson from a top-notch coach. One professional dancer was actually indicted for assaulting his partner during a practice session."

Sarah's eyes widened and she made a "whew" sound as she heard about the partnering violence. "Sounds like dancing is a contact sport."

"Amateurs put a lot on the line when they walk out in front of an audience, as well as a half-dozen judges standing on the edges of a ballroom floor scrutinizing your footwork and everything else about you. The pressure amateurs—and professionals—put on themselves is often enormous. One nervous dancer told me that just before she stepped on the ballroom floor to compete, she always thought, 'This is the point where I wish someone would just shoot me.'"

"When I've seen the ballroom dance shows that come on TV from England, I've wondered how the judging works. Is it like ice skating?" Sarah asked.

"Much of the judging at dance competitions is unfair. There are layers of politics that impact a lot of what happens. Placement is often influenced by whether you take lessons from the right teachers and whether you spend two hundred dollars per hour for coaching from top teachers who end up judging the competitions. It is very subjective."

I could see Sarah was deeply interested. She asked, "How many partners did you have when you were competing?"

"Three. I danced as a beginning competitor with a nice woman who was primarily interested in finding a romantic relationship because she hated her husband. Unfortunately, she became pregnant by him when we just started to compete. The pregnancy ended our dance partnership and her marriage.

"My second partner was Alicia, a tall Polish immigrant. She was talented in a clearly athletic way and she was as competitive as they come. Alicia treated ballroom competitions like they were the next major battle that her people had to fight in Europe. Her desire to make it in the U.S. was obvious with every step she took on the dance floor. She once lost her shoe during a dance. As she stumbled in her white sequenced gown, she hung on me for dear life and took me down to the hardwood floor with her."

Sarah laughed at the image of this elegant accident. "It sounds like this partnership did not work out either."

"Right. Then there was partner number three—Jane. Jane was dancing on the pro-am circuit. Jane focused more on Latin dances with her professional instruction, but I knew she was also working on the standard dances. She was not at my level, but I knew she was a potential good partner because she was deeply invested in her dancing. She was a professional woman who had the time and money for the coaching and competitions. I also had heard she had gone through a recent divorce after failing to get pregnant. Dancing seemed to be her new love. The ballroom world attracts many who are in some sort of pain—me included.

"When I asked Jane to compete with me, she seemed surprised. It could have been that she felt she was not at my level in the standard dances. But I soon learned that she was surprised that I was willing to ask an African American woman to dance with her. Jane, I learned over the three years we danced together, felt that her dancing career was inherently limited because of her skin color. There were clear but subtle signs of this throughout our partnership. I could see the reactions she had when a pro-am standard dancer she knew was asked by her professional partner to turn pro and dance with him. After congratulating the woman at her professional debut Jane said resentfully, 'That will never happen to me. Only blondes make it in standard dancing.' It was a clear and pointed comment about the color ceiling she felt she was hitting in the dance world."

"This sounds like a particularly American thing," Sarah observed.

"Yes, because Jane's concerns were deep-seated on and off the dance floor. During a break at a national competition in Saint Paul Minnesota, we went to restaurant near the competition hall. The waiter seated us about two-thirds of the way into the restaurant. Shortly after sitting down, Jane got up and said she was going to the restroom. A few minutes later the waiter came over and said to me, 'The lady you are with has asked that I move you both to a table up near the very front of the restaurant.' Without saying anything, I moved. When Jane came back to the table, I had an inquisitive look on my face. All Jane said was, 'It is a family thing.' There was deep-rooted pain just below the surface all the time.

"At first Jane and I took lessons from her Russian professional instructor, Virov. She was paying for most of his weekly salary as a pro-am dancer, so it seemed as if there was an obligation to continue supporting him. I didn't want to alienate him or suggest that she give up her pro-am dancing. I approached him and his coaching with an open but cautious mind. Virov was a talented dancer and had the potential to be a decent instructor. But he had a fatal flaw. He was an alcoholic. Like the ripple effects substance abusers have on families, his addiction put an early, inevitable strain on our newly formed amateur partnership."

"So ballroom instructors are in pain as well as the students," Sarah observed.

"Yes. Virov sometimes wouldn't show up for scheduled lessons. When he did show up, most of time he was irritable. Sometimes he was angry and outright abusive. There was slight physical taunting—little shoves and pushes in demonstrating difficult steps. Most of this was directed at Jane. During these lessons he would slap our rears when he wanted greater movement or height on a turn, all I could think of was the absurdist play by Ionesco. Each dance lesson had that kind of submerged violent edge to it."

"Was Jane upset by this? Why didn't she quit and move to another instructor?" Sarah wondered.

"That's what was interesting. Jane was generally unbothered by any of this. She never reacted negatively to anything Virov did in our lessons. I thought this was definitely odd. But then I did have some context in which to interpret it. This petite, pleasant woman told me that she loved watching boxing and bullfighting. I never had a friend who liked either of these sports. It made me wonder where Jane's attraction to these sports came from and what it had to do with her response to Virov.

"She must have seen an element of dance or beauty in both boxing and bullfighting—probably the quick footwork, poise, and controlled posture the athletes need in each of these sports. There's also the intense palpable connection between boxers in the ring and between the bull and matador. My guess was that she somehow saw an underlying brutal dimension to dance and dance lessons that paralleled the violent edge of the boxing and bullfighting. It was definitely odd. When it came to Virov, she simply accepted the unorthodox rules he set for our lessons. I suspected she had been involved with him off the dance floor."

"For a while I convinced myself that Virov's lessons were

the kind of ballroom boot camp I needed to develop the competitive edge that I never had in sports like baseball. But after about a year, I had enough. I told her that I could not go on with lessons from Virov. I said that it felt too much like an enabling, abusive relationship and that she was getting the brunt end of it. I was happy to step out if she wanted to continue taking lessons from him. Or we could move on together with a new dance instructor.

"Turns out Jane already had her eye on a hot new Italian professional—Gianni—who was now teaching and dancing in New York. She apparently had once tried to take pro-am lessons with him. The good news was Gianni was an excellent instructor. We began making weekly trips to New York for what turned out to be terrific instruction."

I was going to stop with the story there, but after several moments, Sarah asked another question. "How did you do in the competitions? Gio mentioned you did quite well."

"We progressed fast. We won the over thirty-year-old pre-championship level at our first national competition. We then moved up to the championship level and kept moving up the ladder."

"Why did it end? Did you just stop competing or was there some particular reason? Did one of you have an injury?" Sarah inquired.

"Well, we finished a small competition in Stamford Connecticut. We both felt great because it was the best we ever felt on the dance floor. But I knew something was wrong. There were some strange disappearing acts at the event."

"Jane hid from me for about ten minutes or so when we got off the Amtrak train from Philadelphia. She left from a different train door, and when I turned around on the platform to help her with her luggage, she was nowhere to be seen. Eventually she came down an escalator and walked up to me as I was just about to begin searching for her. She said nothing and I didn't ask about her disappearance as we stepped into a waiting taxi.

"The second disappearance was in the ballroom right before we were scheduled to dance. When we were next in line to walk on the dance floor to compete, she was again nowhere in sight. This was out of sync with our pre-competition routine. We usually met a half hour before our event. I would zip the back of her dress; we would warm up in a hallway and practice dance holds and opening steps. We would then stretch and line up awaiting our event. None of this happened this time around.

"The emcee was just announcing our heat number and couples were lining up to dance when she walked up to me, took my hand, and never made eye contact. We quickly walked to the corner of the floor to do our first natural turn in waltz. There was no time to comment on the weirdness.

"When we left the hotel and were in the taxi heading to the Amtrak station, Jane was quiet. When we got into the station and were waiting for the train, she looked at me and said with a clinical sense of detachment: "There is no easy way to say this. I am not going to dance amateur any more with you. We had a good run but I'm getting disappointed that we were not moving ahead faster. And I can see that pro-am dancing is where it's at.

"This was an announcement, not an opening for discussion. She was firing me the way she told me she had fired people who worked for her. We had several upcoming competitions scheduled with paid airline tickets and competition registrations. She withdrew from them all."

"She left you hanging there even though you had given her a great chance to dance," Sarah said sympathetically.

"As much as I thought that this should not bother me, it did. The jolt I felt had everything to do with her way of approaching this decision. It felt completely selfish and dismissive. I was someone who she needed to advance her dancing career and when it didn't serve any longer, it was over for her."

"What did you do? Did you look for another partner?" Sarah asked.

"I never competed again after the event in Stamford, and I quit dancing altogether a few months later. I also admitted to myself that I had taken this sport as far as it could go.

Sarah, still listening intently, asked, "So how do you feel about it all now?"

"The way our partnership ended left a tainted memory of an exciting few years in the middle of my life."

Sarah looked away pensively. It seemed as if she was thinking about herself again. She said, "It's tough but relationships don't always give us what we deserve or expect. My father can't give me and my brother what we need from him. I guess it just takes a while to accept where things are—like you sort of did with Jane."

"Your relationship with your father is much more important than my dance partnership. It does help to realize that our expectations are not always met. Relationships often end painfully for a lot of different reasons." Sarah sat quietly. I could see her eyes filling with tears.

Gio came into the kitchen and started to make coffee. I greeted him with a warm hug and told him that Sarah wanted to call her father sometime before she left. He said sure and began talking to her about what he had planned for the day.

As I got ready to leave, I hoped that the dance story helped Sarah move a little further beyond the painful jolt she felt from her father on this visit. She would need time to gain perspective on his limitations and the deep hurt he caused her. Regardless of its other effects, the conversation created a special bond between the two of us.

It also reminded me that ballroom dancing led to a life's love affair with Sarah's uncle. I came to believe that Gio—and ballroom dancing—came to me by fate at a time when life could have become overwhelming. For that I was deeply grateful.

Chapter Nine

One Sided Affair

The next time I checked my email it was late afternoon on Thursday. There was a short message from a name I at first did not recognize in the header.

Mr. Foxe,

It was a pleasure to meet you on the recent trip back from Denver. When you have time, could you please give me a call?

I am hoping I can employ your services. Thank you.

Cordially,
Daniel Simel
215 765 4304

It was from the dentistry professor at U. Penn. I remembered we had exchanged business cards on the flight back to Philadelphia, but I had a tough time anticipating what service of mine he might want. Maybe something to do with work teams at the dentistry school. Because we were going out to dinner with the Danish family that night, I decided to wait until the next morning to give him a call and find out what he wanted. My interest was piqued.

I sent a short email to Adam letting him know that I visited the Manhattan mediation program and was not only able to observe a mediation but also had an interview with Judge Boroughs from family court. I did not mention who did the mediation. Nor did I say anything about my reactions to any of my experiences there. I thought it best to have those conversations in person. I want to see his reaction when he hears that I observed Thomas Binder. I thanked him for contacting Ms. Wight so promptly and I said we should try to find a time to get together and talk about the visit soon.

On Friday morning I tried several times to reach Dr. Simel. Finally, he answered his phone around noon.

"Hello Dr. Simel. This is Kent Foxe calling you."

Two seconds went by, then my name must have clicked. "Yes, Kent, thank you for calling me. I appreciate it very much. I was hoping you would respond." His tone was exactly the same as it was on the flight. He still had an unmistakable diffidence about him that I now attribute to being very polite and well-mannered.

"I didn't expect to hear from you, especially this soon. I hope you are doing well. It sounds like you need something. How might I help you?"

"Well, we didn't talk in detail about your professional services on the flight, but I noticed that mediation was listed on your business card. I am only familiar with labor mediation. You know, union-management issues. I was wondering what kind of issues you mediate?" he asked.

"I have conducted mediations related to a whole range of disputes including small contract disputes, family and divorce conflicts, neighbor disputes, and community conflicts about town development issues. Most of my cases have been referrals from the courts at the Philadelphia program but I also do private cases as well."

"So, have you done mediations that involved relationship

conflicts?" Daniel asked.

"Well, I am not exactly sure what you mean by relationship conflicts but almost all of these types of conflicts involve relationship issues of some kind. Neighbor disputes can be about a barking dog, but the neighbors' relationship has usually been adversely affected by the dog's behavior by the time the case gets to mediation. Or, conversely, maybe the strained neighbor relationship caused a problem with how to deal with the dog. If there were no interpersonal issues, they probably would have worked out the dog problems on their own. There are interpersonal issues woven into the dog dispute. Does that make sense?"

"Yes, it does. What about intimate couples? Do you work with their issues?"

"That would fall under the category of family disputes. I do mediate cases like that. They are usually related to the terms of a divorce."

"It sounds like you might be able to help us." He paused for a few seconds then took a deep breath before he continued. "I have a conflict with a woman I have been seeing for several months. I think you would be a good person to mediate our issues. I can tell you are a good listener, have empathy for people, and take your work to heart. I can see you working well with us."

"Thank you, I appreciate that," I said, even though I was somewhat unsure how he could assign those virtues to me so quickly. He barely knew me.

"I'm wondering whether you can take this on for me. Of course, this conflict is not a court case—nothing legal will ever come up. I am just initiating your help on my own because it is really important to me. And I think she and I can work this through with the right kind of support."

"I think it might be possible," I said distractedly. I was somewhat confused because I thought he said on the flight from Denver that he currently wasn't dating anyone. That's why he was going to the theater last Saturday to try to meet someone there. Maybe I heard him wrong, or he just left something out of our conversation which he assumed he had included. It nonetheless sounded odd to me.

"That would be great. Do you want to hear more about the issues? I can give you an overview so you know what you are getting into," Daniel said.

"No, actually it is best if I know as little as possible about the issues or your views before I meet with the two of you. This way I don't develop any preconceived ideas or biases. It is better if everything unfolds in the conversation the two of you have in the mediation."

"Sure, I understand. That makes good sense. You can tell I don't know much about how mediation works. I wasn't trying to get an unfair advantage in your eyes," he said.

"I didn't think that at all. I do have a question for you though. Has the woman you are in conflict with agreed to participate in mediation? Does she know you are thinking about this as an option and is she willing to be involved? Mediation is voluntary and not everyone is comfortable with it. It depends a lot on the person and circumstances. Obviously, she would have to agree in order to move forward with it."

"I have not asked her yet. I can do that tomorrow," Daniel clarified. "I am not sure she will be receptive. And I am fairly certain she will have concerns about it though. I am hoping you can address them to her satisfaction. If she talks with you ahead of time that would be a big help. But I honestly do not know how she will respond to this as an option."

"That's fine. Just have her call me so I can confirm her willingness to participate, and she can meet me over the phone. I'll do my best to address any questions she might have. But I won't be trying to sway her either way. What is her name?"

"Celia Franks," Daniel replied. "Do you want her phone

number?"

"No, I'd rather you ask her to call me. Initiating the call is a first gauge of her interest." I then asked Daniel to give me some possible two-hour time slots for the mediation that might work for him next week. I told him I would get back to him with a place for the mediation after Celia confirmed her involvement. I had to give the location some thought. The mediation center was not appropriate for this case because it was not referred from the court. Neither was my home. I had to find a place that was comfortable but also somewhat formal and clearly private.

We said good-bye on the phone, and I walked into the kitchen to tell Gio about meeting Daniel on the flight and the somewhat unusual mediation request Daniel had just made. This would be my second private practice case.

After hearing the story, Gio said he was just glad that I might be able to help this guy out. As he put it, "It sounds like this man is still grieving the loss of his wife and is trying to find creative ways to meet someone. The theater strategy sounds farfetched and expensive. We should try to fix him up with one of our single women friends. Some of them are having a tough time meeting someone and he sounds like a good catch."

I looked at Gio and replied, "I do not have matchmaker service listed on my business card. Dolly Levi I ain't. Besides, he seems to have a relationship now. That's why he's asking for mediation."

I received a voice mail from a woman on Saturday evening. She identified herself as Celia Franks. She left a phone number. She said she had some questions about the mediation that Daniel wanted to set up. Daniel had obviously talked with her about participating in mediation. I tried several times to reach her but did not leave a voice message. In the meantime, I thought about where I could hold this mediation. Steve, a friend of ours owns a restaurant nearby—La Terraza—that is closed at lunchtime. There is a small room in the back with comfortable chairs and round tables. I called Steve and asked for the favor. He was happy to give me the space for this mediation. I thanked him and told him that Gio and I would come by for dinner soon. I didn't think Daniel and hopefully Celia would mind making the trip over the bridge to New Jersey. Maybe it would introduce them to a promising new restaurant destination. Our friend loved having customers who came from the big city across the Delaware.

I was able to finally reach Ms. Franks by phone in the late afternoon. She sounded somewhat hesitant about participating in the mediation and she raised a couple of pressing, but not unusual, concerns. She wanted to know if mediation is private. Would I be reporting anything about the mediation to anyone? I assured her that it is totally confidential. I would not be taking any notes and I report out to no one about the case or what is disclosed during the session. She also wanted to know if this is in any way a legal process. I told her that I had training as a mediator, not a lawyer, and that a legal background is irrelevant for mediation. I said, "Since the case did not come from the courts, there is no sense in which the issues or outcomes are treated as legal agreements unless the two of you decide to draw up a formal contract. I will not be giving you legal advice of any sort even if a legal issue comes up."

After about 20 minutes of discussion about these points, her concerns seemed to be allayed, although there was still a note of caution in her voice. I gave her the place and time for the mediation. I scheduled it for Tuesday at one p.m. at the restaurant. It was anyone's guess whether she would go through with the plan that Daniel had initiated. I gave it a 50-50 chance.

After I hung up the phone, I called Daniel and left a message on his voicemail giving him the arrangements. I kept thinking that this was an unusual request, at least the way Daniel described it.

I spent the rest of the weekend with Gio and the Danish family members. They were scheduled to head home on Monday. Late Sunday night Sarah had a phone conversation with her father. At this point, her expectations were low and, although I did not hear the conversation, she seemed somewhat relieved afterwards. Apparently, some connection was restored. Gio and I felt better for her and Linus. They would be leaving the U.S. with some good memories of their visit and a realistic sense of who their father was and wasn't. I took some solace in the thought that, given the distance between them and him, the paternal deficit might mean less and less as they grew older. Hopefully, with time and an adult appreciation of human weaknesses they would outgrow some of the pain. And there's always the possibility that Bill will acknowledge his issues and seek help.

When I got up Tuesday morning, I felt slightly uncomfortable having agreed to mediate Daniel's and Celia's conflict. It occurred to me that they may be asking for couple's counseling rather than mediation. But the distinction between mediation and counseling seems blurry to me even when there are clear divorce terms to be settled. In divorce cases, people talk about each other's personal and parental qualities as well as past behaviors in their marriage as they discuss how joint custody should work. These same issues might be addressed in some forms of talk therapy, but they are clearly relevant in mediation as well. They influence the spouses' views about the terms of the divorce agreement, just as they had in the divorce case that I saw Binder mediate in Manhattan.

The situation with Daniel and Celia might hold unique challenges because it is not a divorce case. If there are no divorce terms to address, then what, concretely, could be negotiated? Maybe the confusion about therapy doesn't matter as long as there is conflict of some sort between the two of them. Adam was always quick to point out that conflict is always emotional. The expression of emotion is not just under the purview of therapy. But I need to be careful not to cross certain therapeutic lines. I reminded myself that I am not a sex therapist. I would have to be careful to back away if things boiled down to carnal discussions of orgasms, premature ejaculations, or contraceptives.

I arrived at the restaurant early so I could arrange the room and collect my thoughts. I learned from doing prior mediations that it takes some meditative time to garner the right mediation mindset. Thanks to Adam's training, I usually say to myself once or twice "I am a mediator. I am here to support both parties equally so that they can have the best conversation possible and make the best decisions for themselves." This is the mantra I want to sink in before starting. It is one way to tell myself who I am—and am not—in the mediation room.

I also had to dispel any remnants of Binder's judgmental interventions which were still fresh in my mind from the trip to New York. Importantly, I had to remind myself that I needed to let Celia know how I knew Daniel. I didn't want her to think I knew him well and that the cards were stacked against her as a result. This was important especially because I decided not to use a co-mediator. I wanted to follow my instincts without the interference of anyone else. No one at the center was moving toward a view of mediation that I was adopting. But without a woman and man mediation team, Celia might assume that male bias is going to be at play right from the start. I knew I would have to work against this perception by providing balanced interventions for both of them and showing that I am attending to her views as much as his. In an odd way, being gay sometimes helps reach that goal.

I placed three small bottles of water on the table where the three of us would sit and I put a box of Kleenex on the table next to me. I moved the extra chairs away and spaced the remaining three chairs equally a part around the table. I laid a note pad and pen in front of me although I most likely would not use it unless they wanted a written agreement of some kind. Adam warned several times in his training that any writing during the mediation process can interrupt the flow of the parties' conversation and turn the parties' focus on the reason behind the note taking. People start to wonder what the mediator is taking down and why. This then takes the parties' conversation off track.

Daniel arrived at the restaurant first. I wondered whether the couple would arrive together. He was dressed impeccably, although more casually than on the flight from Denver. He had on a lime green polo sweater over a white button-down dress shirt and chinos. After shaking hands, he said, "Thank you for doing this. I am sure it will be helpful. I hope this doesn't upset you."

Before I could ask him what he meant by the caution he gave me, he continued speaking, "Before I forget again, I want to discuss your fees. I am happy to pay whatever your rate is. I just don't want Celia to pay anything. Please do not accept anything from her. That's important to me."

"We can discuss costs afterwards if that is okay with you," I said. I was hedging because I had not thought about a fee. There is a set fee—only 30 dollars—that the disputants split at the Philadelphia program. I knew that good mediators charged considerably more for private practice cases. I needed to contact a colleague about fees and determine what range would be appropriate. It wasn't a big concern of mine. I was happy to have another private practice case. I saw it as more valuable experience to build on. But I did need to figure it out to convey a sense of professionalism. I have learned that if you don't charge an appropriate rate, clients don't value the work as much. And clearly Daniel could afford top dollar. Who pays could possibly be an issue for Celia, so I reminded myself about not being biased about this payment issue when it does arise.

Ten minutes later a tall attractive woman entered the

restaurant. She walked across the main part of the restaurant and toward the small party room where Daniel and I were sitting. She wore a tailored rose-colored suit jacket and slacks over a pale pink, silk blouse. Her blond, shoulder-length hair was pulled to one side of her head in a small clasp. As she came closer, I could see that she wore a butterfly brooch on the right lapel of her suit. Her make-up was clean looking, although perhaps a little heavy for an afternoon meeting. Although dressed rather formally, there was an air of sportiness about her, like a confident professional tennis player. She moved quickly and gracefully as she headed to the table and sat down. I thought to myself that even I could see why Daniel wanted to work through whatever conflicts they might have.

I shook hands with her at the table and gave her my name.

"Celia Franks," she said in response. Her tone was professional and deliberate. She then looked at Daniel and said, "Good afternoon Daniel. I hope you are fine."

Daniel replied, "Hello Celia, I hope you are doing well too." Both of their greetings seemed sincere—with no edge of hostility or anger. They were said, however, with some noticeable distance, like two co-workers who don't know each other that well.

As soon as Celia took her seat, I thanked them both for being willing to mediate. I then told Celia that "I met Daniel on a recent flight, but he had not mentioned your name or talked about you to me." I asked if either of them had been involved in a mediation before. Both nodded no. I then explained that "As your mediator, I am here to facilitate your conversation about whatever issues or topics you want to discuss. I do not evaluate your suggestions or views, nor do I give you solutions to your problems. Instead, I help you to become clearer about your own views and to understand each other better." I then emphasized my confidentiality and asked if they, too, wanted to keep their conversation confidential. They both had a puzzled look on their faces, so I clarified my question. Did they want to keep their conversation private, to keep things just between them?

Daniel said, "I think it is important that both of us not talk to anyone including family or friends about what we discuss here."

He then looked at Celia and waited to hear her views on this topic. She nodded yes and said, "I agree. This point about confidentiality is very important to me, as you know Kent. We talked about it on the phone. I wouldn't be here without adequate assurances about this. Kent has made the confidentiality here a top priority. We both should not discuss things outside this room with anyone else."

The only other point I made about the mediation process is that "If either of you feel uncomfortable with the way the conversation is unfolding, please raise your concern. We can talk about how you would want the conversation to change if you feel it should be different." They both seemed a little confused by this comment. I was inviting them to set their own ground rules by mentioning what they liked and disliked about how they are talking to each other. I decided not to get into it further at this early point. I could always bring it up later again. I felt it was more important to let them begin talking.

"Who would like to start the conversation?" I asked looking back and forth at each of them for several seconds. Daniel then said he would start. Before he began speaking, I looked at Celia and asked, "Is that okay?"

"I'd prefer that," she said, as she nodded in agreement.

Daniel started by looking at me and saying, "Celia has become close to me. I did not expect this, despite knowing myself. Maybe I should have known better given my tendency to fall hard and fast for someone I meet, but I didn't anticipate this or think it through as a possible danger. Maybe this is because there were other more obvious dangers to think about with our relationship. I was focused elsewhere."

Daniel's comments were puzzling. Not easy to see where

he was going. He was choosing words carefully, almost hesitantly, like someone who was about to reveal a well-kept secret.

"I thought about the danger of other people finding out about us." he continued. "I also thought about this relationship reducing my interest in other more available women, but I did not think—I didn't anticipate—that I would fall in love. That came as a total surprise to me. You see, Kent, I met Celia through an escort service in Philadelphia eight months ago. We have been seeing each other at least once a week through the year. It has been good for both of us up until recently."

I glanced at Celia. She was looking at Daniel with an attentive expression on her face. There was no indication that she wanted to speak yet. She seemed to be monitoring how Daniel was describing their relationship and was ready to correct anything he said if she felt it was somehow off. She did not interrupt or seem upset by what Daniel had just revealed. I made every effort not to have any reaction show on my face, even though I was wrestling with what Daniel just said.

"But for me it has turned out to be something much more than paid sexual favors," Daniel continued. "Even to use an expression like sexual favors is deeply troubling to me as I sit here today. After the first time with her, it was something very special and personal. More human and more engaging than perfunctory sex. We spent hours talking and getting to know each other well. More so than some spouses who have been together through years of marriage."

So now my head cleared some and I was beginning to understand what Daniel told me on the plane. He was still looking for a spouse at the theaters, but he did have this escort relationship with Celia as he searched. He just never mentioned it to me. Why would he reveal something like that to a total stranger or even a close friend for that matter? I also now understood Celia's deep concerns about confidentiality. There were unique risks for her in revealing her work to anyone.

Daniel stopped speaking. I glanced over at Celia and gently offered her the opportunity to speak with just slight eye contact and a small head turn. There was no need for me to say anything at this point. If I did interject or asked a question it would have changed the dynamic of their conversation and perhaps inhibited an instinctive response from Celia. I wanted the conversation to be primarily theirs not ours.

Celia looked up at me and started to speak with a firm, but not harsh, tone. "I made it very clear to Daniel eight months ago when we met that escorting is a business transaction. That is why he pays me. Do I like Daniel? Yes. Do I love Daniel? Well, no. The problem is that I can't make myself into someone he does not like, otherwise the escort relationship would not work. That is the catch twenty-two of doing this kind of work. You have to be likeable, but not loveable. It's a high wire act that I sometimes cannot pull off well. I admit we have had many deep conversations and part of that is my fault. I try to give clients what they want. Most men just want the sex. But I sensed that Daniel wanted and needed intimacy more than sex. I'm sure he would say that was true."

Celia stopped speaking and looked away. She pushed her chair back from the table slightly, just enough to be able to cross her legs. I left a short pause and then I said solemnly, "So it sounds like the two of you are in different places with your expectations about your relationship—what it means to each of you." I paused and glanced briefly at each of them. Both nodded in agreement. I waited a few seconds for one of them to begin speaking again.

Daniel then looked at Celia and said, "You opened up to me about yourself, about your parents dying in a car accident when you were fifteen and the struggles you had keeping your life together over the years. We also talked about your life goals now and how your work is hopefully just a means to a much better end. These talks led to strong feelings for you.

These feelings were not about a business transaction between us. How could I have interpreted them that way? I want to help you reach your goals so you can move on with your life. And I can never thank you enough for making me feel wanted and somewhat happy again."

Celia responded directly to Daniel. "You have treated me well—respectfully and supportively. As I have told you many times, I appreciate that." She then hesitated briefly, looked at me and raised another issue. "He has been overpaying me. I know it is a way to keep me with him. It's a problem, even though I need the money and it helps me to have fewer clients. But I fear that taking the extra cash contributed to his deeper expectations. I see the error of my ways now but it's hard to turn that around. It has made things more awkward overall."

"The money is a gift," Daniel protested. "I would buy gifts for anyone I really cared about. Why wouldn't I do the same for you? You never made me feel like it was inappropriate or condescending. I appreciated that very much. And it was not meant to restrain you in any way."

I looked at Celia and said, "Celia, it sounds like you are concerned about accepting additional money from Daniel even though in some ways it is actually helpful to you."

Celia immediately responded, "That's it. I have to be firm that I will not accept more than we agreed to from the beginning. Otherwise, we end up where we are now."

When I mirrored what Celia was saying back to her, I could hear myself talking as if this was like any other dispute over a financial contract. But the interpersonal relationship, as Daniel had indicated on the phone, was the crux of the matter. I had the urge to ask how much the fees and overpayments were but realized I would be asking for information that would address only my own curiosity. They knew what the arrangements were and what mattered to them. I did not want to lead them where I thought they should go. They knew where they needed to go and I didn't want to get in the way as I had in the teens' conflict at the Center. I was getting clearer about what I believed about the parties' capabilities, but it was difficult to hold back enough. I felt the persistent pressure to solve things for them.

For a moment I wondered if I should keep mediating this case at all because prostitution is illegal in Pennsylvania. But I thought, mediation is always said to be "in the shadow of the law." This situation seemed to be squarely in that ambiguous shady place. It would have felt wrong to stop the mediation for this reason and it would have sent a message that I was judging them and their situation on legal grounds. That was the last thing I wanted to do, given the statements I made to Celia before she agreed to mediate. It would have felt like a betrayal, and it might have triggered deep fears in her.

Daniel then looked at Celia and said, "I am offering you the opportunity to stop drifting dangerously through life, to have the kind of life you thought you would have. Why can't you just take that offer as a caring expression of my feelings for you?"

When I looked at Celia, I could see that her mood had changed. Her eyes were glossy and her face softened. She was quiet for several minutes as she seemed to hold back tears. I let the silence sit in the room until she decided to speak.

She spoke slowly, somewhat softly as if she were thinking out loud. "I don't know any more what my feelings are for you. You have been so kind and generous. I am confused. I want to think..."

Daniel interrupted her and looked at me. I was not sure he heard Celia's last statement. His mind seemed to go elsewhere, and it was clear that he was in deep thought before and as he spoke. Looking at me, he continued: "Sometimes I think I have I deluded myself into believing I love her. I wonder if I believe I am safe loving her because I know she can't love me back. Is this tied to a submerged fear of losing another wife? Does this relationship only work for me because I know in some strange

way that it can't work? This is an unsettling concern of mine."
Daniel picked up the bottle of water on the table, opened it,
and drank several swallows. He probably would have drunk
as much if the bottle were filled with Jameson's whiskey.

As I listened to Daniel, I became concerned that we were
heading toward deeper therapeutic issues for him. But clearly
his concerns about the source of his attraction to Celia were
related to the terms of their relationship moving forward. He
was raising these issues; I was not taking him there. Perhaps,
I thought, mediation is also done in the "shadow of therapy"
or at least in the shadow of the subconscious. After a short
pause, I decided to comment.

"It sounds like both of you are still trying to define your
relationship for yourself and each other. Daniel, you have
concerns that the feelings you feel for Celia may be coming
from someplace other than your attraction to, and emotional
connection with her. Celia, you are somewhat unsure about
what your feelings are for Daniel. Both of you have some
ambiguity about the relationship. Do either of you want to say
more about that or do you want to bring up something else?

Celia responded, looking directly at Daniel. "I do feel a
connection with you. To be honest, even the sex has been
different with you than other clients. It seems secondary to the
feelings that are between us. Maybe I am holding back as well.
I have never told you this, but I have intense fears of getting
personally involved with a man whose wife has died of breast
cancer. I know it is rather crazy and superstitious. But my fear
is real. I have known several women who married men whose
wives had died from it. They found out soon after the
remarriage that they had breast cancer too. It happened to my
sister so it's very close to home for me."

I thought about the sense I had that both people were
saying some important things to themselves and to each other,
things that were only being articulated for the first time. The
conversation seemed to be moving to a profound place, one

that both were benefitting from albeit in a painfully difficult way. I tried to keep suppressing my curiosity about where this was going to go from here. I kept telling myself that my curiosity does not matter, only their decisions about what to say or not say to themselves or each other. I kept saying to myself, "Stay out of their way. Avoid the temptation to ask questions that only serve to lead them in a direction you think they should head." People will go to the places that are important for them. Leading them can easily take them off the track they want to be on.

"It seems like the escort relationship is preventing us from finding out whether we can work things out in any other way," Daniel said, using his index fingers to put "escort relationship" in quotes. "Could we drop the escort part and just date for a while so we can find out what, if anything, is actually between us? There may be a lot, or there may be nothing. Either way, it would be tragic if we didn't find out. I hope you feel the same way, Celia."

"You know, Daniel, if I started seeing you more, I would still have to keep working," Celia said. "The bills won't stop coming in just because I date you without being paid. I'm not sure you'd be so happy knowing I was working two or three times a week while dating you. I don't see how that can happen. It would be unfair to you. I wouldn't want you to have to live with that."

Daniel picked up the water bottle again and took a drink. Looking at me he said, "It's really all about perception, isn't it? How each of us looks at the money I give her. What do you think, Kent? Do you see a way through this?"

Daniel's direct question to me took me back a little. I responded quickly, "I think the two of you can find the best path for yourselves. You are both sharing a lot of personal feelings right now and are wrestling with tough issues. But you seem to be headed toward some important realizations. Daniel, you were saying something important about your and

Celia's perceptions of the money you give her. I wasn't sure whether you want to say more about that."

"Right. I see the money I give her as a small gift, while Celia sees it as a contractual payment with bonus money attached. This seems to be a clear stumbling block for us. Although not the only issue, it is key to where we are stuck right now."

"I might feel better if you weren't paying me but paying the people I owe money to," Celia said with some enthusiasm. "Something about the money transactions with me stands in my way of seeing you differently. I wish we could somehow get past that."

"You mean it might feel better if I paid your bills for you?" Daniel asked.

"Yes, something like that maybe. I don't know."

"Well, that could certainly be worked out, and I would be fine doing it if it allows you some room to explore our relationship," Daniel said expectantly.

After a discussion about how to exchange payments, Daniel and Celia planned the details about which bills he would pay and how he would get the bills in the first place. Celia made no promise that she would not have other clients. She did say she would take only the number of clients she needed "to make ends meet." She used the phrase without noticing the pun. Daniel said he would still conduct his theater search but his motivation to look for someone else would be much lower as long as he is seeing Celia regularly. She was enough for him. She was what he was looking for.

In some ways, nothing had changed between them. Celia was still an escort by profession and Daniel was going to give her considerable sums of money—perhaps more than he had been providing—by paying her bills. But in another way, everything had changed. From their perspective, they would be dating as any other couple might and she would be getting generous gifts from him on a regular basis behind the scenes.

It was all about a shift in perception, a shift that they wanted to create. They made what was real, unreal but oddly believable.

In the end, though, I reminded myself that this was only a conversation between them. Mediation is about people talking to each other and sometimes making commitments that they may or may not keep in the future. They both seemed more at ease with themselves and each other than when they started talking. But, I thought, neither they nor I knew whether they would ever see each other again once they walked out of my friend's restaurant.

CHAPTER TEN

Muskets and Malpractice

On Wednesday morning I saw an email from Adam saying he had time in the late afternoon to talk if I could make it to his office. I wrote him back saying I was free today about four p.m. and that it would be great to chat about the "Manhattan Project" he gave me.

Adam was just returning from class when I arrived at his office. After welcoming me, he talked for a while about the mixed response to a recent article he wrote about the Catholic Church. In it, he criticized the male domination of the institution, including the exclusion of women in the clergy and the use of terms such as "Father" to refer to priests. Several people responded positively, he said, but a few conservative Bishops were irate and wrote a reply piece about the importance of relying upon Biblical interpretations of current institutional practices. They also reminded Adam, and those who agreed with him, about the grounds for excommunication from the Church. That did not seem to faze Adam in the least. He always seemed to know the risks he was taking.

I never asked him what prompted his decision to go public with his views about the church. I was somewhat afraid to find out, although I am sure it was tied to both personal experience and a well-developed philosophical position. It seemed to me that he was beating his head against a brick wall and getting bad publicity from it. Those who try to change the church from within often find they need to step outside—or they are pushed aside.

After his short update on Catholicism, he immediately brought up my visit to the Manhattan mediation program. His sincere interest in what happened there was evident from the intense look on his face.

"So, how did the Manhattan visit go? Were you welcomed and treated well?" he asked.

"Thank you for setting it up, Adam. Thelma was very accommodating and friendly. She clearly wanted to be helpful to you. The visit was surprising in many ways to say the least. One big surprise was that the mediator I was allowed to observe is someone you know."

"Is that right? Who?" Adam inquired.

"None other than the infamous Thomas Binder—your conference nemesis."

"Really!" Adam exclaimed. He looked genuinely surprised, almost shocked. I could see this was news to him, not something he had arranged or even thought possible.

"Did you know he was a mediator there? Or was it just the luck of the draw?" I asked.

"Actually, I knew he lived and worked in New York, but I wasn't sure exactly where. He may be a traveling mediator. There are programs in all the New York boroughs. He might work part time at every one of them. He probably patches together his work from the five courts and adds private practice cases to garner a livable salary. That's what a lot of practitioners do if they are not hired in-house as a full-time employee of a mediation program. But I am as surprised as you are that Binder was the mediator you were able to observe. A stroke of luck maybe. So what did you think? Was it good luck or bad luck? Did he live up to your expectations?"

"Well, let's just say it was an eye-opening and mind-blowing experience. I guess you would call that good luck. I

learned from the shock of what he is like and how he
It certainly made me understand why he was irate when ᵤₑ
heard you were giving the conference keynote speech. His
whole process is about controlling and protecting the parties.
Controlling how they talk, when they talk, and what they talk
about. Protecting parties from what he believes are their own
bad instincts. His mediation session was a master class in how
to discourage people from taking the reins in their own lives.
It was quite amazing and rather disconcerting. And it left me
wondering how common that type of practice is in the
mediation field."

"So, you were able to see first-hand what the academic
fuss is all about for me. He is the tip of the iceberg. There is a
lot of mediation practice like Binder's out there. Many
mediators who work this way never even let the parties sit in
the same room together. They don't get to talk to each other.
Why? Because the mediator cannot tolerate being with intense
conflict. They believe that anything the parties say with anger,
or any emotion is counterproductive. That's because they are
not trained to work with it. So, I'm extremely curious. What
gave you the biggest jolt?"

"Two things actually. Binder set a tone right at the outset
of 'I know the judge' and 'I know what the judge will do with
your case.' The implication being that the parties might just as
well do right then and there what Binder thinks is best because
it is what the judge wants anyway. It puts Binder in the
driver's seat from the get-go. And then there was the sharp
challenge he made to what the parties themselves wanted to
agree to. The couple had a proposal for the future of the
business which Binder outright rejected. They thought it
would work for them and he didn't agree, so he dissuaded
them. It was tough to watch.

"Wow, you were given quite a show. Those intervention
moves are classic and are based in some pretty common
conscious and subconscious assumptions that many mediators

hold as they walk into the mediation room. Can you imagine what might happen if a socially conservative mediator who followed Binder's practice was involved in a custody case involving a gay father and a straight mother? He, and not the parents, would know best what would work for the child. He would probably claim he had to protect the child from the parents' bad instincts."

"I'd rather not think about that scenario. Binder's control was more out in the open than I thought it would be. I think his defense would be that it is the mediator's responsibility, not just to get an agreement, but one that he felt was workable. But I should be careful. Who am I to critique Binder on his protective but misguided mediation urges? I've been there. You saw my notes about the girls' gang dispute."

"Maybe you shouldn't punish yourself too much for assuming at some level that the parties lack good judgment or capability," Adam suggested. "Do you remember who Richard Holbrooke was?"

"I believe he worked in the Bush administration," I said.

"He negotiated the Dayton agreements for Bosnia. In his account of these negotiations, he makes explicit his assumption about people's incapability. He basically says that people who lived as long as they did under dictators like Tito, are unable to make good decisions for themselves. They needed to be pushed, cajoled, and tricked into an acceptable peace agreement. He knew best and they didn't. He could see what needed to happen. The parties could not. Actually, many prominent international affairs experts contend that most international mediation efforts are just round-about ways to implement American foreign policy. Top-down control by a U.S. sponsored mediator to align conflict agreements with existing political ideology."

"I think that what scares me the most is that the mediation process—with these harmful judgmental moves by the mediators—is done behind closed doors. People are vulnerable to the pushes and pulls of the mediator and no one is checking on it. Not even the judges. Which leads me directly to the very enlightening meeting I had with Judge Boroughs in Manhattan."

"Boroughs has been a supporter of mediation for a long time," Adam said.

"Maybe the place to start is just to let you hear what Borough's favorite motto is. He said he learned from being on the bench so many years that 'If you don't tell people what to do, nothing happens.' A comfortable assumption for a judge but not so much for a mediator. He made an upfront case for a purely economic justification for supporting mediation programs. In his view, mediation exists solely to save the courts money. Boroughs didn't even know how his mediators practiced. He has never observed them or took mediation training himself."

From what you have seen do you think that the Philadelphia program is run like the Manhattan program?" Adam asked.

"I think the judges in the Philadelphia courts are not that demanding. I would guess they are satisfied with fifty or sixty percent agreement rates. This seems to me about right. From my limited experience, parties can get there on their own with the help of a mediator about half of the time. This more reasonable view of settlement rates gives mediators the ability to work with the parties, rather than telling them what they must do and not allowing them to talk."

"I did go out on a limb and asked Judge Boroughs if he knew you. He said he never met you but heard about your book. Binder told him it should be burned—as in Fahrenheit 451."

"Great, burn baby burn," Adam said sarcastically. "Or maybe it's kind of like that old sixties title Steal This Book by Abbie Hoffman. Maybe I should have entitled my book Buy and Burn this Book. It has come close to that in some places apparently. I hear students in an Australian graduate program in conflict management are not allowed to cite or quote the book in any papers or theses they write about mediation. Amazing, isn't it?"

"It's dumbfounding," I said in true disbelief.

"I was going to say that the economic incentives for mediation are only one part of the picture," Adam said. There is another important reason why mediators practice in such a top-down, controlling way. The need to be directive comes from a deeper, more personal place than just financing court programs. I think I told you about the mediation program we set up for the National Employee Relations Program—NERP. But I probably didn't tell you what happened at the training we did for people who were going to train mediators so that NERP had a national mediation crew available."

"No, I haven't heard much at all about the NERP program. All I heard was that it was a huge national project that hired several hundred mediators."

"Yes, the NERP organization was going to roll out a mediation program across the entire country. The plan was to supply mediators to small and large organizations to address conflicts between managers and employees. The organizer of the mediation program had read my book and decided she wanted all the mediators in the program to practice with its principles. She said that her employee relations organization had enough top-down programs and people who tell people what to do or how to act. She wanted the mediation program to be different. She wanted the program to have, as she said, "upstream effects." She thought this approach to mediation would allow people to not just settle specific conflicts but learn how to deal better with conflicts that arise in the workplace after the mediation. Upstream effects meant getting a positive impact after the mediation. She wanted employees to gain confidence that they could successfully handle future conflicts, er working through a conflict successfully in mediation."

"The head of the NERP program had a clear rationale for using a non-directive approach to mediation, and she saw that approach in the model of practice you advanced," I said.

"Yes, she had seen other mediators do their work and did not like it—too much of the controlling, 'I-know-best' approach. She did have one request for us though. She asked that we work with a particular mediation program in Savannah, Georgia. She wanted us to have a few of their mediators and the director of the program to be part of the roll out of the NERP mediation project. Apparently, she owed them a favor. We knew it might be risky to bring people on board that we did not know but we agreed to her request. She was, after all, our supportive client.

"I sent the director of the Savannah program a copy of the book and made a trip to meet her in Georgia at her program. When I talked with her, she said she enjoyed the book very much and agreed with its core principles. She went so far as to say that the mediators at her center already practiced in a way that was consistent with all the recommendations in the book. Based on this response, we invited her and three of her mediators to be part of the team that would learn how to train mediators across the country with our method.

"The only hesitation I had while I was there was that for some unknown reason she had two antique muskets carefully hung on the wall behind her desk. No one who entered the building could miss them. The guns were about three foot long and were made of wood with metal triggers. On the handle of the guns, I could see the word KADET etched in capital letters. They were carefully mounted on black wrought iron hooks, no more than four feet from the top of her head. Very strange as an adornment for a mediation director's office, I thought. I tried to explain it away as either some sort of Southern trophy, maybe from the civil war, or nostalgic family heirlooms that she wanted to prominently display. Either way, it was unsettling to see polished guns prominently displayed in a community mediation center, a place that is presumably dedicated to non-violent means of conflict resolution."

As Adam described the strange office ornaments, I tried to think of other reasons why antique guns would be hung in a mediation center. It was difficult to come up with any defensible reasons, unless it was a joke of some kind. That seemed doubtful, however. I then said to Adam, "Because it was a national program there must have been a lot of opportunities to make money attached to this project. A program that big and well-funded is uncommon in mediation circles."

"Right, it was going to be a huge program with a lot of paid training and mediation work. That's why the Savannah mediators jumped at the chance. The training for the trainers was a three-day event in Washington, D.C. The first day covered all of the theory and ideological principles that underlie the practice. The Savannah team was engaged and agreeable throughout the first day. They were familiar with the conceptual material from reading the book. They participated enthusiastically in the discussions and exercises. Day two was devoted to learning some of the core practice skills. In the early afternoon after the lunch break, we then showed a video example of a mediation based on this approach. We had created the video as a prototype mediation so people in the training could get a clear sense of what the practice was.

"After the forty-minute video was shown, we opened it up to the trainees for discussion and questions. Within minutes, the director of the Savannah program stood up at her table, raised her arm and pointed to the video screen. With a deep southern drawl, she disdainfully announced to the whole group: 'That video is a clear example of mediation malpractice. I would never let my mediators practice that way in Savannah or anywhere else. I don't know why you would mislead us this way and have us make this trip here for nothing.' She then grabbed her materials off the table in front of her and turned to her three staff members sitting next to her. Without letting them say a word about how they themselves reacted to the video, and without explaining her views any further, she told her colleagues to leave the training with her. All three followed her out of the training venue, like a line of ducks quickly waddling across a treacherous street. The room fell silent as people looked uncomfortably at each other around the room. We called for a half hour break to process what had just happened and why."

"Maybe she did have her uses for the muskets that hung in her office," I joked. "I am wondering what set her off. Was the mediator in the video that radically different? Were the parties on the video out of control or verbally violent?" I asked.

"No, the example of a mediation we created is quite understated. It depicts two professional, well-educated co-workers. They are in conflict over their different work styles and the challenges that this difference created for each of them and the quality of their work product. There is no swearing or abusive language—only an intense and honest discussion about why they were having problems working together. The man and woman do interrupt each other. The man at one point accuses the woman of becoming "galvanic." And the woman accuses the man of trying to steal her job from her. They express tough criticism and suspicion about each other during the course of their conflict. But nothing that could come close to being called abusive or violent.

"When shown to untrained mediators, the novices had no problem with the video at all. It was what they expected conflict would look like between two professional co-workers. As one new mediator in the training group put it, 'If there was no heat generated by the parties, there would not be any conflict that needed mediation.' But for the Savannah group, or at least the director, this mediator was clearly guilty of letting things get out of control. He let the man and woman talk freely about what happened in their past. Nor did the mediator enforce interaction ground rules that would have eliminated what the Savannah mediator saw as destructive conflict interaction. She was clearly uncomfortable with the conflict that unfolded on the video. For her, this was intolerable mediator practice because the mediator allowed the parties to speak freely and to focus on what they thought was important."

"It is interesting that the Savannah director controlled her mediators the way she probably controls the parties in a mediation. As you might say, Adam, this is who she is." I said. "It just seems to me that the more experienced mediators, the ones trained in other approaches, are uncomfortable being with conflict. They have been taught to squelch it rather than work with it."

"It is ironic, isn't it? But I think there is truth to it. The whole controlling approach to mediation never gives mediators a chance to be with intense or emotional conflict. It prevents mediators from feeling the parties' difficult emotions through their own senses. People who avoid emotional conflict in their own lives cannot let themselves experience others' emotional conflict during a mediation. They haven't built a deep enough capacity for it."

As Adam said this, I thought of Gio's ability to be comfortable with open conflict and my own reluctance to enter the fray with people. I thought of something I long realized. He may be better cut out to mediate than me.

"In our approach you have to learn to be with, and work with, the conflict and not shut it down." Adam continued. "So, this is why mediators can think they believe in people's capability but when they see the practice that flows from it, or is consistent with it, many freak out. It's like the difference between reading about a strict diet that looks appealing and then trying to hold to it meal by meal. Or as they say in Spain, 'It's easier to watch a bullfight than to be in the bull ring.'"

"Does part of the negative reaction stem from the fact that experienced mediators believe it is too difficult for them to learn how to do it? They would have too much unlearning to do?"

"Yes. In some ways it is the most natural way for a mediator to be in conversation with the parties, but it is often perceived as more difficult if you are trained differently. You have to hold back your instincts to control, protect and direct the parties. Instead, you learn to *proactively follow* the parties. For many experienced mediators this is much more difficult, like learning how to drive a stick shift after driving an automatic car for years."

"There is a song from Sondheim's *Anyone Can Whistle* that I think captures what you are saying. The song suggests that what should be easy becomes difficult if you convince yourself that it is hard."

"Nice. You seem to have a Sondheim insight for almost any occasion," Adam observed.

"It just happens. He captures many truths so perfectly. His thoughts just come to me because they are often so clearly relevant and highly insightful."

Well, I need to wrap this up for today, Kent. Do you need a ride home or to the Center?"

Thankfully I had my Subaru with me. I was glad I wasn't being treated to a tank ride today I thought. One's luck only lasts for so long.

As we exited his building I said to Adam, "I want you to know that I think I did much better in the last mediation I did. It was not as tough as the conflict between the two gangs though."

"What was it about?" Adam inquired.

"It was a conflict between a female prostitute and her male client."

"Kent," Adam said, "I need to hear about that one over a bottle of superb wine. I'll buy."

CHAPTER ELEVEN

I'm Not Crazy

I got home in the early evening. After leaving Adam's office I stopped at Target to pick up a kitchen item that Gio requested. He needed the utensil for pasta that looks like a large claw. This handy tool makes it easy to lift servings of pasta out of a large cooking pot or serving bowl. Can't be without one or two of them in an Italian household. It is the only appropriate way to handle pasta. When I arrived home Gio was sitting in the breakfast nook chopping zucchini and eggplant. He looked somewhat distraught.

"Hi. What's going on? You don't look too well," I said.

"Bill called about an hour ago. He wants to come over to see us tonight."

"Why? What's up with him?" I asked with concern.

"I am not sure. He sounded upset—maybe angry—on the phone. It wasn't clear. It's unusual for him to call me. As you know, I am the one who usually checks in with him a few times a year at the holidays or on his birthday. That's about it. There is some reason why he wants to talk."

"Did he say what he wanted to talk about?" I asked.

"Not really, but he did mention something about Rosa and his kids' visit. The rest was pretty incoherent. I don't really have the remotest idea yet. If you remember, he said so little to us when all those events happened. Who knew what he was

144

thinking through it all? Remember he just walked away from us on that street corner in South Philadelphia and said nothing. He just let Rosa rave and did not try to calm her down. I probably should have called him to see what he was feeling after those horrendous couple of days. He may have been in a different emotional place than Rosa."

"What if Rosa... Do you think Rosa is going to tag along with him?" I asked. Gio could undoubtedly hear the protest in my voice.

"Don't worry, I made a point of telling him that she is not welcome here. I am not ready to deal with her issues yet. Maybe never after the way she acted toward us and the Danes on their visit."

"I know that I cannot be around her yet. Are you sure he heard you and is going to come here alone?" I asked, seeking reassurance.

"It sounded like it. I will not open the door if she is with him. That's how I'll handle it."

"Good. This is a little strange. It's unlike Bill to want to talk about anything except his research project," I said. "Lately I had become less tolerant of his far-fetched ideas. Talking with him about his hidden airplane bunkers feels like I am contributing to a harmful collusion. And questioning him only prolongs the conversation. I managed somehow to avoid the topic with him entirely when he was here for dinner. He sought me out, but I kept ignoring his commentary. I felt I was being rude but didn't see a way around it."

"I think you handled it fine. Bill has some severe issues, but he is not stupid. He picks up on a lot more than he is willing to talk about. He did well in school and in the army. He learned Danish well while he was living there. And I hear it is one of the tougher languages to grasp. Communication is not his strength but still waters do run deep sometimes. I wish I knew more about how he thinks of things. It might help in knowing what mental state he is actually in. It is just too hard to tell. I can see that he has developed coping strategies to deal with his own instincts and issues. He knows when to change the topic and when to ignore something that is said to him. He can hide his issues very well at times."

About a half hour later the doorbell rang. It was Bill. He was thankfully alone. I wasn't up for a confrontation with Rosa, even through a closed door. He looked disheveled and a little out of it. His orange and black plaid flannel shirt was only partially buttoned, and it was out of his baggy, well-worn jeans. His hair was uncombed and looked as if it hadn't been washed in several days. One of his shoes was untied. I noticed his face looked slightly red and he had a couple of scratch marks on his left cheek.

Gio and I gave Bill a cautious hello as he entered the kitchen and asked if he wanted anything to drink. He said no quickly without thinking if he did or didn't want something. He clearly was on a mission that was not to be delayed by an act of hospitality. Gio lowered his voice somewhat and said, "What did you want to talk with us about, Bill? I can tell from your call that you are upset. What's going on?"

"It's good you are both here. I wanted to tell you both. You are both to blame," he said without looking at either one of us. He wanted to make sure he was talking at us, not with us. His voice was a monotone and he talked in short choppy phrases that made him sound like a fumbling newscaster.

"What do you mean? Blame for what?" Gio asked with a degree of annoyance. It was clear we were going to have to pull the issues out of him, maybe because he himself was unsure of what he wanted to say. Or he was afraid to say what his agitated instincts were prompting.

"You guys have ruined things for me. Both. You can't deny what you've done. You were forcing me to see my kids by myself when they were here. That wasn't it at all. I could have spent time with them and Rosa. Together. We could have been a whole family. You are to blame. Getting Rosa so upset. Now

146

she takes it out on me. She won't stop. It's like she's become a different person. I don't know who she is anymore. Terrible. Just terrible. You don't know. And you didn't care about what you did."

I could see Gio was getting increasingly irritated as he listened to Bill's rant and tried to make sense of it. "Wait a minute, Bill," Gio said sternly. "You've got it wrong. Your ex-wife and kids from Denmark decided to visit and we offered them a warm reception. They stayed with us. We even invited Rosa to dinner with them on Sunday night. We did you and Rosa a big favor by being so welcoming to your Danish family. I don't see why you have a problem with us. Your criticism is off base."

"Why did you include Rosa for dinner?" Bill said accusingly. His hand started to tremble some. "You must have wanted her around everyone. She came to dinner. Then suddenly, she was cut out of the plans. Boom, then that's it. That was a mixed message. Confusing to me and insulting to Rosa. She has not gotten over it."

I wanted to speak up and support what Gio was saying but I also did not want Bill to feel that Gio and I were ganging up on him. Feeling somewhat tentative, I said, "If we hadn't invited Rosa to dinner, she would have been insulted. It would have been ultra-rude on our part. You know we're not like that. We wanted to include everyone. We tried, even though it was a mistake. She was so rude to your kids. She intentionally insulted them as foreigners."

"Bill," Gio quickly continued. "We were not calling the shots. You know your two kids really wanted to spend time alone with you, especially after Rosa kept insulting them and Brigid. They just wanted to connect with you more while they were here. Rosa clearly wouldn't let that happen. You didn't see that? It was obvious to me and Kent and to your kids as well. I don't see how you could have missed it. Or maybe you didn't want to see it. Rosa was the one who made it too tough on you. I understand you were caught in the middle. Not an easy place to be. But it wasn't our fault."

"I don't believe it. You insisted. You both were insisting that I be alone with them. You were putting that thought in my kids' heads. They wouldn't have come up with that. Not on their own. They didn't care one way or the other who was there. Who went where. Why would they? Especially Rosa. She's my partner as you gays say. She has a right to be with me at any time."

"No Bill. That's not right. We were not the ones insisting. We were just a voice for your two teens. We were letting you know what they were feeling and wanting. They hadn't seen you in years and they are both at a critical stage of their lives. They need a father now during their adolescence. It has been missing for most of their lifetimes because you backed away and barely kept in touch with them. That's the reality that may be hard for you to face," Gio said.

I was a little worried that Gio was being too tough. But Gio's pointed last comments seem to register someplace in Bill. Bill's voice became noticeably softer, almost apologetic, and his hand trembled less. He seemed calmer and was somewhat reflective. He said, "So now Rosa is mad at me. I have missed the chance to get closer to my kids. Could have while they were here. I can see you were both involved in making this happen. For better or worse. Someone has to be responsible for this. It's just wrong. It just doesn't happen by itself. Someone out there wants me to be a loser and alone. I know it. I feel it. But I don't know what to do about it."

Gio and I both looked at each other and held back saying anything. An argumentative response at this point seemed inappropriate. Just listening was a better reply. We needed to hear how he was thinking and how he saw the events that transpired with his Danish family. He seemed to be working himself through his own confusion and sadness.

Bill continued. "I am very alone. My two brothers live near

me. One hasn't talked to me since shortly after our mother died. The other took me out on his boat once or twice but rarely answers my calls. You know why, Uncle Gio, I am sure you do. But you aren't saying. My kids are not here, and Rosa is tough to live with. Kent, you won't even talk with me. It's like you don't care about my research project anymore. That is the one thing that is all mine. It is a part of me. And I have no one interested in it anymore. And now I am sick, I've just found out I have a heart condition. My doctor says so. All this stress is not helping. I feel I am getting worse with chest pain."

Bill's emotions seemed to keep changing quickly, almost as often as an overly tired two-year-old's. His eyes teared up as he talked about his heart condition but then he became accusatory again when he brought up his research project. He still needed to say more. His tone became angrier and more pointed.

"If Rosa is doing this to me, she will have to pay for it. She is evil. She could be a devil in my life. There are other things she has done. I am convinced that she is bad blood." Bill pointed to the scratches on his face. "I must do something but need to be careful. Bad karma strikes back. I know. I need to be careful."

Gio and I increasingly looked at each other as Bill spoke. His last comments began to concern us both. Was his condition progressing? Was there violence with Rosa? Could he become violent with others? Was he even capable of hearing how disjointed and dangerous he sounded in this conversation? I felt unsure of how to respond. Instead, I gave Gio a long look that said, 'You have to say something about his current state.'

"Bill, you are losing control. You need to get professional help. I've been telling you this for the last few years now. I am afraid of where you are headed. And I don't think you realize it. Some illnesses progress through life. That is clearly happening to you and you don't want to admit it. Do it in memory of your mother. You know she would be insisting that you get help if she were alive today."

"I know that everybody thinks I am crazy, but I am not. I don't need psychological help. I need support for my life. I need people who care," Bill pleaded. He seemed unreachable.

"Listen, we care, your children care, and even Brigid cares," Gio said. "Brigid is in the social services profession in Denmark and cares about you as the father of her children. In her own way, Rosa cares too, otherwise she would not stay with you. You can help her to get stronger. She may have not let you be alone with your kids because she was afraid you would leave her for Brigid—someone you once loved and had children with. Do you understand this? Did you see her jealousy and how it affected her behavior while your family was here?"

"Maybe that's what did this to me. I don't know." Bill said, looking away from both of us.

Bill paused and looked concerned and somewhat agitated. He squirmed in his seat and looked more uncomfortable as he tried to make sense of what he was thinking. Little was resolved for him and in fact Gio's comments may have contributed to even more confusion. He looked down at the table for a few minutes. He was distraught, as if the whole conversation was too much for him to process.

"Well, I need to get back. I am sure she is getting madder every minute I am gone. She is afraid you two will turn me against her even more. Could I take a bottle of water with me?"

"Yes," Gio answered as he stood up and went to the refrigerator.

Asking for the water made me realize that he must have walked the two miles over to our house. He was probably low on gas money. And he was sweating from becoming so intense.

Bill took the bottle and plodded slowly toward the back

door. On the way out he said, "See ya" but did not turn around. Bill and I both only said, "Bye Bill." It felt like we just followed someone through a hall of mirrors—disorienting and a little frightening.

As he walked away, I thought about how lost he was. He was adrift in thoughts that were only partially in touch with reality. He is intelligent but he was losing his grip and his emotional life was in turmoil. He seemed paralyzed with confusion and indecision. The haunting words from Sondheim's gut-punching ballad Losing My Mind flooded my brain. I worried about him walking home alone in his current state, especially since he said he was having heart problems. I asked Gio whether we should give him a ride home.

Gio shook his head slowly and said, "The walk may help him. He probably needs time to sort things through before talking with Rosa when he gets home."

I wondered how involved Gio thought we should be. After the incidents with Rosa, it was far from tempting to step in again. But caring from a distance is not helping. And our overwhelming urge was to make things right with him. I felt the need to protect just as I did in the girl gang mediation. Once again, I wrestled with the dilemma of trying to protect someone when protecting means taking control from the outside.

Gio and I stood in the kitchen for a few minutes saying nothing. It was tough to digest it all and to absorb the hurt, anger and loneliness Bill was expressing to us. I spoke first. "I hate to suggest this but is there some way we could have him admitted for professional help? It really would be for his own good. He's getting a little scary. He might be a danger to himself or others."

"That would be tough. I've investigated it. There is a lot of red tape, and he could only be held for a very short time—a matter of days—against his will. I would not want to take that on. I do see, though, that he is getting worse. But I still don't think he is violent."

"I don't know. You could be right. He almost seemed too confused to be dangerous. Although something happened between him and Rosa. It's just that we see what's going on and feel helpless without his cooperation. There are wonderful drugs for psychosis that could make a huge difference for him, better his life."

"If he did get better through drugs, he may not be able to stay with Rosa. He may see her differently—more realistically. Then where would he be? Off on his own somewhere? At least Rosa has steady disability income that helps support the two of them. Remember that Bill blew the inheritance money from his mother on his Nazi research in Europe and a ridiculous car that ran for only a couple years. Without Rosa's support, he would probably be on the streets—a homeless soul. Remember that Eliza Doolittle could never go back to her family after she was transformed by Professor Higgins. Bill might be worse off if he did change too much. I wouldn't want to be responsible for that outcome."

"That's a possibility," I said. "It's sad that positive change could lead to worse outcomes for the guy. The stability of his day-to-day life might be gone. Or we'd have to provide a lot more support. We would feel more responsibility for him."

My misplaced interventions in the teen gang mediation came back to me. Like then, I was now looking for the grand solution to a complex problem. And I wasn't fully realizing that only Bill can take the steps that would make a difference in his life. When you care about people or want to help them, this is a tough realization to hold on to. Trusting that people have what it takes is difficult, I thought, especially when you don't sense much capability on their part.

We both had enough drama for one night. When Gio asked about the meeting with Adam, I gave him an 'it's-too-late-to-talk' response and went to read a few pages in Sondheim's biography before falling asleep.

CHAPTER TWELVE

The Deal

Two weeks went by without hearing anything from the Mediation Center in Philadelphia. I hadn't done a case since I mediated the girls' gang dispute. I wondered what was going on. They may have trained a new crew of mediators and were giving them the chance to practice while their skills were fresh in mind. But usually, they asked a more experienced co-mediator like Karen or me to assist them with their first cases. Sometimes caseloads were low, depending on how busy the courts were overall. I decided to stop at the Center and talk to Anita to find out what was happening.

Anita was on the phone when I entered the reception area of the Center. She seemed to be talking to one of the court's administrative judges who was the acting director of the mediation program. She was discussing the case referral process. Something about setting up a tighter schedule, more aligned with the judge's dockets and schedules. When the call ended, I walked over to her desk.

"Hello Anita, how are you?"

"Fine," she said in her usual impersonal voice. She looked as if she would rather not continue with any conversation.

"I was wondering what was going on with the mediations. I haven't been assigned a case for about three weeks. Are the caseloads lower than usual? I know they fluctuate at different

153

times of the year. Or have I missed something?"

"Anita's face changed before she responded. She looked serious and sounded apologetic. "I was going to call you, but I have been putting it off. We've had some bad news. I got a call from one of the court administrators last week. She told me that one of the young girls from your last mediation was critically wounded in a terrible knife attack not far from her home. They are pretty sure it was related to the ongoing street gang activity in north Philadelphia. She told me to be sure to tell you when I could."

I flinched hearing this disturbing news. "My God, that's horrible. Do you know which girl was injured?"

"I believe they said her last name was Charles," Anita said.

"That was Latisha, the one who had her infant with her at the mediation. She was very worried about the safety of her child. She didn't want to put her baby girl at risk amid the street violence. I hope her baby was not with her. This is disturbing. Do you know if they think she will make it or if her child was hurt?"

"The last we heard she was in critical condition at Temple University hospital. We decided it was inappropriate for anyone from the mediation center to reach out now that it is a criminal case being handled by the police. There would be no reason to get in touch. We could not give them any information because of the Center's commitment to confidentiality. There may have been something in the news about it but I haven't seen anything. I thought you may have seen something if it was covered by the media. These types of attacks happen so often they aren't considered that newsworthy anymore. It's sad. If I do hear anything else, I will let you know."

I was thrown by this upsetting news. The mediation with the teen girls and their mothers came back vividly to me. The commitment to retaliation, the futility of practical suggestions, the elusive source of the conflict, and the mothers' fears of losing a child. More than anything, I relived the helplessness I felt sitting at that table wanting to do something that worked. That helplessness allowed for more violence to occur.

After a few minutes, I started thinking about why I had stopped by the Center in the first place. I wondered whether this tragic event had anything to do with why I wasn't being called to mediate. This seemed like a sensitive issue, and I hesitated to ask Anita. I was not sure I wanted to hear the answer. Could the judge who referred the case think that something that happened in the mediation—or something I did as the mediator—triggered the violence? There are judges in the court who are skeptical of mediation in the first place, especially because the court does not monitor what happens during the sessions. For all the judges know, bringing these girls together face to face rekindled the flames between them. They could be thinking I had a role in the escalation. Reluctantly, I decided I had to inquire about this issue. I needed to know more about why I hadn't been called to mediate.

"I am not sure you would know this, Anita, but does this violent attack have anything to do with why I have not been called to do a mediation for the past couple of weeks? Do you happen to know if this is related to my case assignments?" I knew Anita would know but I wanted to give her a way out of answering directly if she wanted to take that route. She seemed hesitant to talk about the whole issue. I could see she was balking, and it worried me.

Anita looked down at her desk momentarily and said, "You probably know that Judge McGinny—our administrative judge and director—is very sensitive about any bad publicity that the court or the mediation program might get. He himself has been under investigation recently so any bad news really hurts his reputation and makes him a target of political attacks. His assistant asked me to hold off giving you mediations for a bit just in case the press or police start following up on what happened in the days prior to the attack. You did write a court report after the mediation that included something like "the parties did not agree to stop the escalation of their conflict." Someone could interpret that as implicitly accepting future violence among these girls. I certainly know that was not what you meant, but the language is there. Unfortunately, it is a little unclear."

I could feel my face redden as my blood pressure started to rise. I was not at all confident that Anita would come to my defense with the judge or his administrator. She probably would just as soon leave me in a vulnerable position. I said to her, "I thought a statement like that was actually helpful to the court because it suggested that the case still needed judicial monitoring. It was an honest appraisal of where the parties were at the end of the mediation. I did not sugar-coat the situation. I am trying to think about why McGinny might see this as a failure of mediation or some sort of malpractice on my part, God forbid. Who knows what these judges think happens in mediation? They are not very invested in finding out."

My own prior feelings of inadequacy and failure with this case flooded in again. Who was I to work with such a difficult and dangerous set of issues? Maybe I should have ended the session as soon as the violent past was revealed by the girls. But talking at least provided a chance for change. And they did express that they wanted to protect their babies. I could only hope that these young girls held up their maternal commitment to each other in this recent violent attack.

"I wouldn't go so far as to think you were in any way responsible," Anita said. "But I think the judge would just as soon not have the media even know about the mediation you conducted. It could be interpreted as a mistake by the court for even sending the case to mediation in the first place. It might be seen as a bad judgment call on the court's part. That would have nothing to do with you. In any case McGinny would not want you to say a word to the media about any of it. I think he is just trying to prevent that possibility. The press might pursue you if you are around the mediation program. They could put you on the spot. Even not talking can be interpreted negatively."

"Of course I wouldn't talk to the press. It would violate the confidentiality promise that mediation is based on. That could destroy the whole program if I revealed anything publicly or to the judges." I was annoyed that I even had to say this to defend myself, especially to Anita. But she is a key intermediary in protecting my reputation. The court officials may be putting pressure on her to protect themselves. They could be looking for a convenient scapegoat.

"There are some changes that the administrative judge wants to make in the program. These may or may not be related to the gang mediation. I'm not sure, but I think you should know about them anyway. One policy went into effect this week. McGinny said that I should assign only one mediator per case—no more co-mediation. He is recommending that another mediator or some outside neutral person observe each case and give feedback to the mediator and possibly the court for each session. These case monitors would not be paid of course. An observer's feedback form is being developed for this process. I am working on it for the judge."

"So, these observers take on a monitoring and assessment function for the court?" I asked.

"Yes, basically," she said.

"What else is coming down the pipe? Do you know yet?" I wanted to know what other ripple effects there might be from the teen mediation.

"It looks like the court may set a time limit for each mediation session with no return sessions possible, even if the clients ask for one. The judge feels these multi-session cases are taking too much time. He wants case management streamlined."

"Really?" I said disbelievingly. "Some of the mediations require two or three sessions because the parties need to consult with their counsel or obtain information in between the sessions. That will no longer be possible. How much time is going to be allowed for a single mediation session, did he say?"

"He is talking about a thirty-minute time limit. He wants cases finished quickly, one way or the other. This way the cases can go back to court the same day if no settlement comes out of the mediation. It ensures that the parties have it all over in one day. I think that is actually a benefit for the program. We cannot be accused of delaying the court's schedule."

"I bet he is setting up a batting average system as well," I said facetiously thinking about the judge's record keeping in Manhattan.

"A what?" Anita questioned.

"Oh nothing," I said. "I was saying the judge will probably start watching the success rates for each mediator."

I walked away from Anita's desk and sat in a chair in the reception area. I started thinking again about Latisha and her comments during the mediation. It was as if she knew she was going to be the next target of violence and was trying to ensure that her child lived through it. I had a strong urge to call Temple Hospital to find out her status but knew that the HIPAA guidelines would prohibit it. There was no possible way for me to reach out. Clearly, according to Anita, the judge did not want this anyway.

I was still wondering how responsible the judge felt I was and how responsible I should feel. I did believe after the session that I failed by some standards, but I have come to see that people in mediation are only going to support an agreement if they create it themselves and commit to it. Stopping a cycle of violence is a tall order for mediation. It only happens when the people involved are "ripe" for it, as they say in some conflict theories. The girls' conflict was not ripe enough yet. They were not ready to end the violence on their own. Maybe the judge needs to hear this I thought. But the futility of making any arguments to court officials seemed obvious to me. Or, I thought, maybe I was rationalizing my way out of confronting the judge.

I realized that the new policies that Anita described were going to turn the mediation program into a case disposal mill. We were headed toward the Manhattan set up and perhaps even worse. There wasn't a time deadline for the cases in New York as far as I knew. For many cases, a half hour is barely enough time for the parties to be comfortable just being in the same room with each other. The issues are complex enough in many cases that even a settlement-oriented, negotiation expert would have trouble resolving several issues in 30 minutes. To me, it sounded like our judicial director was giving up entirely on the mediation program. Adam was right that this was the trend. Whether it was due to financial pressures or judicial convenience, now the Philadelphia program was going to be caught up in efficient disposal of cases.

As I sat there in the reception area, I saw Karen Abrams, my co-mediator—or former co-mediator—enter the Center. She saw me sitting across the room and immediately walked over to me without acknowledging Anita.

"Hello Kent. How have you been?" she asked. "I haven't seen you in quite a while. Sorry I could not help you with that mediation you had a few weeks ago. My seven-year-old was at home ill so I had to stay with him. I was disappointed. I was looking forward to co-mediating with you again."

"That was okay, Karen. I understand. I figured you had a good reason for cancelling. Family always has to come first."

"Did you hear that we are now going to fly solo through these cases?" Karen asked.

"Yes. Anita just told me. Mediating alone a few weeks ago was a sign of things to come, I guess. Have you heard anything about that case that I mediated without you?" I asked, wondering how far the story about the teen gangs had circulated.

"No, actually not. Why do you ask?

"Just wondering," I said evasively. I was relieved to hear that my mediation had apparently not become a hot topic of discussion at the Center.

Anita stood up at her desk, greeted Karen and then said, "Your mediation case starts in fifteen minutes in room number two. Both parties—two men—confirmed yesterday that they will show up, so we'll see what happens. We should start the new practice of having an observer for each session. Kent, can you observe Karen's mediation while you are here today? We can do a test run of the new practice."

"Yes, I can do it, as long as it doesn't go over thirty minutes," I said wryly. Anita got the sarcasm. Karen missed it. She thought I was serious. Apparently, Anita had not told her yet about all of the new practices that the administrative judge was imposing on the program.

"Is there an observer's critique sheet I should use?" I asked Anita.

She shook her head and said, "No, the form has not been developed yet. That will take some time. We can do this one informally. Just take some notes and provide Karen with your comments after the session."

Karen and I walked back to the mediation room and waited for the two men who apparently were on their way. Karen took out her notes and three small pads of paper, one for her and one for each of the parties. She placed a pen near all three of the note pads on the table.

Each man arrived separately and close to on time. They were both someplace in their late twenties or early thirties. Both were dressed casually with jeans. One had a Philadelphia Eagles sweatshirt on and the other had on a Grateful Dead long sleeve T-shirt under a light grey jacket. It was easy to feel the tension in the room as each man decided where they would look to avoid eye contact with each other in the small and somewhat stuffy space we were in. The pads of paper on the table became an easy focus for both of them.

Karen greeted them and asked for their names. One was Carlo and the other was Robin. She then introduced me and told them that I was a mediator who was going to observe the session. I stood up and shook hands with both of them then pulled my seat back away from the table. It was a much warmer welcome than Binder had given me as the observer in his mediation.

Karen started the mediation by stating the goal she had for the session. "I hope you are able to fully settle your dispute here in mediation this afternoon." She added that she knew nothing about the issues that brought them here, only that their case had been referred to mediation by a judge. Karen was a strong believer in establishing clear ground rules for the session, so she went over the usual set of behavioral expectations: confidentiality, no interrupting, take notes on the pad of paper so you remember what you want to say when it is your turn, no foul language or insults, there might be a caucus with each person if needed, the terms of settlement will be sent to the court to finalize the process. She covered these ground rules in a far less imposing manner than Binder. But I noticed that both men seemed to tune out as she went through these process prescriptions. They probably heard very little of what she said. They were most likely just mentally rehearsing what they were going to say to the mediator and perhaps each other when things got started. They did seem to understand that this was not a court hearing.

Robin did ask one question. "Nothing we say here goes to the judge, right?"

Karen immediately replied, "Only the final agreement between the two of you if there is one. Anything else you say here is kept confidential. I will not report anything you say.

The two of you can decide whether you want to keep it confidential as well."

Neither man said anything about their own preferences regarding confidentiality.

Karen then asked Carlo, the man with the Eagles shirt, to start by telling his "side of the story." I wasn't sure why she chose Carlo to start first. It seemed random or maybe it was because he was the better looking of the two men. I noticed that Karen was sometimes slightly biased toward men she found attractive. Although I usually agreed with her assessments, I was concerned about the obvious impact this could have on the parties. It was too subjective and insulting a point for me to raise with her. It is so much better just to ask the parties who wants to start and let things unfold from there. A process point I took from Adam's training. Obviously, Karen had not thought of this, or she just preferred to make the decision for the parties.

Carlo started with a polite, but firm thank you then said, "It's rather simple. Robin owes me money, a significant sum of money. I leant it to him about six months ago and I have received none of it back. Zilch. I need to be repaid now."

Karen jumped in quickly as Carlo paused. She asked him a series of questions, "How much money exactly did you lend him? When did you expect Robin to pay any or all of it back to you? What are your expectations now?" As Karen asked these questions, I thought of how unnecessary they were at this early point in the discussion. But these questions served a definite function. Karen was determining what information was needed for her to get somewhere with the negotiations. The questions were guiding the topics and focus of the two men's conversation. Maybe this kind of control is what it would take, I thought, to finish every mediation in 30 minutes. But clearly it put her, as the mediator, in the driver's seat. She is taking them where she thinks they need to go.

With little hesitation Carlo answered Karen's questions. It

would be difficult not to, I thought. "We are talking about twenty-six hundred dollars. Robin and I discussed that he would pay it all back in three months or less. I have received none of it so far. Robin knows this so he better not change the story here today," he said.

I saw that Robin was looking down at his notepad as Carlo spoke. Robin wrote the figure $2,000 on the front sheet of his pad and emphatically underlined this amount.

Karen then asked, "Was this an agreement you both made in writing about this financial arrangement?" With this question I thought Karen sounded like a persistent Judge Judy. She was trying to get to the facts of the case, to pin down the tangible evidence. This is quite futile because, as Adam pointed out in his training, there is no way for a mediator to assess what really happened in the past. In mediation, it can only be about what people say to each other. There are no tests of evidence or testimony to verify anything that is said or claimed by any of the parties. Someone could bring a written document and a mediator would have no way of verifying its authenticity.

Carlo replied, "No, there was nothing in writing. It was just our word, a verbal agreement that should count as much as any signed paper. It should not matter how the agreement was made. This is the typical way we do this."

Karen then asked, "Is there anything else you want to say at this point, Carlo?"

Carlo thought for a few seconds and said, "Not really, I just want to hear when he is going to pay me back. I don't want to listen to more excuses, that's for sure. The bluffing and hard luck stories have to stop. There is no point to that anymore. I've had enough. I want him to know that I may need to take matters in my own hands if the payment is not made soon. What else can I do? I need that money. I have debts to pay off too."

Without commenting on Carlo's last ominous comment,

Karen then turned to Robin and asked, "Robin, what would you like to say to Carlo about the financial agreement the two of you made?" When I heard this question, I thought about the recommendation the instructor made in my first mediation training. The trainer said it is always important to encourage the parties to talk to each other, not to the mediator. Clearly Karen's question was trying to make this happen. After taking Adam's training I now see this move for what it is: a method of mediator control. It tells the parties who they are to talk to and when. It feels forced, like when a mother tells her ten-year-old son to look into his younger brother's eyes and apologize for something.

Robin continued to look down at the notepad as he started to talk. "I know I owe you money. You know it is only two grand though." Looking intently at Carlo, he then added, "And I told you that I would get you the money as soon as I have it. Why don't you believe me? You know it has been rough out there this year. I've had a tough..."

Carlo interrupted Robin and said, "It's twenty-six hundred dollars, not two grand."

Karen quickly reminded both men, through her own interruption, that they should not interrupt each other. "I will ask each of you to speak when it is your turn to talk," she said, raising her voice slightly. "Robin, let me ask you, when do you think you can return any of the money, regardless of the amount? There is clearly a disagreement about the amount you owe which we can deal with soon. But a payment plan of some kind might be an option."

Robin thought for a few seconds and then looked directly at Karen for the first time and said in a firm, steady voice, "Mediator, you should know something. The money I owe Carlo comes from a drug deal he and I did a while back. These type of cash arrangements sometime take time and Carlo knows that. It's not like we're talking about a rental payment that is late or a mortgage check that bounces. This is more relaxed, more flexible. These deals always are. There is a lot of obstacles along the way. But I am known as an honest guy on the street. And I will get the money to Carlo when I have it. It's just that it has been tough for me lately."

I looked at Karen as Robin disclosed the nature of the transaction the two men were involved in. A few uncomfortable seconds passed. Karen seemed to be stopped in her tracks. She fidgeted with the pen in front of her then sat back in her chair, looking as if she was overcome by what she just learned. Suddenly, her rules about interruptions seemed almost comical. She was worried about trivial turn taking in the conversation while these two guys were probably negotiating for their lives. I tried to anticipate what she was going to do next, and I thought about what I would do if I were in her mediator's seat. I was sure that having my eyes on her made her even more nervous about how she should respond. I tried to look away. This was a tough call, and I could see that she wanted to get it right.

Karen gathered herself for a few more moments and then nervously said, "I need to stop this mediation at this point. Mediation is not a place for settling illegal debts. I will send the case back to court and only indicate that no agreement was reached here. I will say nothing else to the judge about the issues. I will keep confidentiality. Please leave through the reception area as soon as you gather your belongings."

Both men slowly pushed their chairs back from the round table and, looking somewhat confused, left the room. Karen did not ask them to complete the mediation feedback forms that she had placed in front of her at the beginning of the session. I had the feeling that she was now actually somewhat afraid of having the men anywhere in the vicinity. Her tone of voice changed just as the tone of a piano changes when someone plays Prokofiev after Chopin in a concert. She now had a completely different and unsympathetic view of the two men. And her body language revealed her discomfort and agitation.

After the men left the Center, Karen looked at me and said, "Can you believe that? Did they really think I would facilitate the negotiation of a drug deal? Why would Robin even bring it up? Didn't he realize I would have to stop the mediation?" Her voice did not reflect the in-decision I saw on her face a few minutes before. It was almost as if she was defending herself after enduring a personal insult. And she was obviously looking for confirmation from me that she did the right thing.

I hesitated for a moment, then thought out loud, careful not to sound antagonistic. "Well, I think Robin wanted you to know the nature of the deal and assumed you would still continue to mediate their issues. Otherwise, he would not have brought it up. I can see where he was going with this. He was trying to say that the context of the deal mattered. Things are not that cut and dry in street transactions—no written agreements of course and no real deadlines for payments. That needed to be understood in order to understand why he hadn't paid off his debt yet. It was about the terms of accountability for him at that point in the discussion. He felt the information surrounding the deal mattered."

"I hear what you are saying, Kent, but are we supposed to just look the other way when we hear in mediation that something illegal is going on? Aren't we an accomplice of sorts then?" Karen contested.

"You're saying this is more than a 'shadow of the law' issue?"

"Exactly, this is within the sunlight of the law," she insisted.

"I still think that my instinct would have been to continue mediating after Robin talked about the drug deal," I said somewhat tentatively. I was feeling more confident about my inclinations than I let on to her at the moment. It felt like she could become defensive if I expressed myself more assertively. After all, I was supposed to observe her practice with this case and write something about her performance. I did not want this to turn into a confrontation between us.

Karen looked incredulous. "Really? Why would you have continued?"

"Because this case would not be identified as a drug case even if it does go back to court. Robin knows it would be foolhardy to tell a judge about it. So, it would be treated as a financial verbal contract if they take their money issues back to the court—which I doubt they will. But if you had successfully negotiated a deal between them, you may have prevented next week's drug-related homicide in West Philly. The fact that they were both willing to come to mediation to talk about what was between them is a huge positive step. Why not build on that? We can't fix society's drug problems in mediation, but we may be able to prevent murders over drug deals."

Karen was silent. She seemed to be stymied by my views, as she collected the small pads of paper she had placed on the table. Her confusion was understandable. My reactions were prompting her to think about who she was in the mediation room and why that matters so much. Adam would love it, I thought. The case had put the question of how Karen saw the parties front and center.

After I left the mediation room I spoke briefly with Anita. I had to account for not giving her my observations of the mediation. "I am sorry, but I cannot give feedback on this session. I really would need a standardized feedback form to do it right." Although this was only a cover for not saying how I felt about how Karen handled the case, Anita seemed unusually receptive.

"Don't worry about it. This new observation policy is just getting rolling anyway. We can skip it this time. The court is not looking for these until next week. What happened in the mediation? I did not get to talk with Karen before she left. Was there an agreement?"

"Actually, there was no agreement because Karen ended the session." I hesitated for a second and then added, "One party told her that the money issue they were disputing involved a recent drug deal." I held back telling Anita what I thought of Karen's decision. I started walking toward the reception door to end the conversation when Anita said more.

"Oh really," Anita said with a curious tone. "The fact that it was a drug deal should not have stopped the mediation. It sounds like these guys needed a chance to work things out." Anita's commentary was somewhat odd. In my experience, rarely did she opine about the outcome of a session.

As she spoke, I remembered that she hadn't given Karen the court intake paper for the case. "Anita, can I see the court's intake sheet for this mediation? I'd like to see if there was any hint of the drug connection in the write-up."

"You should know, Kent, that something like that would never show up on an intake sheet," Anita admonished.

"It's unlikely, but maybe there is something there between the lines. I am just curious."

"Well, I don't have the form any longer. The court likes me to return those sheets the day of the mediation. You know how on top of things I am. Sometimes I can see that my efficiency actually annoys you. But the court appreciates it and I feel good about keeping up with the details."

Before I left the building, I decided to stop at the court administrator's office and ask to see the intake sheet for the mediation I had observed. The court clerk looked through her files for about ten minutes and said that there was no intake record. I told the clerk about the case. She said she would investigate it and told me I could call her back to find out what she discovered.

As I left the courthouse, I saw two men talking in front of the building about 20 yards to my left. I wasn't sure but I thought it was Anita's boyfriend talking to Carlo, one of the men in Karen's mediation session. I waited about halfway down the block and saw both men go back inside the building together. They did not look toward me.

Chapter Thirteen

Bad Wind

After I left the Philadelphia Mediation Center, I checked my messages. There was a voicemail on my cell phone from Bernadette Foy. She is the HR representative at the financial firm in Denver. She originally called me about the team-building session for the IT group at her firm. She said she wanted to talk with me about a possible follow-up assignment with Elliot Susskind—the manager who did not attend his senior staff team building session that I conducted. I wondered what Bernadette wanted. HR representatives can be unpredictable because they are often caught in the middle, representing and advocating for employees at times but also holding them accountable to company standards and policies. It was difficult to surmise what her call was going to be about. I immediately thought of two possibilities. Elliot may want to blame me for the fallout that may have followed the team building session, the kill the facilitator phenomena. Or perhaps someone in the group told Bernadette about giving me an executive coaching engagement with Susskind. The team seemed to be hoping for the coaching.

I called Bernadette the following morning. It turns out her request was for something rather serious. She told me that there is a lawsuit filed against Mr. Susskind by one of the employees in the IT group. He was not one of the senior leaders who attended the team session. She said it was an employee who worked directly for one of Susskind's senior managers, one tier below Susskind's direct reports. This employee did have direct contact with Susskind in working on a couple of high-priority technology projects. In his lawsuit, the employee claims he was injured by Susskind in a closed-door meeting with him when no one else was present. Bernadette wanted to know whether I would mediate this conflict.

My first reaction was to walk away because I thought that this could be dangerous. Too high wire. I would not want to have to fight a subpoena to testify in court if a business dispute like this went to court. I knew that has happened to other mediators. They had to hire their own lawyer to fight the court's demand for testimony. After intervening in the girls' gang dispute, the thought of stepping into another violent conflict was not appealing. I decided to ask more questions before making any decision about the request.

I asked Foy whether Susskind and the employee both agreed to mediate their conflict. Bernadette said she hadn't approached either one of them yet but wanted to know my professional opinion about whether mediation was appropriate to offer. I said personal injury cases are sometimes mediated but this one sounded out of the ordinary. The employee is contending there was a physical altercation of some kind. I asked if she knew whether something injurious had actually happened. She said that Susskind denies it. He says there was no violence or injuries. He claims there was no physical contact at all between him and the employee and he was outraged about the bogus lawsuit.

Foy added that the corporate attorneys have been involved in the case and have talked to both of the parties involved. One of the attorneys suggested that the two men try to mediate their issues. She was not told why they made this recommendation for mediation. She was just following up on the recommendation.

The background Bernadette offered alleviated some of my biggest concerns. I thought that if the lawyers were recommending mediation, they must have thought that a conversation between Susskind and the employee could be helpful. They probably thought it would avoid an expensive court case. I told Bernadette if they both agreed to mediate, I would be willing to do it. I heard a lot about Susskind at the team session but only talked with him on the phone once. I knew it would be a real challenge to remain objective about the issues. I would let the employee know that I had met Susskind and had done the team development work for his group.

I also mentioned that because there is a law suit underway, the employee may ask whether his lawyer can be present in the mediation. I said to Bernadette, "Please let the employee know that I am fine with his lawyer being there so long as Susskind is comfortable with it. If Susskind is not comfortable, then we would not be able to move forward if the employee insists upon having counsel there. Also, let both of them know they can talk with me to find out more about mediation if they feel they need more information about the process before deciding to participate."

Bernadette said she was comfortable asking them whether they would agree to having a mediation, based on the corporate lawyers' recommendation. She would get back to me with their responses. I said I would send her a proposal for the work, and I asked her what the employee's name is in case he contacted me ahead of time with questions. She said that his name was Enzo Morales.

It did not take long for Bernadette to get back to me. Two days later, on Friday, she called and reported that both men were agreeable to mediation. We set up a two-hour time slot for the following Tuesday afternoon in Denver. Afterward she sent me a text. She had forgotten to mention that neither man wanted to have lawyers present at the session. I thought that was a good sign, although predicting what will happen in mediation is a dicey game to play. Anything is possible, as I have learned.

My flight from Philadelphia to Denver on Tuesday morning was late. Air traffic tie ups over Philly. I was worried I might be late for the mediation session, but we made up time in the air and the flight was uneventful otherwise. There was an empty seat beside me, so my claustrophobic threats were low. I was relaxed as I left the airport and got into the limo that would take me to the company. I found myself wondering whether both men would actually show up for the mediation. It was possible that one of their personal lawyers would pull them out.

I asked Bernadette for a comfortable meeting room for the mediation, someplace away from both Susskind's and Morales' workspaces. The room she found was not ideal. It was next to the entranceway of the building and is probably used as a waiting area for vendors and other visitors. It housed an oval table with six swivel chairs around it. Although the chairs were comfortable enough, they were too low for the table. Sitting straight up, the table came only to chest level. It made one's presence in the room shrink, as if you had to look up to see over the table. The light in the room was almost all natural but somewhat harsh. It came from large floor-to-ceiling windows and a huge skylight over the table. I checked and found that the windows did have blinds that closed, reducing some of the afternoon's sun glare and providing needed privacy. I wasn't too pleased with the room overall but decided to live with it. I did not know the building well enough to know what the other options were. I did worry, however, that we would be interrupted repeatedly by those familiar with the space as a quiet waiting area by the entrance. I told the building receptionist at the front desk that we would be meeting in the room and should not be interrupted for two hours. His unintelligible grunt indicated he was non-committal.

Mr. Morales arrived on time. I introduced myself and asked him how he would like to be addressed. He said, "Enzo is fine. No need to be overly formal." I held off talking about the mediation with him and instead asked him several questions about his role and work history at the firm. He was in the IT department for four years and before that he worked for another financial firm in Salt Lake City. He said he was originally from the Dominican Republic but went to school at the University of Miami. I asked him if he missed the island culture. He replied, "Dis is something I miss every day, sir." I noticed the remnants of his Caribbean accent when he spoke. As we talked, I saw that his whole demeanor was calm and non-aggressive, maybe a little overly polite. He conveyed a sense of steadiness and confidence without being abrasive or arrogant.

Twenty minutes went by, and Susskind had not arrived. It occurred to me that he might decide not to go through with the mediation. I called Bernadette's office to see if she could locate him. She was not there so I left a voice message. After almost 30 minutes, a slight, almost gaunt-looking man in his mid to late thirties came through the door. It was Elliot Susskind. I recognized him from the company photo Bernadette had sent me. He was dressed somewhat formally for an IT manager. He had on a blue and white pin-striped shirt and a navy-blue tie. He was much younger than I expected, although he did not look in shape or vigorous.

"Mr. Foxe," he said knowingly. "Sorry, back-to-back meetings never work out."

The uncomfortable aura in the room became considerably more uncomfortable with Susskind's late entrance and his weak apology. He did not look at Morales when he offered his excuse for being late. Nor did he extend a greeting to him, although Morales tried to look directly at him. I was left in the awkward position of having to ask Susskind something we all knew the answer to.

"You know Mr. Morales, don't you?" I asked. I immediately thought that Wittgenstein would say that the actual function of my request for information was a request for action. It told Susskind to acknowledge the other person sitting in this room. He accepted my indirect command. He looked at Mr. Morales for the first time since he entered the room.

"For sure, I do. Hello Enzo," he said with light sarcasm, as he took the seat across from his employee. He clearly wanted the higher ground in the conversation that was about to happen. He was not going to make a cooperative gesture until asked to do so.

There was something immediately unlikeable about Susskind. He had an air of superiority and over-confidence that was as much about defensiveness as status. He was younger than I thought he'd be but he tried to convey that he was older—or more mature—than he was. I quickly told myself that I had to be careful. I could not let his current negative vibe or the prior reactions of his senior staff in the team building session lead me to become biased in this mediation. Being aware of possible bias helps, but it is tough, as a mediator, to distance yourself from your own emotional reaction, whether that reaction is dislike, sympathy, anger, repulsion, or attraction. Bias slips in easily and is difficult to overcome without staginess. I reminded myself that this is one reason to have a co-mediator on hand to take the lead in a mediation if you sense your emotions are getting to you.

I also noted to myself that Morales did not seem offended by Susskind's behavior. Either he was used to it or he expected worse. It was helpful to recognize that Morales's reactions mattered more than my own.

I started the mediation with my usual short opening that covered my role as the mediator, the goals for the session, the promise of confidentiality, and the possibility of private separate meetings with me if requested. I added that I had talked to Susskind on the phone once in preparation for a team-building session I conducted with his senior staff. I assured Enzo that I had never discussed him with Susskind at any prior time. I also said that Bernadette had given me a short overview of the dispute and that she said the firm's attorneys had recommended mediation. I made it clear that was all I knew.

I told both men that if they wanted to speak to me privately at any point, I would do that at their request. I opened the conversation by asking who wanted to speak first. Enzo immediately asked if he could start. I looked at Susskind and waited expectantly for a response. He lifted his shoulders slightly and tightened his brow as if to say "whatever." Another flash of dislike went through me. Hold on, I told myself, he is probably scared and acting out at the thought of being sued by the employee sitting across from him. The thought of legal action would put anyone on the defensive.

Enzo started by talking about an important IT project that he headed. "I was project manager for a large conversion effort dat is affecting de entire firm—de office here in Denver and de one in San Francisco. I report to a senior leader under Elliot, Joe Wong. But for dis project it felt like I was a direct report of Elliot's. Dis project was that important. It was de most high-pressure project I have ever worked on here. Huge visibility in the firm.

"I would have dese meetings with Joe and Elliot and sometimes I would have update meetings just with Elliot. Dese meetings were always at his request and always dey were intense. Lots of pressure. For de last year, every time I met with Elliot, I told him dat we did not have the human resources to complete de technology conversion on time. I told him dat de November first deadline dat Elliot set for de project was way off-base. It was just not enough time. Every time we met, Elliot insisted the deadline was reasonable. He would forget dat the conversion project was only one of many projects that my IT group had on its plate."

There was a short pause, then Elliot jumped in. "I insisted about the deadline because it was possible to meet it with the right organization and planning. It is a project management issue, not a human resource issue," he said emphatically. He looked intensely at Enzo in what was a somewhat intimidating stare. It was clear that he would not be hesitant in challenging any claims that he felt were misrepresentations.

Enzo looked at me and responded, "Well, dis is where we have de disagreement. I was very detailed in my conversations with him about what was needed and why. I specified de capabilities and limitations every time we met. Dese were the facts. Dat was all I could do."

As Enzo paused again, I felt it was important to highlight the differences I just heard from the two men's statements.

"So, the two of you have a strong disagreement about the conversion project and the resources needed to complete it on time. Enzo, you feel the deadline was unreasonable because of inadequate resources. And Elliot, you believe the resources were adequate to meet the deadline if there was sufficient organization and planning for the project." I paused and looked back and forth at each of them as they thought about the divergent views I had summarized.

"That's right," Elliot said. Enzo simultaneously nodded in agreement. My summary gave them both a chance to think about what they were saying and where they disagreed.

Enzo then continued, "De real problem came in when I met with him on October fifteenth, and I told him dat we definitely would not be able to meet de November first deadline he had set—and I never really agreed to. When I told him dis news, Elliot became very angry and slammed dis heavy project manual down on de table. He was sitting less than three feet away from me and I could feel a large puff of air come at me when de manual hit de table. And de slamming noise was so extremely loud dat it injured my eardrum. I have been having trouble hearing in my right ear ever since dis violent incident happened in his office. My doctor has confirmed dat I have hearing loss. I am seeking compensation for dis physical damage. It is dat simple. I think I deserve it. No one should have to go through life with bad hearing."

It took me a few seconds to digest what Enzo just said. I sensed my own skepticism about Enzo's claim but knew I had to reflect his comments as neutrally as possible. But before I could say anything Elliot, now clearly agitated, started to speak again.

"That is ridiculous," he said indignantly. "Do you expect me or some judge to think for one minute that your hearing was hurt by the slam you heard in my office? It is preposterous. Your lawsuit is preposterous. It will never hold up in court. I don't know why you are wasting your time and money. We are in a tough business, and you are making it tougher on yourself." Susskind's claims were delivered with more nervous intensity than outright arrogance.

Looking directly at Susskind I said, "You believe that Enzo's hearing could not have been caused by the sound you made when you slammed the manual on your desk. Is that right?"

"Exactly," Susskind said emphatically. "I am not denying I threw down the manual, but it was not thrown at Enzo. Not even close. It landed on my desk three feet away from him. And I had every right to be mad. I was under pressure to make sure that the deadline was met. At the end of the day, the buck stops with me. I am the one who has his ass on the line for these big, important projects. That is the way this place works."

"My ass is on de line as well," Enzo said assertively, looking directly at Elliot. He was holding his own against Susskind's aggressiveness. He sounded convinced of his own arguments and was not about to let Susskind gain unwarranted ground.

There was a long pause that I did not want to interrupt.

Both men seemed at a loss of what to say next. Their blunt comments pointed precisely to the chasm between them. I resisted thinking about or suggesting any grand solutions—I was learning from past mistakes. Follow, don't lead the parties.

Enzo then asked me a question. "You said, Kent, dat either one of us could ask to have time with you alone if we feel we needed it. I would like dat private time if it is okay with you."

I looked at Elliot to gauge his response to Enzo's request. He shrugged his shoulders again in the "whatever" reaction. I said, "I am happy to meet with you alone as well, Elliot, if that is helpful."

He replied, "It's not necessary. Bernadette would like us to meet separately after this session for coaching anyway. I can talk with you then about all this."

The coaching was news to me. I didn't recall Bernadette mentioning it. Perhaps I was too wrapped up in planning the mediation to recall it at the moment. I made a mental note that I needed to confirm this with her before meeting with Elliot after the mediation was over. And my time would be limited because of my flight schedule.

I said to Elliot, "Please step outside the room but stay close so I can reach you when we are finished. Usually, the separate meetings last about ten minutes or so." Elliot walked out leaving the door open behind him. I got up and slowly closed it. I could see that he was sitting on a chair in the lobby looking at his phone.

I told Enzo that this separate meeting was confidential. I would not tell Elliot anything that he said during this private conversation without his permission. Enzo nodded and then began talking slowly.

"I know dis is rather peculiar but dere is something important to say about my response to Elliot's behavior at dat meeting in his office. I said dat when he threw down de manual I was hit by a puff of air. I was sitting close enough that I could feel it. That was true. Well, in my culture we have a deep belief about bad wind. We believe dat when you get hit by wind from the expression of someone's anger, you have seven years' bad luck. The negativity stays around you dat long. I think I deserve something for dat risk he has left with me. Dat is why I have the lawsuit. My hearing is bad, but I am not one hundred percent sure dat it is all due to Elliot's slamming de manual down. It could be though. I don't know definitely. My question for you, Kent, is should I tell Elliot about my belief in bad wind and tell him dis is why I am so upset with him? Why I am suing him. It is tough for me to bring this issue up to the lawyers or Elliot. I know they will not understand."

I paused for a few seconds and decided to emphasize Enzo's own instincts. "That decision is yours. There are risks either way—of talking about it or not bringing it up. But I can help you think it through. What specific concerns do you have about telling him?" I asked.

"Well, I think he might see it just as a foolish superstition. For me it is more than dat, it is more like religious belief. To be cursed with bad luck is a serious threat for my people, like losing your faith in God's protection. We have needed that protection over the years in my vulnerable country. I don't know if he can understand this point. It is not in North American culture. Bringing it up might just make me look backwards in his eyes."

"So you seem to be saying you don't want to tell him because he may not understand your cultural and religious beliefs," I said. "What would you like to do? What do you think is best?"

"I don't want to be the one to tell him, but I want him to know about it. Is it possible for you to tell him? If he hears it from you, I won't have to deal with his negative reaction. I could avoid being insulted further," Enzo asked.

"I am not comfortable doing that in the context of this

mediation," I replied. "I don't reveal anything you say in this separate meeting. Also, if I tell him in a separate meeting now, it doesn't protect you in the way you want to be protected. If I do act as an executive coach for him after the mediation and I have your permission, I could give him this information as feedback for him. It might have an impact, or it might not. I can't say either way how he might react but at least you would not have to deal with his reaction in person."

"Dat might work best," Enzo said. "Please tell him why I am so upset with him when you meet with him alone. You can let him know dat I gave you my permission."

"Anything else you want to talk about before I go and get Elliot?" I asked.

"No, not really, but thank you for this conversation," Enzo said.

I called Elliot back in the room and asked the two men whether there was anything else they wanted to say to each other or any topics they wanted to discuss.

Elliot said, "I've been thinking during this time. What is most important for both of us is that we get the project completed as soon as possible. Can we talk about that? It might be the most productive way to spend your time with us, Kent. Other things will just have to work themselves out over time. If there is legal action, we will have to deal with it outside this meeting anyway."

I looked at Enzo to see what he would say.

Enzo brightened up a bit and replied, "Dat is fine with me." It seemed like both men wanted to avoid further uncomfortable discussion and instead make some progress on the project they had to finish. In a way, it was escapism from the tough issues. But it was their choice. Maybe they could have a more productive conversation about the work than they ever had before. I was careful to tell myself that it was not up to me to decide where their conversation should go next.

From that point on the two men discussed the details and

plans of their rather complicated IT project. A lot of the topics were too technical for me to retrace for them, so after about 30 minutes I asked them each to summarize what they thought they were agreeing to. Both seemed to have similar interpretations of what would happen going forward. They set no new deadline for the project but agreed to talk about it again in a week. Neither was completely happy with the results of their discussion but they both seemed to appreciate the opportunity to talk civilly with each other about what needed to be done and by when. They seemed relieved to focus just on the details of the work plan in a way they hadn't been able to recently.

As the discussion wrapped up, they both thanked me for conducting the mediation. I told Elliot I would be willing to talk with him now, but I needed to confirm the coaching engagement with HR first. Elliot said he would be in his office for the rest of the afternoon. He said he had already agreed to the coaching and Bernadette would confirm it.

CHAPTER FOURTEEN

The Coaching

When I called Bernadette, she apologized for not being clear about the coaching engagement for Susskind. She said she thought she had talked with me about it. I knew she hadn't otherwise I would have already sent her a proposal with fees for the coaching. I told her I had some time to get started today and Susskind was expecting that to happen. She said she appreciated my flexibility. She wanted a high-level commentary on the mediation and the coaching in a few days—just any accomplishments which were achieved. I told her I had to be careful not to break confidentiality for either the mediation or the coaching assignment. I did say that both men were fully engaged in the mediation process. I knew she wanted to know whether the lawsuit was dropped, but I did not comment on it. The truth was I didn't know what Enzo would do from this point on. There were clear pros and cons of continuing to pursue a lawsuit on what appeared to be shaky grounds. It may depend upon what Elliot did or did not do after this mediation. But I could not predict where things would go from here.

After talking to Bernadette, I called Susskind to confirm he was still available. He said, "Yes, come up to the second-floor reception and the woman at the desk will escort you from there to my office." When I arrived at Susskind's door, he inted me toward a chair at a small round table on one side of the room. He stayed six feet away at his desk. There were two other chairs at the table which he chose not to take. Whether it was conscious or just intuitive on his part, he clearly established his status—and a sense of personal distance—by this awkward seating arrangement. I knew immediately that I would have to confront him about this move before this first coaching session was over. His office seating arrangement was a concrete illustration of how he made people feel distant and manipulated right from the start of any meeting with him. It was a physical embodiment of the symbolic messages he consistently sends to people.

I told Elliot about the coaching process and the promise of confidentiality. I said that HR would ask only for a set of goals we decide upon for the coaching. I told him I had about 45 minutes today and would then need to head to the airport. We should plan for two-hour sessions in the future.

"I am not exactly sure how this coaching will work. I'm suspicious," Susskind said. "When someone is assigned a coach at this firm, it is usually a sign that he is on the way out. After he is fired, HR can then say we tried to rehabilitate him with coaching, but it didn't work. So don't get your hopes up that you will make a big difference in my case. The outcome may already be determined."

"That is not my sense of why I am here to work with you. Coaching is an investment the firm is making in you," I said, feeling slightly unsure of my own claim. "If I learn that the outcome is pre-set, I will stop the coaching immediately. But I have nothing to make me assume this is a futile effort. The results are more likely to be determined by how you view the coaching engagement and what changes you decide to make. So how do you want to use the time we have today?"

Susskind thought for a few seconds then said, "I'd like to talk about the mediation we just had with Enzo, since you were there and saw it all firsthand. Is that okay?"

"Sure. That's fine," I replied. I was glad he wanted to go there.

"It was helpful to finally talk productively about the project again," Elliot said. "I'm not sure we could have done that on our own. Or done it in as constructive a way as we did. If Enzo had kept that intense focus on the work rather than demanding more people for his staff, he probably could have met the deadline. Instead, he went astray by going after me and accusing me of inappropriate behavior. That story he made up about his hearing damage was preposterous. That's just insane and any judge will see through it in a minute. HR knows that as well, that's why they suggested mediation. I am sure of it. They wanted him to give up on this foolish claim. It was good we talked about the project. That was a sensible use of the time at least."

"Why do you think you were able to make progress today and not before?" I asked.

"That's easy. He wasn't arguing that he could not do the work on time. He did not set me off with his weak excuses. He focused on what needed to be done."

"It might be good to think about how a change in your behavior enabled him to keep focused. What were you not doing that allowed him to change? It is easy to miss that a change in our behavior makes possible changes in someone else's."

I wasn't going to let Susskind stay in his safe place. He was too willing to overlook what mattered. "I am glad you found the last half of the mediation useful," I said. "But I think I missed a huge opportunity when Enzo discussed the aggressive behavior you engaged in during that one-on-one meeting with him in your office."

"Really, how so?" Elliot asked somewhat defensively.

"Two points actually. First, you did not take any personal responsibility for your behavior. Nor were you self-critical about it. You left the clear impression that you felt your behavior, especially slamming the manual down on your desk, was warranted and acceptable. Second, you missed a chance to find out what made Enzo so upset. Why he would go so far as to contend that you had caused his hearing damage, a rather outrageous claim, as you suggest. There were possible revelations in that conversation which you did not explore or benefit from. In a way you actually shut them out."

As I spoke, I heard the switch I had made from an unbiased mediator to instructive coach. I was no longer a neutral facilitator. The difference in goals and language sounded quite stark to me and hopefully to Susskind. I was there now to help him reflect on his management and communication styles. I didn't want to be judgmental but I did want him to think in new ways, to become more aware of his blind spots and inadvertent messages.

Elliot looked puzzled and a little annoyed, as he asked, "What kind of revelations from Enzo did I miss? He was quite direct and had every opportunity to speak his mind. And I got what he was saying—I had heard it all before. Maybe he said something to you in the separate meeting that I didn't get to hear."

"Well, Enzo has some deeply held beliefs that stem from his cultural background," I explained. "One is that when you get hit with what he called bad wind you will have seven years' bad luck. The manual you slammed on the table did not hit him, but the air it moved did. The bad wind came from your expression of anger towards him that day. He wants compensation—and maybe a sincere apology—for that bad luck he truly believes lies ahead for him. He asked me to tell you about this belief and why it matters to him so much. He was afraid you would belittle him if he raised this with you directly. He did not want to deal with your likely reaction."

"Although it is a little out there, that makes more sense than the hearing damage story," Elliot said. "I know about some superstitions like never pointing at a rainbow or never having a dinner with thirteen people, but I never heard of the bad wind belief. I don't think I should be held accountable for not knowing about his culturally based superstitions and for damages that have not happened yet. This still sounds out there someplace."

"That may be true, but the conversation you had in mediation was a time and place where you could have learned about his belief and responded to it in a way that respected his assumptions, even if you held different beliefs. My sense is that this is why he was amenable to participating in mediation in the first place. He had hopes for greater understanding that could have taken the edge off for him. Maybe it would deter him from continuing with the lawsuit."

"I see that now. But his superstitions are not mine as well. They don't have to be. I did not intend to cause the bad luck. And I did not injure his hearing."

"It's not about the validity of the superstition as much as it is about the interpretations that are assigned to your behavior. Especially the meanings that get assigned to what you say and do that you are not aware of. Your angry behavior was interpreted as causing bad luck for him. Finding that out matters whether you agree with that interpretation or not. And there may be a lot of messages you send that get interpreted in ways you are not aware of. We need to explore this more in the coaching."

Elliot began to look somewhat concerned. A serious expression came over his face as I began to see a different emotional side to him. I decided to broaden the discussion somewhat and focus more on how he wanted to use the coaching moving forward. "So maybe we should talk for a while about the specific goals you want to set for this coaching engagement overall."

Elliot paused. He still had a somber look on his face. "You should know my history here because it may come to an end soon. Ever since I started here nine years ago I beat my brains out for this place. My days at work were endless and I knew how to master the competitive game that this place cherished. I went overboard in every way to move up the hierarchy. I was so competitive that someone once said: 'Susskind would eat his twin at birth if he had to.' Once I started running on this competitive track, I jumped every hurdle in front of me. It didn't matter how many people I knocked down along the way. I was ruthless—but effective—just like my mentor."

"Who was your mentor? Was it someone here at this firm?" I asked.

"James Cathcart. He was a former army colonel who led IT here with an iron hand before me. He is retired now. I adopted his ways—how he got things done, mostly through disguised intimidation, silent threats, and sheer bullheadedness. People feared rather than respected him. I thrived on his strong man methods and learned to imitate his style perfectly. We were both highly rewarded for effectively tackling any difficult project at this firm. We were almost revered for it by senior management. No one gave a hoot about how we got it all done or how many people left the firm because of us. They just assumed we knew best. We were given a long leash."

Susskind stopped briefly and seemed slightly hesitant to continue, as if he might not want to hear what he was going to say. His words seemed more for him than me. I left the pause and he decided to continue.

"When Cathcart retired, I was the young clone who was next in line to preserve the tight-fisted culture. I sat on top for a while and continued to enact the militaristic management moves. Now, recently, the firm's leadership has changed and so has its culture. The firm has found Jesus—and I am practically an outcast Saint. I am now the Judas Iscariot who betrayed the culture. My competitive drive is now seen as aggression, and I am close to being fired. I look back and ask myself how did I get here? How did I become what I have become? I have a lawsuit against me, two of my senior staff—

talented people—left last week and blasted me in their exit interviews. I am sure you heard an earful at the team session. I am about to be demoted to head of software development rather than running all of IT. That will make me lose face in the entire firm. And I have been warned by my manager, who you will have to meet, that I will be fired on the spot if I have another outburst of any kind with an employee. They have told me flat out that I am not indispensable. I already feel like a lame duck manager. I don't see how I can stay. And when I think of how I was when I first started, I am a different person now—someone I don't really like."

"That's a lot," I said. I let the lull in the conversation remain as he and I both thought about all he had just revealed. I pondered whether his gaunt appearance was due to the stress he was obviously coping with. Maybe he was not eating normally or was severely ill. Clearly there was a link to his current physical appearance. The pressures he described had taken a noticeable toll on his body.

"There's more. My wife left me about a year ago, after fifteen years of marriage. She said we had no life together anymore. She was right. She was not at the top of my list for years. It was too late to try to revive the marriage. I don't think I am fit for any close relationship anymore. But that goes way beyond this coaching, doesn't it?"

"I am sorry to hear that," I said sympathetically. I could not help but feel badly for him after listening closely to his disturbing confession. "It sounds like the coaching might help you decide who you want to be from this point on—whether you stay at this firm or move someplace else from here. That could be a main goal of this coaching assignment," I suggested.

"Right. How do I keep my intellectual strengths and strong ambition but not be the asshole I have become? How is that for a coaching goal? Can you help with that one? You probably haven't had to deal with someone who is caught in such a self created down-turn."

"That goal for the coaching may be linked to where you want to end up, what you're working toward. A smart consultant once said, 'Ambition is a path, not a destination.' It sounds like you may need to recalibrate your definition of success and think about how you want to walk whatever path you decide to take from this point."

Elliot thought about it and nodded slowly in agreement. Although we hadn't talked long, I felt he was overwhelmed by what we had discussed. He probably was never this open with anyone before and just telling where things stood for him personally and professionally was emotionally exhausting. Although in some ways, it seemed to be a relief for him. He was able to admit to himself where he was and how he felt about it. He seemed brutally honest about himself.

I was slightly hesitant to give him one more piece of negative feedback, but I felt it would help him realize that coaching was about changing his behaviors and eliminating unrealized and unwanted interpretations of them. I decided to go ahead with it, at the risk of turning him against me and the coaching.

"We need to wrap up soon because I have to catch my flight. The airport is not close. Next time we should talk about who you think I should get feedback from, who can make sure we are not missing anything important. But first I need to give you one thing to think about based on what I saw today."

"You might as well. I need as much help as I can get," Susskind said submissively.

"You need to know that I have been somewhat uncomfortable through this entire meeting with you."

"Really, why?" Elliot asked, looking ill at ease. "Did I say something offensive? I tried to be on my best behavior for you. Maybe I was too blunt."

"No, it's not anything to do with what you said. I was uncomfortable from the start because of the seating arrangement you set up with me in this office. You sat me here at this table by myself across the room from you as you sat there behind your desk. It would be good to think about what kind of relationship this seating arrangement establishes with people even before any conversation starts in this office. It is not a positive frame to put around people. In effect it says 'I will talk at you—not with you. You cannot share space with me. I will keep you at a distance.'"

I could tell by the concerned look on his face that he had never thought about this before. It was a definite wake-up call for him. It reinforced the sense that he is missing other people's negative interpretations of his behavior. I knew by his reaction that his decision to sit across the room was intuitive, not strategic. It reflected who he was—or had become.

All Susskind said was, "I can see you are not afraid to hit a guy when he is down."

His violent metaphor made me uncomfortable. Giving feedback should wake people up, not injure them. Susskind was not as tough as he led on. He might be facing more than he thinks he can handle.

As I wrapped up the conversation all I said was, "Thank you for being willing to think about some tough issues." While I gathered my things, Susskind turned to his computer and began typing intensely. The message from him was that the meeting was over. We ended without saying good-bye or offering well-wishes. It was a reminder to me that corporate cultures have a way of making simple civilities seem inappropriate.

CHAPTER FIFTEEN

It's a Wonderful Fight

When I got back from Denver late Tuesday night, Gio was asleep. I was exhausted but still somewhat restless, my usual response to being confined on a plane for over three hours. I decided to watch an old movie. I checked the TCM channel and, although it was only early November, the popular holiday film *It's a Wonderful Life* was on. I was not ready to start thinking about the holiday season yet. It seems to start earlier and earlier every year. I left the channel on and, as I watched the movie, my mind kept drifting to the mediation and coaching I did today.

I kept hearing the title "It's a Wonderful Life" as "It's a Wonderful Fight." I thought that the conflict between Enzo and Elliot had the unrealized potential to be a wonderful fight. People are often in a state of valuable wonder when they hear or realize something about someone else or themselves that they hadn't thought of before. They come to appreciate themselves and their perceived enemies in ways that are surprising and profound. It was too early to know how the Susskind-Morales conflict was going to turn out. Susskind might work through his deep regrets over who he has become and find his true value, like Spencer Tracy does in the holiday movie. He is obviously a smart and successful guy. He might see the positives he has contributed to others' lives and what he could do with the rest of his career that would be of value to him. Understanding Enzo's cultural background might be the first step in that empathetic direction, like a preschooler who realizes for the first time that the toys in the kindergarten are for everyone's use.

My wandering thoughts began to make me realize how much was at stake for Susskind. Further influenced by the plot of the Wonderful Life film, I started thinking that Susskind, in despair over the demise of his professional and personal life, might try to take his own life. Now the coaching took on greater significance, perhaps too much significance. I would have to watch for signs that he might need therapy more than executive coaching. Or was my tired mind just letting my imagination run wild? I would need tomorrow's clear head to put this all in perspective.

Gio got up before me the next morning. I awoke to the smell of an Italian family favorite breakfast: fried potatoes and scrambled eggs. There was a subtle way of mixing the two together that I never quite mastered. Gio frequently let me know that it was a cooking skill that I did not have. One time I added chopped green peppers to the mix and was severely chastised for ruining the dish. It tasted fine to me, but I've learned that tradition is paramount in Italian family cooking. There is never a written recipe but, God forbid, you should change things slightly. It's cause for debate and sometimes divorce.

I asked Gio if he missed me while I was in Denver. He said it was fine because I was gone for only a day and a half. I told him this was highly interesting work and worth the travel time. He asked what went on at the Denver firm. I gave Gio a summary of what transpired the day before. After hearing both sides in the mediation, Gio stood behind Susskind more than Enzo. Analytical neutrality was not a skill Gio had mastered. He easily saw the rights and wrongs in most situations. Sometimes too easily. I often tried to slow down his judgmental tendencies, but he relied heavily on his first instincts. These were often quite valuable to hear.

"The employee just went too far in making the claim about his hearing damage," Gio said. "That was just foolish on his part. It was too obvious a ploy for a lawsuit."

"I know it was absurd in one sense, but people do things like that when they feel they have been treated unfairly," I responded. "They just don't want to lie down and take undeserved abuse, so they find a way to get back, even if it is a far-fetched tactic or a totally transparent lie. Just the threat of a lawsuit, no matter how preposterous, got corporate HR attention. It gave Enzo an impactful voice in the organization. That is definitely worth the risk of being seen as overly litigious."

"I do think that the manager deserves to be demoted," Gio added. "He seems to be scaring away the firm's best talent and demotivating the people who stay at the company. No one should be allowed to undermine an entire division out of personal greed and career ambition. You heard enough from the disgruntled employees about Susskind at the team building session to know this was happening."

"I tend to agree. But here again, things are complicated. These large firms demand extreme competitiveness and even condone aggressiveness as long as it is adding to the bottom line or saving great expense. Sometimes they set up co-heads in a division to see who outshines the other as they both vie for the top spot. The firm says it values cooperation but rewards extreme competitiveness. Then it happens. One day, someone like Susskind steps a little too far and someone higher up in the firm is outraged. The leadership becomes afraid that Susskind is exposing the tip of the dangerous iceberg. He then becomes a scapegoat for the firm. They use him to warn other people in the firm. It reminds me of the Mike Tyson fiasco."

"Mike Tyson, how so? He was a boxer, wasn't he?" Gio

asked.

"Yes, a champion boxer. Do you remember what happened? Boxers can punch the hell out of their opponents. Concussions and brain damage of any kind are just fine. But whatever you do, don't bite the other guy's ear as Tyson did in one well-publicized fight. There is an artificial line drawn. Aggression is aggression, but some of it is expected and rewarded while some is punished. God forbid you don't see where the line is. Knock someone out and you are a revered champion. Bite an opponent's ear and you are a monster. Susskind bit the organizational ear and is now an outcast in his own professional boxing ring."

"It does seem like the manager, Susskind, wants to change," Gio said. "It sounds like he really opened up to you in the coaching and wants to be someone other than himself. He seems to hate the culture that made him what he has become. It sounds like there is some positive motivation there."

"That is half the battle in coaching. When people want to change because they have a real incentive, then the coaching tends to be successful. When the coachee resists their current situation or the feedback they receive, nothing much happens. As a coach, I see myself as someone who points out how and why people's behavior is perceived as non-normative—out of the bounds of the organization's expectations. It is up to the coachee to then decide whether he wants to stand outside the norms. But the risk is theirs to take, not mine. I get to walk away from the situation. My only risk is their reaction when I give them negative feedback that lets them know how they are perceived. This can be deeply threatening to people. The feedback process is one of the most tricky and delicate aspects of coaching. I may have offended Susskind with some of the challenging feedback I gave him."

"Have you ever coached someone who decided not to change and ended up bucking the norms and taking the risks?" Gio asked.

"There have been several people. I worked with a woman who headed one of the investment banking areas in a large Wall Street firm. She was African American, was from the South originally, and was educated at Harvard and Wharton. The coaching was suggested by her senior manager—a VP for banking—who had been at the firm for over thirty years. When I collected feedback about her from the VP and other senior leaders, the comments were quite positive. Only a couple people had any constructive criticism, and that feedback was quite vague. They referred to "cultural fit" issues with the firm. When pressed, I could only get any helpful clarification about this from one or two people. Others seemed reluctant and too embarrassed to explain what they meant. The few who did clarify their feedback said that people talked about her personal style not fitting the staid, formal image that the firm had of itself. Pressed further, they talked about the colorful clothes she wore and the amount of jewelry she had on every day. When I told her that people in the firm saw her personal style as non-normative for the organization, she looked at me and said unapologetically, 'That's fine. I am not changing a thing.'"

"Did she succeed at the firm?" Gio asked.

"Yes, but only to a degree. She definitely hit a cultural ceiling at her conservative firm. At least she was clear about her choices and their consequences. Her eyes were wide open. She was willing to challenge entrenched male racism within the organization. She felt older white men had no right to dictate how she dressed. She was willing to take the risk of not changing."

"Interesting coaching assignment. I can tell you had your head on straight as her coach."

"It was enormously helpful in defining my role as a coach. I was not there to tell her to change, but rather to give her an opportunity to change if she wanted it. Her reasons for not changing were clear and principled. Who was I to question them? I wanted to make sure she did understand the risks of not conforming though."

"Getting back to yesterday in Denver, were there any problems doing both mediation and then the coaching with Susskind? Was there any conflict of interest in taking on the two roles?" Gio inquired.

"No question, I had to be careful. It was awkward in some ways, although not really a conflict of interest. It meant being totally transparent about my involvement in each process with both people and with human resources. Stepping dramatically from a truly neutral role in mediation to a guiding voice in coaching is not that rough for me. Although the mediator's role was tricky, it was actually a great opportunity to see Susskind interact with his employee. Even though he was probably on good behavior in front of me in the mediation, I could see his impervious, condescending style in the raw. This was valuable for the coaching. I had firsthand observations to draw on. "

We finished breakfast and went our separate ways for the day. Gio headed out to his office, and I stayed at the home office to think about where things stood with several projects that were on the back burner and what I had to get done this week. I looked out the window and saw that we were just starting to feel the ominous effects of a fall Nor'easter storm up the New Jersey coast. These storms come roaring up the coast from the south and tend to produce more wind than snow or ice at this time of year. I still thought it would be fine to plan for a workday out tomorrow. Maybe a trip to the Mediation Center in Philly.

I decided to call Anita at the Mediation Center to see what my status was there and whether they were even thinking of me for any upcoming mediation cases.

When Anita answered the phone, her voice was solemn, "Kent, there is more bad news," she said. The young girl—

Latisha—died last night from her attack wounds. It is in this morning's paper. It turns out it was the boyfriend of the other girl in the mediation who attacked her. Very sad. Unfortunately, the article mentions that the two girls had been to mediation but with no positive results. Judge McGinny is a little freaked out. He wanted to know how the sensitive information about the mediation leaked. I assured him that I said nothing to anyone about the case. Do you want to talk with him? It might be a good idea."

"Don't tell me he thinks it was me who talked to the media. That's outrageous. Let me think about this for a while," I replied. "I am too upset about this tragic news."

I knew I was too defensive to talk to the judge. It seemed like my mediation effort was being singled out as a factor in the violent attack on Latisha. I am sure the judge would not want to hear my views about that. And I might not be able to hold back about the changes McGinny was making in the mediation program. But I should be able to hold back about my views and, with the girl's tragic death, I don't want to sound callous.

"I just feel terrible about Latisha," I said to Anita. "Such a waste of young life. So senseless. And it is happening all over this city and others across this country. I don't know what would make a difference, but something needs to be done."

I took some quiet time to grapple with Latisha's death and what was happening with mediation at the program. I had images of the two young girls sitting across from each other in the mediation session. And I saw their mother's helplessness in the face of where they knew things might end up. Self-doubts began to rise up in me again. I got into this work because I thought I could help people. Now it seemed like I was only a witness—perhaps a contributor—to a mindless murder.

I started feeling down and decided that I should put my mind elsewhere or take a few hours off. The day was far from over, but I did not want to get caught up with what was happening with court annexed mediation in Philadelphia. I could feel the ground shifting under me and I needed to stabilize myself. Whenever I feel unsettled, I start to think about how time passes. Time seems to have stopped since the teen mediation, even though I was very busy. My mind was not moving completely forward, past the tragic event. I decided to listen's to Mahler's first symphony. It always awakens a sense of hope in me in the darkest of days.

Around three-thirty I got a call from Gio. He was on his way home. Something was going on with Bill but he couldn't give me details right then. "I'll tell you as much as I know when I get home," he said. I could tell he was upset.

Gio looked beside himself when he came through the side door of the house. He was clearly distraught. I could always tell when something bad happened because Gio would tend to talk past me rather than to me. His focus was on the event, not the telling of it. It was always apparent on his face that he was coming to grips with whatever had happened.

"I got a call from Rosa," he said. "She said that the Cape May police called her. Bill was in the hospital close to the shore after being rescued from a boating accident near Ocean City."

"A boating accident? He doesn't own a boat and who would be out in a boat with the Nor'easter storm that's moving up the coast today?" I asked dumbfoundedly.

"I have no idea what happened, Kent. I only have limited information at this point."

"Do you know if he is seriously hurt?" I asked.

"Rosa was too upset to be able to clearly describe Bill's condition on the phone. She wants to head down to the hospital as soon as possible. Her beat-up car is not reliable enough to make the trip. She asked if I could take her in my car."

"What did you say?" I asked.

"I said I would pick her up around five p.m. I was hesitant but I felt trapped. What was I supposed to say, no I won't drive you? When it comes to situations like this, there is no other way. I'm just going to have to deal with Rosa and shake off some of the past, at least for the time it takes to get to the shore to see Bill."

Gio's values were always clear. His family commitments were always a priority. He could draw a line when he needed to, as he did when Bill's brother Sammy had repeated drug offenses. But in a crisis like this there is no question that he would do what's needed, even if it meant having to support Rosa. You just had to be there for family in a crisis. It was an admirable quality, but one that sometimes caused him and us thorny problems. Somehow, though, he always managed to maneuver through the issues and still be loved by all of the 30-some family members he had.

"Do you want me to come with you?" I asked unenthusiastically.

"It's probably best if you stay here until I find out what's going on first," Gio said.

I didn't want Gio to think I didn't want to go with him because of Rosa. But truth be told, I didn't want to go with him because of Rosa. "Are you sure?" I asked sincerely. "I am worried about you making the trip in the storm. I am sure I can handle it."

"Well, if I need to go back tomorrow you can come with me then," he said. He was kind enough to spare me the ride to the shore with Rosa. Now that is true love, I thought. I hoped he didn't feel like, if I went with them, he would need to manage me and Rosa.

Gio quickly ate a sandwich and started to head out to get gas before picking up Rosa. I hugged him and asked him to call me as soon as he arrived at the hospital. I was worried because the storm had not completely passed yet and I knew it would be worse at the shore. The shore towns flood quickly, and power lines and trees go down easily in the wind.

Getting to the shore from our place usually takes about an

hour and a half, depending on traffic. The traffic on the Atlantic City Expressway would be light this time of year, but Gio would likely hit rush hour traffic heading over the bridge from Philadelphia to New Jersey. I wondered what kind of company Rosa would be for him. Just thinking about the whole situation made me edgy.

Gio texted me around seven to let me know he just arrived at the hospital. He didn't call back until eight to let me know what was going on.

"Apparently the boat Bill was in capsized in the storm, overtaken by strong winds," Gio explained. "Bill is being treated for hypothermia and a broken arm. They are also monitoring his heart because of his cardiac condition. Hypothermia can aggravate it. I noticed his breathing is shallow and they have him on oxygen. So, it is quite serious."

"Is he conscious? Can he talk?" I asked.

"Barely. He comes in and out of it. He mumbles a lot but it is mostly unintelligible. It may be the medication he is on for the hypothermia, or he still may be in shock."

"And Rosa?" I asked, taking a deep breath.

"She barely said anything the whole trip down here. I sense she feels resentful for needing my help in this situation. There were no expressions of appreciation from her. At the hospital she was close to hysterical before the doctor came in and gave her more positive news about Bill's condition. I tried to calm her down several times while we sat in Bill's hospital room. I hope she took enough of whatever drug she is on before she left their apartment. She was understandably anxious, but her emotional state was way over-board. It was hard to be with her."

"Sounds like you have not been able to find out much about what Bill was doing out in a boat in a storm. There are so many questions. Was he alone? Whose boat was it? Did Rosa know where he was? There's a lot to find out about what happened, isn't there?"

201

"A lot of this doesn't make sense yet. Rosa said she had no idea he was at the shore. She thought he took on an extra shift at the restaurant where he works. But who knows if she is telling the truth? For all I know she could have sent him away. I need to talk to the police to find out more of the details. Let me head over to the Cape May County police headquarters now to see what I can find out. God knows what I will hear from them. It's hard to believe it's not criminal in some way."

"Okay, call me back no matter how late. I will stay up," I said.

Gio called back around ten-thirty. In some ways, the details of the accident were more upsetting than the medical report. The boat was his brother Anthony's. Apparently, Bill stole the boat earlier in the day.

"He knew all the keys for the boat and the storage shed were in Anthony's car glove box," Gio explained. "He got the keys by breaking into his brother's car last night. He headed down to the shore this morning on the train to Atlantic City. Then he took an Uber to the docks on the bay in Ocean City. He remembered which boat was Anthony's and he was able to get it going. He took it into the bay and then the ocean. The local Coast Guard had an eye on him because he was out in the boat as the storm was headed up the coast. They track this kind of risky behavior. No one should have been anywhere near a boat today. They knew something was not right."

"Wow. This is bad. Why would he do such an insane thing?" I asked.

"Because he is very unstable. I think he must have had a breakdown of some kind. I told the officers about his untreated mental condition. I also told the attending doctor at the hospital. The doctor said she would have the staff psychiatrist examine him first thing in the morning. I am sure there will be legal charges against him because the Coast Guard had to go out to rescue him in stormy weather. They put their lives at risk trying to save him."

"He was lucky the Coast Guard saw him out there," I said.

"Yeah, if it had gotten any darker out, he would have been a goner," Gio agreed.

"What are you going to do? And what does Rosa want to do?" I asked.

"There is nothing more I can do here tonight. I am headed back to the hospital to check on him one more time. Visiting hours were over at nine though, so it may not be possible to get in. Then I'll head home."

"And Rosa?"

"She said she was going to spend the night at the hospital. The floor nurse approved it."

"Well, be careful driving home. You must be exhausted," I cautioned. "Are you sure you just don't want to get a motel room for the night down there someplace?"

"No, I'll be all right. The storm seems to have passed. Things have quieted down," Gio said. "My adrenaline is still pumping. The ride home will calm me down."

I tried to stay awake until Gio returned home. I could not last that long. I heard Gio enter our bedroom a little after midnight. I was too tired to wake up fully. When he got in bed, we hugged then rolled over so we were back-to-back—the best arrangement for much-needed, uninterrupted sleep. I was sure he was exhausted.

I woke up before Gio and made a pot of loose-leaf, jasmine tea for us. My first thought in the morning was about Bill and why he did what he did. It was so hard to figure out. Was he on a planned suicide mission? Or did he need to relieve deep anxiety by taking a dangerous, self-destructive adventure? Or was this somehow wrapped up in his World War II bunker project? Was he on a sea-crossing mission for his research? Any of these were possible explanations. We may never know or understand why it happened, I thought. I realized that the more immediate question is how involved should Gio and I be with Bill and Rosa and their current problems? The stakes had now risen dramatically.

Gio and I talked for quite a while after he got up and took his shower. There were a lot of decisions we had to make. I told Gio about the possible explanations I had come up with for Bill's reckless behavior. He agreed that all of them were feasible. "We don't know what he is like day to day but his last conversation with us was disturbing," Gio said. "He was coping with a lot of anxiety and seemed confused and lonely. Things probably just built up in him and the build-up resulted in his self-destructive actions yesterday. It could have been much worse."

"Right, but it was bad enough. Are you going back to the hospital this morning?" I asked.

"I probably should. This way I can have a conversation with the doctors about his precarious mental state. I am a little afraid that Rosa will interfere with or at least not support any medical plans for help they recommend for his condition. I am sure Bill has convinced her that he doesn't need psychological help. She did not hear me mention Bill's issues to the attending doctor last night. I am not sure what she will do or whether she will get on board with any suggested treatments. She is not his wife, so she does not have a final say. This is in some ways an opportunity, an opening for finally getting him the help he's needed. Let's try to be optimistic about it."

"Yes, there may finally be an opening," I said. "I want to go with you today. I want to keep you company and I want Rosa to see that we both are part of Bill's family. If she loses it again, I can deal with it now that I know what she is capable of. I won't be shocked or defensive. I will just not respond to her." No time for a wonderful fight with Rosa, I thought to myself.

"Okay, I am so glad you are here and not away on a work trip. Do you see why I press you on the amount of travel away time you take? You never know what a new day will bring and why I might need you close by," Gio said. "I want you to watch how involved I am getting in their lives. If Bill doesn't accept the advice from the medical experts and if Rosa does not cooperate and treat both of us decently, I will walk away. Don't let me get sucked into something that is hopeless or degrading. When it comes to blood relatives, I sometimes lose perspective."

Gio called his nephew Anthony to see if he knew what had happened. Anthony received a call last night from the police. They told him his boat had been stolen and was damaged in the storm. He did not know that his brother Bill was the thief. Gio gave him that distressing news on the call. Anthony was irate and unsympathetic. "The guy needs serious help. We have all known that. But I will have to press charges. He stole property. Maybe this will wake him up, get him what he needs." Anthony said he had no interest in going to the shore hospital to see Bill. That was probably for the best. There would be nothing wonderful about a fight between two brothers in a medical ward.

Gio and I arrived at the hospital in the early afternoon. Rosa was there with another woman who looked as if she was closely related. There was a strong family resemblance. Gio and I both said hello. Rosa said nothing and the woman sitting next to her said "Hello, I am Rosa's older sister Bonnie." Bill was much more alert, and the oxygen was removed. His heart monitor was still on. Gio asked Bill if the doctors made their rounds yet. He said, "No, I've only seen the nurse and the guy who takes blood. He was here very early. Before it got light out."

Without asking about the details of what happened with the boat, Gio laid it on the line with Bill and Rosa.

"Look Bill, you are lucky you are alive today and I am glad you made it. Kent and I are really concerned about you. I have talked to the doctor last night and told her that you have psychological issues. They are going to examine you and I am sure they will recommend treatments—some may be extensive or require prescription drugs or admission to a psychiatric facility. I know you have concerns about taking drugs or getting treatment. You say they make you feel like someone is controlling you. But you need to follow their advice and deal with your problems once and for all. You know there will be legal charges against you for what you did yesterday. If you refuse medical testing or treatment, your punishment could be a lot worse. So you need to welcome any help they offer you here. Do you follow me?"

Bill nodded slightly and looked away. It was a clearly non-committal response.

"And what about you, Rosa? Are you behind the idea of getting Bill the help he needs?" Gio asked.

Rosa turned to her sister and flippantly said, "These are the guys I told you about. They think Bill is mental somehow. If they give Bill drugs, he will be afraid of being captured. He has these fears of the government and what they know about him. They should leave him alone and let us get back to our lives. That's what we need most right now. We can handle things."

Rosa's sister said nothing. She looked confused by what she was hearing.

Gio stiffened, became louder and spoke forcefully. He spoke directly to Rosa. "We are not two guys; we are Bill's uncles, and we love him. You will be partially responsible for what happens from here on out. If yesterday's events don't tell you he needs help, then you need more help yourself." Gio then turned again to Bill and said, "Kent and I are going to leave now. You have my phone number. Reach out and let me know what is going on. We are there for you. But you have to be there for yourself."

Gio stepped back and said to me, "We should be on our way. I have sent the message we wanted to send, nothing we might say next is more important than that. There is no more we can do here."

As we left the hospital room, I heard Bill softly and sadly

say, "Thank you, Uncle Gio." Gio was ahead of me and did not hear him. Rosa deliberately looked away, as if to invalidate Bill's gesture of gratitude. To me, leaving the room felt like the ending of every mediation session I have done. You leave not knowing what the people will do and whether you will ever hear from them again. And you hope that you have somehow helped them, or at least made them feel as if you respectfully tried to improve their situation.

On the drive home we stopped in Ocean City and walked on the boardwalk. It was a crisp, clear fall day and the ocean was calm and bright blue after the storm. The boardwalk, still wet from the heavy rain, was nearly empty. Only a few joggers putting in their miles before winter sets in. As we began to relax, we chatted about the sad turn of events with Bill. I said, "It really is hard to talk with him. Nothing seems to get through. He seems like he is just trying to hang on—manage a day-to-day life—with forces that are nearly overwhelming him. It's so frustrating. The conversations seem futile."

Gio asked me, "Have you ever mediated a case where you thought that one of the people was incapable of making decisions? What do you do then?"

"There has to be a baseline requirement," I responded. "But it is tough to determine. Little is usually known about the parties before a mediation starts. And there is a fine line with some people. Many are not clinically diagnosed but have significant issues. A mediator could not make an assessment on the spot. The other party would have to make that call and decide for themselves whether to continue with the session."

Gio did not comment further. He was deep in his own thoughts. I knew he was thinking about Bill and his issues. And I could see that he was still conflicted about how to respond. Bill would always be family whether or not we were involved in his life. We could only hope that better days were ahead.

Just then, a small boat glided slowly past us not far from

the brown sandy shore. It barely made a ripple on the glassy surface. My eyes followed it until it was out of view. I thought that all boat trips should be as peaceful.

CHAPTER SIXTEEN

Mediation Follies

Two weeks passed since Bill's boating incident. Gio and I heard nothing from either Bill or Rosa. We talked several times about whether we should reach out to them to find out what was happening. That is a tough call given how we left it with them at the hospital. We have not made an intentional decision either way, although we know that our indecision is also a decision. Nothing feels quite right. There could be a lot going on with him medically and legally right now. The pressing question will then be how far do we get involved with their issues? When it comes to family obligations, is there ever truly a point of no return? I sensed this dilemma was tearing at Gio. I encouraged him to get advice from his older sister in California.

We did make a call to Denmark to tell Brigid and the family what had happened. They were concerned but not surprised. They now understood enough about his condition to know that destructive behaviors were possible. We left the door open for them to talk with us about the situation and we promised to provide an update if we heard anymore from Bill or Rosa. Brigid said she was concerned about Linus. He had become more withdrawn since he returned to Denmark. She was afraid that his normal introverted personality was turning into depression. She asked whether we thought he should see a therapist. Gio said it couldn't hurt. It was important, Gio added, to be sure to let Linus know that it doesn't mean he has the start of his father's severe condition. It could be common teenage angst. Brigid agreed.

I had not heard from the mediation program for almost two weeks. I called Anita to see what was happening with case assignments. When I reached the office, someone said "Hello, this is the Philadelphia Mediation Center. May I help you?" It was not Anita.

I asked, "May I talk to Anita please?"

"She is not here. Who is calling?" the unfamiliar voice asked.

"Kent Foxe. When do you expect her to be in the office?

"She is no longer employed by the courts. Did you say Kent Foxe? You are one of the mediators here, correct?"

"Yes."

"I was just about to call you. There is a mediation scheduled for you that I wanted to confirm."

Still trying to make sense of what the voice on the phone had just told me, I asked, "When is the session scheduled for?"

"Next Tuesday at two-thirty. Karen Abrams will be your observer."

"Thank you. I will be there then."

After saying goodbye to the unfamiliar voice, I thought about what could have happened to Anita. Did she quit? Was she pushed out by the nepotism that ran through the court appointments? I then remembered her boyfriend talking to Carlo—one of the parties in the mediation Karen terminated. My curiosity got the best of me. I decided to call Judge McGinny's administrator, the woman who was checking on the intake papers for Karen's mediation. She would surely know what happened to Anita.

McGinny's administrator answered my call on the first try. A rarity for that office. I told her that I had just called the Mediation Center and was told that Anita no longer works there. I asked whether she was transferred somewhere else in the court system.

"No, Mr. Foxe. She no longer works anywhere in the courts. She was terminated three days ago."

"Can you tell me what happened? I thought she was a prized administrator for the court's mediation program."

"Yes, she was very good. I really can't say much about what happened. But because you sparked the investigation by asking for the intake papers for that mediation case, I can give you the basics. This is strictly confidential. You cannot pass this information along to anyone else, even family members. Do you understand?"

"I understand," I said sincerely.

She then told me the story. "We found out that Anita had set up the mediation you observed. It did not come from the court at all. Anita convinced the two men—Carlo and Robin—to come for a mediation. She was the one who put the session on the mediation schedule. The court knew nothing about it. She assigned Karen to the case and asked you to observe her. It turns out that Anita's boyfriend was a friend of Carlo's. He was also part of Carlo's drug dealing ring. Anita wanted to help Carlo get his money back. This way her boyfriend could get paid as well and no one would get hurt in the process. You can see why we had to let her go. She set up a fraudulent mediation case that the court knew nothing about. Not to mention that the conflict stemmed from an illegal drug deal."

I was stunned. All I managed to say was, "This is beyond shocking. Hard to believe, actually."

"Right," the court admin said. "In a way she was trying to have these men work things out without violence, but she stepped across the line. Thanks to you we found out about it. Remember you can't breathe a word about this to anyone."

"Yes, I promise to keep it to myself," I said. I was sure others would find out somehow as well, although everyone would let on as if they knew nothing.

"By the way, the judge and I are looking for a permanent replacement for her. Would you be interested in her position? We could work something out. You could split your time between administration and mediation work."

"Thank you for the offer, but I am not interested." I quickly replied. Although the full-time position in Philadelphia would have made Gio happy, I was so opposed to what McGinny was doing to mediation in the courts that I couldn't even consider it.

"Give it some thought. You have some time. We don't have a good candidate yet. Thanks again for bringing that mediation case to our attention."

After we hung up, I felt uncomfortably edgy. A nagging guilt came over me. Was I responsible for Anita's demise? If I knew she had set up the mediation, would I have reported it? Was it that serious of an offense? Or was Anita just wrong to do what she did and needed to pay the price? I had told Karen after the drug deal mediation that we should be willing to mediate such cases. Wasn't Anita simply facilitating the same goal? How could I be critical of her? I'd have to think all this through alone because I agreed to not even talk with Gio about it. I did feel sure about one thing. If Anita found out that I asked the judge's administrator for the intake form, she would think I was out to get her. There is a good chance she knew that my inquiry triggered the investigation and her ultimate departure.

On the following Tuesday I met with Karen at the Mediation Center about 15 minutes before my mediation was scheduled to start. Karen was going to observe me, as the new policy required. Karen had heard that Anita was no longer there before she got to the Center. She asked me if I knew what happened. I had to lie.

"No, there are some rumors floating around but I'd rather not pass them along. How many years did she work here? Do you know?"

"I don't know for sure, but I think it was about five years. I can't imagine why they would let her go. She seemed to do everything they asked of her," Karen said.

I quickly changed the topic. "So, you will be my official observer and critic today."

"Yes. Whatever that means. We all have to figure out what these new policies are doing to us," Karen added.

"'Right, but they aren't improvements in my view." I stopped short of elaborating further.

The mediation that I was assigned, and that Karen observed, was in some ways a classic business contract dispute, with a few twists and turns. The parties were two males in their early thirties. They had been friends since college and stayed in touch with each other as they pursued separate careers in accounting and healthcare management. Three years into their chosen careers, each of them became disenchanted with their prospects. Moving up the accounting ladder in a first-rate CPA firm is a long grueling process and healthcare management has turned into an insurance driven nightmare. They decided to step away from their onerous career tracks one year ago. They started a joint entrepreneurial adventure, an international retail business. Their product was medicinal stones.

Over the past nine months, they traveled together to several African and Asian countries to search for and then sell stones and crystals that they believed had great beneficial health effects. The man with the health management career said he came to believe in the healing power of certain stones when he felt their mitigating effects on the asthma he had since childhood. They had done substantial research on the gemstones, and they identified promising markets globally—especially in Asia—that were willing to carry and sell their healing products. They each entered this business with great optimism and a sense of adventure.

At the beginning, they were both highly committed to their

joint business endeavor. Both men contributed substantial money to the business—$100,000 each. It was obvious that they both left lucrative positions when they decided to change their careers. The gentleman's agreement between them was that they would stay with the medicinal stone enterprise for at least three years before giving up on the business for any reason. Neither one could bail out before then. Now, a year later, one of the men wanted to leave the business. He had had a rough 12 months. He was recently divorced, was diagnosed with manic-depression and was pessimistic about the prospects for the new business. He felt he did not have the enthusiasm or energy needed to make the project work. The other man was furious about his partner's decision to leave the business early and didn't want to return any of the initial investment he had made in the project. These issues drove the first 20 minutes of their discussion. But there was more to their story.

Just as some revealing underlying issues were brought up in the session by one of the men, Karen, observing from the back of the room, interrupted the mediation saying that the court allotted time for the session had expired. When she said this, I looked at my phone and saw that it was twelve-thirty. The 30 minutes were indeed up. It felt like an incredibly short period of time. I did not say anything after Karen called time. The two men looked disconcerted because they knew it meant going back to the courtroom for the judge to render a final, impersonal decision based on little information. They knew it would be impossible for them to gauge how the judge would rule on their case. The 30-minute time limit forced them to give up control of the outcomes of their dispute and they were clearly concerned about it.

It was obvious to me that the men did not have the time they needed to delve into the issues that complicated their contractual arrangement. Just before Karen said time was up, one man said that the other was spending money frivolously and that his spending was undermining the success of the business. The man who was recently divorced accused the other partner of having a romantic interest in him that changed their friendship and undercut the trust that had supported their relationship all along. The other man did not deny his romantic interest in his business partner. These topics were brought up during the last five minutes and could not unfold in any depth during the limited time allotted for the discussion in this mediation. A lot was left unsaid about a whole range of issues that the two men raised.

I was tempted to buck the imposed time constraint and continue with the mediation despite Karen's notification. I realized that this move would circulate, and I might be excluded from any future work if I wanted it. Instead, I handed the men the mediation feedback forms and asked them to complete them and give them to the receptionist on the way out. I thanked them for participating and I apologized for the limited time the court allows for a session. I believe they could tell I was upset by the imposed time limitations on the mediation process. I did not want them to think that these limitations were my choice, or that I was dodging work.

After the men left, Karen and I talked about the mediation. She gave me feedback that she thought would be helpful and that she was going to write up on the observer's form that Anita had designed.

"Kent, your approach was too open-ended to get anywhere near a settlement in the thirty minutes you now have for a mediation session," Karen argued. "It is going to take a streamlined approach. You needed to spell out their underlying financial interests and separate them from possible solutions. Then keep a tight focus on the tangible issues and give them a five-minute warning at the twenty-five minute mark. This way they feel the pressure to come to an agreement before the buzzer goes off and the session must end. They will drop the secondary background issues knowing that their time is limited. It was clear that this case was going to come down to how much money Man X was going to return to Man Y. It probably would end up someplace near the mid-point of $100,000. You should just make that proposal to them because they won't get there on their own. They need your immediate advice and counsel."

I was in total disagreement with Karen's analysis and suggestions for the mediation session. It felt like, as the observer, she was the timekeeper in a soccer match. Her suggestions were way off-base. They totally bought into the new efficiency policies of the judge and program administrator. And they were an affront to any belief in the parties' capabilities.

I felt I had to be careful in how strongly I disagreed with her. I didn't care what the court thought but I've learned that it is better not to burn bridges behind me.

"I followed where the two men wanted to go in their conversation," I said to Karen. "I was allowing them to get into other important topics that they brought up and that they felt were relevant to reaching a satisfying outcome for them. Clearly, there were concerns raised about issues beyond the dollar amount for leaving the business. These background issues undoubtedly take more time to discuss but, without that time and discussion, I don't see what the point of mediating is. They might as well let the judge hear the case and rule on the money issues in twenty minutes."

"I would just ignore the underlying issues," Karen insisted. "I'd get them back to the issue of the investment in the business. The question really is: Who will settle for what amount and why? It's all about the money from the courts point of view. That is all the judge will deal with. You might as well steer them there. They need to know, and accept, what is fair."

Karen's commentary was getting me increasingly agitated. I wanted to hold my ground while not trying to be too dismissive. I didn't want her to think that I cared about what she was going to say in her review of the session. I said, "It could be that the man's divorce and his subsequent depression is something that is affecting why he wants out of the business after only one year. He might offer information that his partner may or may not want to consider when he is deciding how to settle the financial terms. But that decision about what to consider or not consider should be up to him. If there was adequate time, he might have suggested that the depressed man take three months off and go for therapy, paid through their joint business funds. I don't know where this could have gone but there are many possibilities. The last thing I want to do is to tell them what I think is fair for them. That steps way beyond a mediator's role."

I didn't say anymore to Karen, but her views made me realize that I could not in good conscience mediate in this court program anymore. I could not accommodate the new restrictive policies the judge had imposed, and that Karen was more than willing to accept. They were unfair to the parties, and they undermined any respectable mediation process that I would be willing to conduct. To satisfy the requirements and follow Karen's suggestions, I would have to become a Thomas Binder.

I said very little to the temporary new administrator on the way out of the Center. I gave her my mediation summary form on which I checked the "No-Agreement-Reached" box. Under "Reason for Not Reaching Agreement" I wrote only two words: "Insufficient time." The new admin looked over the form and all she said was thanks. I felt a sense of relief as I headed out the door in the reception area. It was the same relief I felt when I left the Manhattan Center. I could stop defending my views of practice and relax. But I worried that once again I was not being confrontive enough. There was so much more to say to Karen about her views on how to conduct mediations. I had held back again as I did in the Manhattan program when Boroughs and Binder aired their troublesome views.

CHAPTER SEVENTEEN

The Romantic

When I got to my car, I checked my voice mail and listened to my messages. One was from Daniel: "Hello Kent, this is Daniel Simel. I was wondering if I could treat you to lunch in Philadelphia some day this week. Just suggest a place and time and I am sure I can accommodate your schedule. Hope all is well with you. Take care, Daniel."

He did not say anything about mediation or any type of consulting, so I assumed, perhaps incorrectly, that he was requesting a social visit. My curiosity about his relationship with Celia led me to un-hesitantly accept his invitation. I called back and offered tomorrow afternoon at one p.m. I suggested we meet at one of my favorite seafood restaurants in center city Philadelphia—the Oyster Bar on Sansom Street.

When I arrived at home about six, Gio was out for the night. I remembered he was speaking about his antique car collection at a Sons of Italy dinner. He had left meatballs and red gravy for my dinner. He did not arrive home until late, so I had little time to talk with him. He was in an upbeat mood. Getting to show off his antique muscle cars always gave him a high.

When I arrived at the Philadelphia restaurant in the early afternoon the next day, Daniel already had a table for us. I forgot that this restaurant gets quite busy and noisy at lunch.

A little tough to hear when conversing, but I thought that the noise may help to keep the conversation upbeat. Daniel seemed somehow different to me, a little more relaxed and content than he was at the mediation. That was surely understandable. As we began to talk, he asked me a lot of questions about how my work was going and whether I had any follow-up projects with the financial firm in Denver. Without breaking any confidentiality, I gave him a broad overview of the mediation and the coaching I had conducted. Although I felt his interest in my work was sincere, he also was being polite in asking about me and my work before discussing what was happening with him. Something I sensed he clearly wanted to do.

"Besides the work, my spouse and I have had to deal with some difficult family problems as well," I said. "Gio has a nephew with a psychological condition, most probably he is schizophrenic. He seems to be getting worse as he ages." I felt comfortable opening up to him and stepping beyond small talk in the conversation. Maybe it was because I knew so much about him already through the mediation. It felt like I was reciprocating the self-disclosure, not initiating it. To do less would have seemed unbalanced, as if I were in the intervention seat again.

"My sister was a schizophrenic. I know how tough it can be. She tried to commit suicide several times in her forties," Daniel revealed. "The good news is there are more effective drugs now that can control severe psychotic episodes."

"Yes, that's true but they are helpful only if the person can see and acknowledge they have an illness," I said.

"That's right. That can be the stumbling block. Fortunately, my sister accepted the help. She is over fifty now and leads a normal life. She has married and holds down a decent job."

"So how are things going with you?" I asked. I wanted to ask him about himself without implying that he had to talk about Celia or his romantic pursuits. That seemed almost impossible even though I asked a broadly worded question. The universe of responses was somehow limited. Inevitably, his response was clearly shaped by the revealing personal knowledge he already shared about himself on the airplane and during the mediation.

"It seems to be over with Celia," he said somewhat regretfully. There was a sense of distance in his voice. He sounded like he was reporting objective facts that were unrelated to himself. "We went on one date after the mediation, and it just was not there for me. I kept thinking about the insight I had during the mediation. I wanted her when I knew I couldn't have her. I wanted a relationship when I knew that a relationship was impossible. Then, when she was truly open to having a somewhat normal relationship, it fell apart for me. It's perverse. I feel horrible about it. But I am thankful that your mediation gave me the insight. It was a breakthrough for me. Thank you for that."

"You came to that realization on your own." I said, refusing to take credit. I wanted to keep the tone of the conversation light, so I said, "There is a song from a Sondheim musical that captures perfectly what you experienced with Celia. I know you are a Broadway musical buff. Do you happen to know it? If you do, I will be amazed."

"If I remember correctly there was a cynical song in the second act of *Follies* that rings a bell. I'll never remember the title or lyrics exactly, but the character was complaining about having the blues over a difficult intimate relationship," he said.

"You're right. Great memory. Sondheim's vaudeville-like song is titled, God-Why-Don't You-Love-Me Blues. He comically observes that we often chase someone's love and then when we get it, we run the other way. Sondheim really understands and often mocks the push-pull of intimate relationships over time. He understands our darker sides well. Somehow when his characters sing about the paradoxes of relationships they don't seem to be disturbed or psychotic. That's where the cynicism comes in. Sondheim always seems to be saying that relationships throw us in the deep side of the pool, so we somehow learn to swim—or we just drown."

Daniel laughed and then looked away with a reflective expression on his face. "So true. I need to spend more time working on myself and what I am ready for before I try to get very close to someone. I've been calling myself a romanatic—a cross between a romantic and a lunatic. I see women through rose-colored glasses, but I know deep down that my feelings are out of touch with reality. I torture myself. I should go to therapy, but it is tough to find the right therapist. I tried two different counselors after my wife passed away and neither one was all that helpful. But I do know I need to look at what is pushing me away from women even when I pursue them."

"You need to find a therapist who is smarter than you. Otherwise, it's easy to outsmart the therapist. That gets you nowhere even if you spend months working at it. Finding the right therapist is as difficult as finding the right life partner." I smiled and then added, "And more expensive too."

"Speaking of expensive, I saw *Hamilton* for the third time last week," Daniel said with a more upbeat tone. "This time it was with the touring company at the Walnut Street Theater. Wonderful show. I enjoyed it more each time I saw it. Maybe it was because I caught more of the complex lyrics each time. I also met a wonderful woman sitting alone next to me. We went out for coffee after the show and had one additional date. Both times things were pleasant enough. But I am definitely holding back. I need to be careful."

"So, you are going to date while you are working on yourself in counseling?" I asked. I was afraid my question may have sounded like a challenge. I did not mean it that way.

"Yes, I want to continue looking for someone, but I want to keep the dating light, nothing too serious."

"I am not sure that will be possible. I think Sondheim would agree with me. He's not very positive about half-way relationships." I quickly changed the subject to not get into his dating challenges too deeply. "Did you know that throughout his long career as a songwriter Sondheim constantly used a thesaurus to find words that rhymed?"

"No. I didn't know that. That takes a little of the magic away."

"It reminds me of that line about genius being ten percent inspiration and ninety percent perspiration," I continued. "He sweated over the details of all his lyrics but made it sound so easy when you hear his songs. And he wrote for so many different genres of music for different plays—from a Japanese historical event to a British operatic gothic tale. I read that he lives by the artistic principle "content dictates form." This guiding rule kept every new project of his fresh and different from all the others he created. It's like Meryl Streep taking on radically different roles and mastering them all. She lets the content of the role shape her acting each time. Lesser actresses bring the same basic persona to each character. They are saying different lines, but you always know exactly who is speaking them."

"That's a good way to understand his greatness. And Streep's as well," Daniel agreed.

"Sondheim also believed in the principle that 'less is more.' He would under-write lyrics rather than over-write them, always respecting the intelligence of his audience. This is a guiding principle for me in mediation as well. Follow the parties and let them hear what they are saying and wanting. Don't crush them with my voice or the perspectives rolling around in my head."

"You are making me a bigger fan of Sondheim's than I already was," Daniel said. "And I did notice your unobtrusive style when you mediated for Celia and me. Very respectful of us both. It encouraged us to have the confidence we needed to find our own way. I appreciated that."

We kept the conversation away from Daniel's love life for

the rest of the lunch. When we finished our flounder stuffed with crab meat and caramel parfaits, Daniel insisted that he cover the check. A friendly gesture, or, I thought, was it that he just likes to pay for all his relationships?

As we left the restaurant together, I said, "Okay, then it is my turn to treat next time. Maybe you could have dinner at our house so you can meet Gio and have some of his authentic Italian home cooking."

"That would be great. I would look forward to it," Daniel said. "Maybe you would let me bring Deborah along."

I had never heard him mention a woman named Deborah. Maybe she was his recent Hamilton date. Or maybe I was jumping too fast again. Deborah could be a new escort. I decided not to ask for a clarification as we said good-bye. It might be more fun to find out over our dinner together.

CHAPTER EIGHTEEN

Losing What Lays Beneath

Kent: "Mr. Sondheim, It's a pleasure to meet you."

Mr. Sondheim: "Please call me Steve."

Kent: "I'm so pleased that you have interest in this project, Steve."

Mr. Sondheim: "A musical about mediation, not meditation, right Kent?"

Kent: "Yes, it will attract a wide audience, everyone has conflict in their lives."

Mr. Sondheim: "What's the plot? Or is it one of those explore-a-theme musicals?"

Kent: "No, actually there is a serious plot. A lonely mediator ends up marrying one of his female clients who he met in a divorce mediation he conducted. The marriage soon runs into trouble when the mediator tries to control his wife the way he did during her mediation. He decides to go for a ten step, mediator deprogramming treatment at the National Judicial College. Through this program he *learns how to talk to his wife without setting ground rules, to stop asking her to repeat everything he says to her, to refrain from reality testing her looks, and to stop insisting that there are six phases of lovemaking that must always be followed. There is a happy ending. The deprogramming intervention saves his marriage in six months.*

Mr. Sondheim: "Great plot, lots of possibilities with that. Do you have any song title suggestions to help me start my composing?"

Kent: "Well yes, I have a few. See what you think of these: They're Writing Ground Rules, But Not for Me... If Ever I Would Leave You Talk.... Some Enchanted Agreement...On A Clear Day You Can See How Mediators Actually Practice.

Mr. Sondheim: "That gives me a lot to go on. I think I'll write the entire musical in waltz time. That will make the score uplifting, but not too sweet. It will be an ironic look at how mediators deal with conflict."

Kent: "Wonderful!"

* * *

Gio woke me up from a late afternoon nap on the couch. I must have been sleeping deeply for at least an hour to dream so vividly at this time of day. The result, I am sure, of having a big lunch with Daniel earlier in the day. There was also no doubt that my amusing dream about Sondheim was the result of the banter with Daniel about Sondheim's music and creative methods.

"I was having a funny dream just now about Stephen Sondheim, Gio. He was willing to write a musical about mediation and he wanted me to suggest song titles and the plot for the show. What a hoot."

"Oh really? That is funny. Haven't you dreamt something like that before? Maybe it's an omen. Maybe you should get in touch with him. He might be interested, you never know. You could start the story line with the Daniel and Celia mediation case. A conflict between a prostitute and her client would get an audience's attention quite fast, I'm sure. If Sondheim can write a whole musical about presidential assassins, I am sure he could pull off one about mediators."

"Yes, and there are so many other options. There was that case in rural Texas where a cult of five practicing vampires came to a community center for mediation for help with their conflicts. That would grab them too."

"Was that for real or just a put on?" Gio asked incredulously. "I don't remember hearing about that one. What the heck was that even about? Was someone stealing valuable pints of blood?"

"It was something about whether the cult should be out in the public more so they could attract new blood, so to speak."

Gio laughed with amazement.

But enough about the Sondheim fantasies. I have to tell you about the lunch conversation I had with Daniel today. I am sure you will find it interesting."

"Oh right, please fill me in with the lurid details in his life," Gio said sardonically.

"To get right to the main development, Daniel is no longer with Celia. It's that old romantic dilemma again. His interest in her waned as she became interested in him. But apparently, he did meet someone at the recent run of *Hamilton* in Philly. He went out with this new woman once or twice and seems to like her. He insisted that he treat me to lunch today so I told him we would have him over for dinner sometime. He liked the idea and asked if he could bring Deborah along. I am not sure if Deborah is the woman he met at the theater. She might be another escort. I didn't ask him. Is it okay with you that I invited him over?"

"Sure, he seems like an interesting professional guy. And it never hurts to know a skilled dental specialist," Gio added.

"Would you be willing to make Italian food? I was thinking something like red gravy and meatballs over fusilli with romaine salad."

"Sure, I'd be fine making an Italian dish, as long as it is not pasta putanesca," Gio said.

"Why not putenesca? It is always so good when we have it. And isn't it relatively easy to make?" I asked.

"Right, that's it exactly. It is very easy to make. But if Deborah is an escort she might be offended, especially if she is Italian and knows the history of the dish."

"Why? How could someone be offended by a delicious Italian dinner?"

"I must have told you that the Italian word for whore is 'putan.' So putanesca was a dish, according to the folklore, created by women who whored around during the day. They then needed to make a fast dinner at night for their husbands. It's quick and uses common ingredients that would always be around the cucina and needed little advance prep. Fast and easy indeed—just right for the busy call girl."

"Oh my god, I don't remember you ever telling me this. There must have been some truth to the story or otherwise why the name? So, okay I agree, no pasta putanesca. If I find out that Deborah is his girlfriend, maybe then we should have the putanesca as a reminder of what he has given up. I'll call him and figure out a date for the dinner."

"Well, enough about whores and pasta," Gio said. "I had a skype call with Sarah in Denmark this afternoon. I wanted to catch up with her and to see how she was doing. She seemed fine although she is a little worried about her brother. Apparently, Linus still is feeling some aftereffects from the debacle with his father. I tried to reassure her that he would be fine, but I do wonder whether he is going to be alright. The good news is that Brigid is well connected to the best social service agencies in their town and can get him appropriate help if needed."

"Good to reassure Sarah. Both she and Linus are at vulnerable ages. All we can do is stay in touch and be supportive. We all have had some turmoil in our adolescent years."

"Sarah mentioned that she started taking ballroom dance lessons. I am sure it was because you told her the story about how we met at the dance studio and about your amateur dancing career. She seemed to really enjoy hearing about it. It gave her some insight into our relationship and the whole ballroom dance world. She also felt she bonded with you because you opened up to her so much about your life. I'm glad you took the time to do that. It meant a lot to her."

"Yes, Sarah was very interested. Retelling the events and seeing my reactions then and now did something for me as well. It kind of put that whole dance phase of my life in perspective. It was more intense than I realized. I was surprised that it did open up some old wounds for me."

"Which reminds me, I've been meaning to ask you about dancing again," Gio said pointedly. I know it is a sensitive subject for you. There are some old wounds there as you say. But why don't you come back to the studio to dance, even if it is just for fun? Do it for your own enjoyment and for the exercise. You loved it so much and it was a good social outlet for you. It doesn't have to be tied to the negative memories with Jane. Just dance socially, not competitively. This way you avoid the whole partnership challenges. It would be good for you."

"Gio, I know. You have raised this with me before. And I know you mean well. Dancing was a true pleasure for me. But I am not sure I could go back to it. I went very far with serious competitive dancing. It would seem like a big step backwards to just dance socially. And you know, I am not getting any younger."

"Is that it? Or do you think you are hanging on to the hurt and resentment Jane caused for you? Are you cutting off your toes to spite your dance feet, so to speak?" Gio asked.

I smiled, "You may be partially right about that. The ending of the partnership with Jane was tough on me and retelling the events to your niece stirred up a pot that I thought was long emptied. I think I did not get over it because I did not understand Jane well enough. She has a difficult background. I never gained a clear sense of what that story was for her although I did hear snippets of it. It was clearly tied to her image of herself as an African American woman and a black dancer in a white ballroom dance world. This issue was somehow linked to her competitiveness, her attraction to violent sports such as boxing and bullfighting, and her acceptance of Virov's punitive teaching style. I am not sure how it all fit together for her, but I always felt that she was enmeshed in a deep web of vulnerability and resentment as I got to know her over the three years we danced together."

"How did this affect you and your dancing memories?" Gio asked.

"It was tied to how she ended the dance partnership with me. Because her story was left untold, I couldn't really understand her behavior toward me without an appreciation of what she carried around with her. But finding that out is not so easy. I often wondered, should I have pursued her story if she wasn't offering it? Would she even be able to tell it if I did ask her and tried to understand it? Or to put it more on me, was I open to considering her issues or was I closed off to it? I might have been afraid that it would lead to an uncomfortable situation. It's tough to assess why it ended without understanding her actions more deeply."

"Sometimes just realizing that there is a back story for someone else can be helpful, even if you don't fully know what it is," Gio observed. "At least you sensed that there was more going on with her at a deeper level. Give yourself credit for that."

"Yes. Even if you don't know someone's unique history, just knowing there is something buried somewhere is enough to encourage you to pause and perhaps qualify or reconsider what's going on. You can see them through a different lens because you know that there is more there than meets the eye."

"It's definitely that way with Bill. We see the undercurrents in his life that he cannot explain or confront himself. He keeps trying to move forward without acknowledging what is holding him back. Maybe he can't see it at all. It's tragic actually," Gio said.

"Yeah, and we don't know Rosa's back story either, but I am sure there is one. Or Celia, the escort, has her own tragic past that Daniel got a glimpse of while dating her. It brought him to have more empathy for her as a person, empathy which he misunderstood as love at first. Enzo, the Hispanic employee at the IT program in Denver, also has a cultural story from his past that Elliot missed. If Elliot pursues it and comes to grips with it, he could radically change their conflict. If he doesn't engage it, their relationship will continue to be strained or it will just dissolve."

"Yes, people's underlying issues seem critical to how conflict develops and how people respond to each other," Gio added. "You don't need to agree with someone to understand and be sympathetic to what is controlling their thoughts and life.

"This all seems somehow related to mediation and what makes it work," Gio commented. "Aren't people given the chance to find and tell their stories in mediation?"

"Yes," I agreed. "It's what mediation can do so well. People can unearth and reveal the stories that are from their past and that are unknown by the other. Telling the story allows someone to see themselves differently and perhaps more honestly. Hearing the story also provides the opportunity for another person to understand someone whom they detest or whose behavior they find intolerable. It gives them a chance to become less judgmental and more compassionate.

"I now can imagine what a mediation between Rosa and Sarah might look like," Gio said. "As tough as it might be for both to sit through it, there would be an opportunity for Rosa to talk about why she is so afraid of losing Bill—what her life would be like without him. Sarah could talk about her life without a caring father and her fears about being rejected by him. The fight over who got to visit with each other when they were here was deeply tied to both of their back stories. And in some ways, their stories are similar. They are both dealing with crippling fears of losing an important relationship in their lives. This might be a possible meeting place for them— a place to at least understand each other. They have similar ghosts looking over their shoulders."

"That's what I love about you, Gio. You intuitively understand this stuff so well. If I wasn't getting so pessimistic about mediation, I'd be encouraging you to take Adam's training so you could volunteer as a mediator. You would have a strong sense of what is important to people. But trust me, you would have to work on your listening skills some. That Italian talk-over style connects with people but does not sharpen the ear!"

"For people in my culture, it is not even felt as talk-overs. It is being close with people when you are talking to them. You haven't said anything about how your mediation went yesterday. I know you had concerns because of the new court policies. How did it go?" Gio inquired.

I took a deep breath and exhaled slowly. "It was worse than I even expected. And it all relates to what we are talking about now. The Philadelphia court has come to a point where all that matters is that the case is off the judges' dockets. They do not care whether people have a chance to talk about their back stories and how the past influences their present. It is impossible for that to happen in the thirty minutes now allotted for a session—one of the new regulations the court imposed."

"What can you do? Do you think the court will actually monitor the time spent in mediation? Can that be strictly enforced? Maybe it will be a policy on the books but won't be enforced." Gio wondered.

"They are doing that now with a volunteer observer assigned to each mediation. My former co-mediator, Karen, did it for my mediation yesterday.

"So where do these changes leave you?" Gio asked looking concerned.

"I have pretty much decided that I can't mediate there anymore. It would be going against all my beliefs about what makes mediation valuable."

"Could you talk with him about a vivid case where great things happened with the parties to get that kind of point across to him?" Gio asked.

"There are several cases that might get him thinking about what is being lost. I don't think I have it in me to call him on what he is doing. These judges make their minds up and that is it, especially when money is the motive. I can't see me challenging the system."

"It sounds like with these new court restrictions there will be a lot of important back stories that go untold in Philadelphia," Gio observed. "Little chance for people to understand the deeper sides of each other and their conflicts."

"That's it." I said. "It is a real loss when mediation falters anywhere. When it goes off track it means there is no place left for wonderful fights."

As we finished our conversation, I noticed that I received an email from Elliot Susskind. I had sent him a message shortly after the coaching, but I had not heard back until now.

Dear Kent,

Thank you for the mediation and the coaching session. They affected me profoundly.

I decided to leave the Denver firm. I need time to find out who I can be now.

If I do join another organization someday, I want you to coach me.

With appreciation,
Elliott Susskind

It was good to know he found the coaching session valuable. I wasn't sure how he had taken it. Susskind's decision to leave seemed predictable given the state he was in—he didn't see a face-saving way out. His message got me thinking about the seen and unseen forces that carried him away from who he wanted to be—at work and at home. He felt he was headed in an inevitable direction but, when cornered, he saw that there were choices along the way that could have changed where he ended up. He seemed to be blinded by his own corporate upbringing.

My thoughts drifted back to Anita and the forces that brought her to lose her job and get involved with drug dealers. I knew too little about her to understand what happened. Had she now come to a point that she gained a life changing realization, as Susskind did? Or was she still moving swiftly down the same treacherous road she was on? Life's momentum is hard to stop. She may not be capable of redirecting herself. Few people have the luxury of taking time away to find oneself as Susskind does. Certainly, Latisha and Tanya could not stop the escalation that ended in such tragedy. Even their mother's best efforts could not divert the girls from the inadvertent and destructive road they followed.

I came to realize, in a way I hadn't before, that a critical challenge in life is to be able to see where you are going. I started to wonder whether the forces directing me now were taking me someplace that I would eventually cherish or regret. Was I seeing where I was going and what influences were taking me there? Or was I blind to what today's events will lead to tomorrow?

For the moment it was reassuring to think that, if done right, both mediation and coaching can help people see where they are headed by examining the choices they are making. That is something worthwhile in this work. I consoled myself by believing that perhaps I was on a good path, at least for the time being.

CHAPTER NINETEEN

Lunch Anyone?

That evening I got a strange message from Adam.

Hello Kent,

I received an email today from none other than Thomas Binder. He wrote just to ask me for your email address. Of course, I would not give it to him without asking you. What do you want me to do? It's your call. I have no idea what he is up to.

Adam

I was bewildered. Why would Binder want to reach out to me? He must have a motive and I could not imagine what it was. For sure, it was not positive. He was so arrogant and self-centered at the Manhattan Center. Maybe he was offended by my aloofness—my effort to avoid talking much with him. Although I was hesitant to give Adam the go ahead, I felt I had no choice. It would be putting Adam on the spot to not respond. I had the feeling that Binder would not give up. I wrote back:

Adam,

Thanks for passing along Binder's request. Go ahead and give my email address to him. I may or may not respond to him if he does email me.

I don't know what to expect but will keep you posted.

Kent

The next morning there was an email from "Bindmediation@netnit.com." I quickly opened it, anxious to see what it was about.

Dear Mr. Foxe,

I was the experienced mediator you observed when you were at the Manhattan Mediation Center. I will be in Philadelphia the next three days and would like to meet with you someplace at a convenient time and place.

Thank you in advance for your positive reception to my invitation.

Thomas Binder

My first reaction was that this was undeniably Binder. The four-line email captured his arrogant tone and off-putting demeanor perfectly—bow tie and all. Then my adrenaline-driven, fight-flight response kicked in. When I am on a keyboard this means either leaping on the delete button or sending off an unedited, scalding response. I managed to avoid either and began thinking about whether I would respond to him at all, no less meet with him.

I started thinking about my long history of not being able

to confront difficult situations. I saw myself as the ten-year-old playing baseball on a junior team and hoping that the ball would not be hit toward me and that I would never have to come up to bat. I never overcame a fear of the sport. It left an inferiority scar that I carried into adulthood. I also regretted never confronting Jane about how she ended our dance partnership. That reluctance may have cost me further enjoyment of dancing, as Gio had pointed out. He sensed the scar from that injury. Then recently there was my fear of confronting Binder and the judge at the Manhattan Center and my hesitancy with Karen as she gave me feedback under the new crippling court rules.

These regretful thoughts led me to quickly resolve that I would not avoid Binder for a second time, whatever came of a meeting with him. Why assume the worst? I asked myself. Maybe he was going to offer me an attractive opportunity in the mediation field. Of course, I knew the chances of that were as great as me becoming Pope.

I decided to ask Binder to come to New Jersey rather than meeting him across the bridge in Philadelphia. This would be a small test of his commitment to his own request. And I wanted to meet him in a quiet place where I would feel comfortable. Our friend Steve's restaurant was still closed at lunchtime, and he was more than willing to let me use the space again. I set our meeting up at 1 p.m. on the second day of Binder's visit to Philly.

I arrived at the restaurant early so that I had some time to myself to think about the meeting with Binder. I was in the same part of the restaurant where I conducted the mediation with Daniel and Celia. Thinking about that event, I inevitably saw a connection with Binder. Binder was, in a way, a paid escort for the judges in the Manhattan court. His service was case disposal—a tension relieving function for over-worked judges. And it appeared that he would do almost anything to satisfy his clients, even though the pay was meager. Before getting into this demeaning comparison further, I caught myself. My cynical side was taking over. I told myself that this was not a picture I wanted to carry into our meeting. Instead, I wanted the scene in my mind of Binder confronting Mrs. D'Antes when she recommended that her husband continue to work for her. This picture represented the core of Binder's questionable mediation work. It was more substantive than malicious. This switch put me in a more relaxed state—I was consciously controlling my reactions and deciding how I wanted to approach Binder.

Binder arrived right on time. The first thing I saw was his bow tie. It was different than the one he had on in New York but equally audacious. I realized the source of my distaste for this neckwear—it has a clear association with clown suits. It makes men look as if they want an audience everywhere they go. A sure sign of self-conscious eccentricity. He also wore the same black beret he had on at the Manhattan Center. This time he did not remove it. It sat precariously on the left side of his head and made him look off balance.

Without exchanging any initial greetings or offering to shake his hand, I stood up when he walked to the restaurant table and, in a neutral, non-effusive tone, I asked, "What brings you to Philadelphia for three days, Thomas?" I could hear that I didn't sound like myself. This was a less friendly, more assertive sounding Kent. I felt like I was acting. But hearing my steady voice made me more confident.

"I am doing a mediation training across three evenings. This important event is hosted by the Pennsylvania Mediation Association," he answered, complimenting himself. He was strategically pretentious. I was sure that his self-congratulatory style was his way of gaining the higher ground in the conversation.

I decided to jump right in—banter or small talk seemed inappropriate. The aura was already serious and unfriendly. "Why did you want to get together with me?" I asked.

"I wanted to meet the real Kent Foxe, not the ruse who came to Manhattan to observe me surreptitiously," he said accusingly. He looked at me eagerly, as if I would not have a good response to his insult. He clearly thought I was defenseless.

Without hesitation, I said boldly, "Let me correct you. I did not come to observe you. I asked to observe a mediator and you were the person Thelma assigned to me. I didn't even know that you worked there. Not everyone knows about you and your questionable mediation methods." I could hear that I was becoming cynical, almost biting. I warned myself to choose my words more carefully. I wanted to stay on the substance. The urge to return his insults was nearly overwhelming though.

"Why didn't you tell me about your relationship with Adam Maurie? You had time to mention it before or after the mediation session or you could have told me later."

"I didn't feel it was necessary. I did not want to be a critic when I was there as a guest of the mediation program. That would have been inconsiderate of me." I then changed the subject quickly and asked, "How did you find out that I knew Adam?"

"I have a network of people here in Philly and one of them was in Maurie's training with you. He told me you were part of his group."

I kept diving deeper. "Have you ever been a party—one of the clients—in a real mediation? A mediation where you were in a serious conflict with someone else?" I asked pointedly. I could hear that my questioning began to sound like a cross-examination. Not a bad way to engage him, I thought.

Binder looked somewhat stunned by my last question. "No, I haven't been a mediation client but that should not matter one way or another. My professional background is all I need. You don't need to have had heart surgery to be a cardiac surgeon," Binder replied defensively, anticipating criticism.

"Then it is not easy for you to see the serious flaws in what you do. You have not felt what it's like to be treated by someone who practices the way you do." My voice remained steady and clear. I was surprised that my mouth was not dry.

Binder was obviously taken aback by my accusation. He was not getting to play the part he planned for this conversation. "What flaws? You are quite inexperienced to be identifying flaws in a seasoned professional's work, don't you think? It's really quite rich." His body became tense as he tried to pull rank on me.

"It doesn't take extensive experience to know when things are not right. You just need a clear sense of the purpose behind the practice—what you are trying to do and why." I kept my eyes fixed on his face as he readied himself to respond.

"You and Adam and the other 'mindful new agers' don't get it," Binder said sarcastically. He wasn't averse to name calling. "The mediator is the only one in the room who is dedicated to reaching an agreement. He is the impetus, the energy behind getting there. You must push, set the parties in the right direction, protect them from their own bad instincts, and keep them focused on getting to the final agreement. You must stop them from talking about the past. You need to use any and all of the tools in your toolbox to get them where they need to go. It is easy to criticize these moves, but they are absolutely necessary. Without them there are no agreements to give the court. That's who we work for, you know. Without agreements there is no mediation."

"Reaching an agreement is only one goal for mediation. It may be the courts' goal, but it may not be the parties' and it doesn't have to be the only goal of the mediator either." Before I could explain further, Binder jumped in quickly.

"I can't imagine what goals you are talking about. Pushing for kumbaya moments? Do you bring incense and candles to your mediation sessions?"

I sensed the sweat starting to form on my neck as Binder increased the ridicule. I bit my lip to avoid reacting to his sarcasm and said, "That means you never really read Adam's book. You just slammed its success without digesting the content. An important goal is to help the parties become clearer about whatever they are discussing—what they want to say or do about their issues. And to help them understand each other so they can make informed decisions. They can then better decide whether there will or won't be an agreement. And if they do reach an agreement the terms will come from them. It will be theirs. The clients are then less likely to sue the mediator for giving unrequested legal advice or representing both parties simultaneously."

"You and the other Adam followers are misfits," Binder retorted. "I do exactly what the courts want, and I am where private practice needs to be. Go ahead and try to make a living doing what you do. You won't eat. Just don't get in the way of what I do. Keep your half-baked new age ideas in their place." Binder then leaned toward me across the table, lowered his voice and said slowly, "Know that there will be consequences for trying to push real professionals like me out of this field. Life is short and sometimes we make it shorter for ourselves by our offensive actions."

This must have been the kind of threatening language that made the conference board encourage Adam to have security at the conference. The comments unnerved me for a brief moment, even though his veiled threats soon sounded hollow. I took them as part of his pretentious staging.

Before I spoke again, Binder slowly reached into his coat pocket and took out a small, high-end Sony tape recorder. He looked at it as he laid it on the table in front of us. I could see that the bright red recording light was on. The mischievous smile on his face told me that he clearly wanted me to see this device as his secret weapon—as the street tool for the ambiguous threats he had just made. Although I was somewhat stunned, I was determined not to let this ploy throw me in the least. I knew that this was a cunning test to see how far he could push me. I reached across the table and moved the recorder closer to me. I wanted him to know that he should record clearly every word I said.

Looking directly at him, I put my arm back on my lap and continued. "Maybe fitting in too well is the root of your problem. Try standing outside the court's grip and ask yourself what is uniquely valuable about mediation and what happens when its uniqueness is lost. Let our professional standards as mediators lead the stakeholders' expectations for how to practice, rather than the reverse."

"You seem to be saying that the owner of a building like the one we are sitting in is not allowed to decide whether his renter can open a restaurant here. That's absurd. The building owner has every right to decide what business he will allow in his building."

"No, I am saying that the owner of the building can't tell the chef in the restaurant how the food should be prepared."

Just as I finished my comment, I could see my friend, Steve—the restaurant owner—heading over to the table with two bottles of water. He politely asked: "Would the two of you like to have lunch? I'd be happy to fix something for you. Maybe a chicken Caesar salad or some fresh calamari?"

I held back any response and looked blankly across the table at Binder. He seemed to be thrown by the generous offer. He looked up at Steve and said curtly, "I've already swallowed too many insults at this table already." His refusal was far from a friendly "no thank you."

Steve just stood there, awestruck by the defensive comment. He knew it was not said jokingly. All he said was. "That's too bad. Let me know if you change your mind." He made quick eye contact with me and walked swiftly away from the table.

Seeing the two unopened bottles of water on the table

made me think again of the mediation with Daniel and Celia in this room. Their conversation was more civil than the one unfolding now. I chuckled to myself when I thought that Binder and I could use a mediator, but we would not agree on which kind. We would need a mediator to help us decide who the mediator should be.

Without saying a word, Binder abruptly got up from the table, picked up his tape recorder and left the restaurant without saying a word. There was a sense—however slight—of defeat on his face and in his walk as he headed out of the restaurant. He was defiant but not victorious.

I continued to sit at the restaurant table and tried to make sense of what had just happened. I saw how Binder revealed his own answers to Adam's two key questions. He is the person who is there to satisfy the courts by reaching settlements in any way possible. And he sees the people who are in mediation as barriers to his success. They can't get there without his invasive, controlling methods. Binder clearly held these views, although I doubt he is fully conscious of them. I thought that they simply define who he is. One thing was certain. Any questioning of them threatens him profoundly.

I also thought about where things stood with Binder and me. I was not worried about the tape recording. Nothing I said would be lethal to my career. I was able to keep my comments short and substantive. No one could accuse me of trying to do him in. He was the one who relied on threats and ridicule. I still wondered why Binder sought me out and saw me as a threat. Why did he think I could be successfully subversive? The only semi-satisfying explanation I came up with was a twisted Freudian one. I was a convenient scapegoat for him. If he couldn't take Adam down, he would pursue me. It was an act of psychological desperation.

There was no agreement reached in our conflict. Nor did there need to be one. In a diverse world, the big challenge, I thought, is to learn to live with difference rather than search hopelessly for elusive or nonexistent common ground. Maybe the best sign of living with difference is that you can enjoy a good Italian lunch together. We were not there yet.

As I got up to thank Steve for his hospitality, I felt a slightly embarrassing sense of accomplishment. Not because I had won the argument. I hadn't. But because I stood up to Binder the way Adam had at the conference. I finally was able to stand in the outfield hoping the baseball was hit to me. I was ready to catch it, no matter how hard it was hit.

CHAPTER TWENTY

Showtime

Two days after my conversation with Binder, I received a voice mail from Adam. The message was simple enough: "Please let me know when you might be able to meet. Can't wait to hear about your encounter with Binder. Also, something has come up and I am excited about filling you in." I was glad he reached out because I have been wanting to let him know about the discouraging developments at the Philadelphia Mediation Center and my decision to stop mediating there. I was gratefully excited to hear some positive news from him. I know that it is a busy time of the semester for him so I assumed that he would not have reached out over something insignificant. I called him back and told him I would stop by his office shortly after his three o'clock class ended tomorrow. "Excellent timing, see you then," he replied.

That night, I told Gio about Adam's call and we both tried to guess what might be going on. We came up with a pretty wide range of possibilities, some more outlandish than others. I guessed that he might want me to teach a conflict course with him during the spring semester. Gio guessed that he broke down and bought a brand-new car—a big truck-like vehicle like a Ford Expedition or Cadillac Escalade. Something that would be a contemporary version of the armored tanks he is accustomed to driving. We also considered other possibilities:

he was invited to speak at another conference, Thomas Binder was arrested for malpractice, he has a contract on a new book and wants me to be co-author, or he has been officially excommunicated from the Catholic Church. Adam always seemed to attract a lot of interesting opportunities, so it really was anyone's guess what had "come up" as he put it or how it was going to involve me.

When I arrived at Adam's office the next day, he was just finishing a conversation with a graduate student about a paper assignment for his course. While I was waiting, I thought about the decision I made to stop mediating in the court program. Although it still felt like the right choice, I regretted that I had to make it. I felt a nagging sense of loss. I hoped that Adam would allay any possible regrets I have about opting out. I hoped Adam had suggestions for how to build a sustainable private practice so I could continue to hone my mediation skills and provide the value of mediation to people who would find it helpful.

As the student left Adam's office, I greeted him enthusiastically. "Hello Adam. How are you today? It looks like the end of the semester rush has started for you."

"Yes, but the winter break follows so I can get through it. Anything new with you?" Adam asked facetiously. He was obviously eager to hear about Binder.

"Binder wanted to confront me about knowing you and about our views on mediation. I held my own in our conversation but of course he dug in. He is still really threatened by the ideas and by the growing interest in an alternative form of practice. He doesn't see that what he does in his practice turns people away from mediation."

"Did he threaten you in any way?" Adam asked.

"There was some of that. He said something about not getting in his way or there will be personal consequences. He secretly recorded the conversation and halfway through he let me know he was doing it. Trying to intimidate. He is one intense guy, and he made some strongly worded statements that were intended to frighten me. It was hard not to stoop to his tactics when he was on the attack. It is so strange that he even took the time to meet with me. The threat level for him must be sky high."

"He could just be a little out there someplace or he could be a dangerous and insecure stalker. If he is the latter, that is worrisome. He is clearly delusional. He sees us having a chance to overtake his territory. That is surely not going to happen. The court pressures are too great. His approach will win out nine times out of ten with judges. Just remember that we are not trying to turn everyone into vegetarians—we can't convert the whole mediation field. We are just hoping people eat less meat."

"Do you remember asking me whether the Philadelphia program was like the Manhattan Program?"

Adam nodded. "Yes, it was part of our conversation about the interview you did with Judge Boroughs while you were at the Manhattan court. The interview that opened your eyes to the emerging state of mediation."

"When you asked me that question then I said that the judges in Philadelphia had more reasonable expectations for the mediation process and its outcomes. They seemed to get its value. Well, that is all changing fast now. Over the past few weeks, the administrative judge in Philadelphia has enacted some significant changes in policies that directly impact how mediation is practiced. Now there is no more co-mediation, and all mediations are given a maximum of thirty minutes, with no possibility of a second session with the parties. If no settlement is reached in a half hour, the parties go back to the judge on the same day for a decision."

"That's beyond unfortunate," Adam lamented. "What does the administrative judge think mediators are—a clan of wizards?"

"Wizards or, more likely, arbitrators. I know there are

more changes to come so it could very well mean that mediators are not paid unless an agreement is reached with all of the expected directive mediator moves associated with that change. I think it is only a matter of time until the administrative noose gets tighter around mediators' necks."

"This news is really distressing, Kent. Even though the courts are overloaded, these judges should have a wiser vision of what mediation accomplishes. An increasing number of administrators don't seem to have the remotest idea of what mediation can provide to citizens, especially the insights that happen for people when they work through difficult conversations. The potential societal impact is lost. That is something the courts should care about."

"I tried to mediate a case under the new thirty-minute rule, and it just doesn't work unless you are acting like Thomas Binder. What is amazing is that the mediators in Philly just seem to be going along with it. What does that say about their professional beliefs—how they see themselves and how they view the parties?"

"I think you know, Kent."

"I do know, and I also know that I can't practice that way. I will not be mediating any cases at that program anymore. I don't see how I could. "

"I respect that choice, tough as it might be for you. But this may be a blessing in disguise. It may free up time for you to work on a project I was going to tell you about today. You know that old saying, 'When one door shuts, another one always opens.'"

"I'm all ears."

"Well, it turns out that the huge mediation project we did for the National Employee Relations Program is doing quite well. They have been collecting data on the effects of the mediation cases. Their research shows short-term and long-term positive results. Companies that have used mediation have saved substantial money because about eighty percent of the disputes have not gone on to expensive legal hearings. NERP has also found that managers who participated in a mediation with an employee have been able to deal better with conflicts that arise with other employees. The managers avoid conflict less and are more comfortable when employees express themselves emotionally. In other words, they are learning how to work through difficult conversations. Mediation shows them what is possible—what they are capable of."

"That sounds great."

"There is an upshot to this good news. NERP would like to produce a video that demonstrates mediation with a real case. They want an expert consultant to work with them over the next two weeks as they develop the video. I have no time to do this so I thought you would be perfect to help on this project. They are willing to pay around five grand for the work and you would hold the rights to show the video in trainings and elsewhere."

"That's quite a project. Are you saying, Adam, that they would want me to be the mediator on the video?"

"Yes, that's it exactly. Be the mediator in a real case recorded live and left unedited."

"Wow, that is quite the high wire assignment. Little room for error."

"That's why it's a big dollar amount!" Adam exclaimed.

"Are you sure you can't do it, Adam? You would be terrific," I suggested.

"I have no time. And even if I did, I would still want you to do it. Your instincts are excellent, and you are more photogenic than I am. They don't need an elderly Clint Eastwood look," he said with a wide smile.

The proposal was highly enticing. "I am excited about doing this, but I am sure I will be somewhat nervous."

"I'm certain with real people as the parties your nerves will recede because your focus will be entirely on mediating. You will forget about the camera within seconds after starting," Adam said reassuringly.

"You are probably right. The lead up will be nerve-racking but the mediation will just be a mediation like the others. And at least I will not have a thirty-minute time restriction."

"There is one other exciting piece to this which I haven't told you about yet."

"It's pretty exciting already," I noted.

"But it does get more interesting. One of the NERP employees who is based in Southern California was contacted by a Los Angeles television producer. He heard about the mediation program and wants to see a sample of the practice. Apparently, he is looking for something to produce that is like the judge shows that are on TV now but with a slightly different twist. You know how these television shows go, if they get one success, they hope to jump on the bandwagon with something that is within the same genre but different enough to draw audience interest. Dancing with the Stars begets ice skating with the stars which begets roller blading with the stars, etc. I think that is what is going on. He is looking for a spin-off."

"Well, that *is* interesting," I said.

"NERP is not interested in getting involved in such a project, but they are willing to turn the TV contact over to us. Once you make this video, it could be used as an initial pilot for the TV series. You could send it to the producer, meet with him in person and see if anything comes of it. What is particularly good is that we will be demonstrating the kind of practice we value. It could set the record straight about mediation in the public's mind."

"I can see how this fits in with the court mediation door that I just shut. It is an opportunity to build a bigger market for private practice, if this is done well and stays true to this approach to practice. Hate to say it but it does remind me of the Sondheim tune Opening Doors from Merrily We Roll Along. The characters are eager young professionals trying to find new opportunities so they can reach for their lofty goals. They don't always make it though.

"Right, it is definitely a new door opening. Who can say what will happen? You know by now, Kent, that I too am very disenchanted with much of mediation practice, especially court mediation. It seems to have a death wish. There are so many ways that it is being undermined by the very people who say they support it. We need to go back to where some of the founders of mediation started. They warned against connecting mediation to the courts in any way. The way to reach the public might be through a sophisticated media presentation. It is a long shot and there are many slips from teacup to lips, as my mother would say, but it's worth a shot and you would be the perfect person to make it all happen."

"Whoa, this is getting a little intimidating—but it is exciting. I feel exuberant about the project, and I will have the time to put into this if it takes off. I could take on less consulting work to do something this worthwhile."

"Without something that builds public appreciation for mediation, the prospects are slim that it will survive. I for one will step out of this endeavor entirely if all that's left is court-based mediation," Adam said.

"I am sorry to hear you say that. And it does put more pressure on making this project successful," I said, warning myself. "I vowed a while ago on that plane ride to Denver that I would do something to correct the public's understanding of what mediation is and how it is different from arbitration. This is a great opportunity for me to try to keep my vow."

"You can only help by trying. And I would be so appreciative if you do."

"Count me all in. I will need the information for the NERP video contact and the L.A. connection. Gio has relatives in Orange County so I can make it a family trip when I head out there. That will make him excited about the work too. Any sense of a timeline?"

"This is going to be fast paced. NERP wants to spend the money ASAP while they still have the funds allocated for the project. TV production people are always looking for something to be done yesterday. They want to get ahead of their competitors."

I left Adam's office and drove home feeling both enthusiastic and apprehensive. Apprehensive about doing the live video and excited about the possibility of engaging the help of a media producer in reaching a potentially huge public audience. If it all worked well, I might have a significant hand in putting quality mediation on the map. This could be a landmark event. Or it could be a final bust that sends Adam into academic no man's land. Because we are both on the brink of jumping off the mediation cliff anyway, it is worth a try. Besides, it is a great trip for Gio to take with me. That should be quite satisfying for both of us.

The next day I called Sandy Halburn, the contact at NERP who oversees developing the video. She was enthusiastic about the project and was glad that I was willing to be the mediator. Adam had obviously recommended me highly to her, paving the way for my involvement. Besides his other fine qualities, Adam is a generous opportunity maker.

Sandy said she has a case for mediation that is already teed up. She said it is a conflict between two professionals who work together in the Philadelphia area. They have agreed to be videotaped but the parties want to be able to review and approve the video after it is made. They each want to reserve the right to cancel use of the tape for any reason they might have. She asked when I could do the mediation, implying sooner would be better than later. I gave her three time slots in the following week, all in the early evening.

The mediation was scheduled for the following Thursday evening. Several days before, Gio made me laugh because he had picked out the clothes he said I *had* to wear for the taping. He wanted me to look "on the expensive side of business casual, not too formal but with noticeable quality from any camera angle." He had good taste—much better than my absent-minded sense of style.

When I arrived at the videotaping studio that Sandy had rented, I saw that the setting was highly professional, and the taping was going to be done with three cameras. The technician told me there would be shots taken from across the mediation table as well as close-ups. Gio was right, the clothes would be seen, and the image probably mattered. Professional but not stuffy or lawyerly. I made a mental note to thank Gio for making clothes a somewhat annoying priority. Annoyance is often appreciated later, when it heads in the right direction.

Sandy arrived at the studio just after I did. She thanked me again for taking on this assignment and she reassured me about the plan for the video. It was going to be used as a marketing piece for companies whose HR departments were considering using NERP's mediation services. That was her company's only interest in making the tape. They were not proprietary at all about the video.

She indicated that "Many HR professionals had the wrong idea of what happens in mediation. They think it is a legal process, like the courts. This video should clarify the difference, regardless of the outcome of this session. As long as the parties have voice and choice, the final decisions made by the parties don't really matter. It's about showing how parties can work through difficult conflicts with the help of a supportive mediator. This is what our research is showing."

"Well, there are radically different ways of doing mediation, so it is important to have a concrete example on hand to show what it is not, as well as what it is for NERP," I said. "In our view, reaching an agreement in mediation is one of many valuable outcomes. The quality of the parties' conversation and decision-making matters most."

Sandy agreed, "That is what makes the key difference. I see it repeatedly."

Sandy said that the two parties should be arriving in about 20 minutes. I took this time for myself to focus on my role as the mediator. I thought about some core principles that help me know who I am and what I want to believe about the parties: I am here to facilitate their conversation, supporting their efforts to have the best conversation possible about whatever their issues are. I need to proactively follow the parties, letting them see where they are going and whether it is where they want to be going. Finally, I kept repeating to myself Sondheim's "less is more" guidance. I am not here to do the work for them. Better to be respectful and careful than pushy and disempowering. Anything I say will probably be given more weight by the parties than it deserves.

The mediation started about a half hour late, although the parties arrived on time. It took time to arrange seating, set camera shots, and test the sound equipment. The technicians were helpful in letting us see how they were going to capture the three of us with the cameras. The cameras were far enough away, and the lighting was natural enough to be quite unobtrusive. Still, I worried that the production context would be hard to ignore. Sandy kept talking to the parties, making them comfortable and giving me the chance to adapt to the awkward surroundings. She introduced the parties to me when they arrived, so it was obvious she had been the intake person who talked to both of them beforehand and arranged their permission for the mediation.

Before I started with my short opening comments, I did review a few points off camera. In talking about confidentiality, I said that their names would never be identified and that when the video was used as a demonstration tape no one would disclose whether the case was a role play or not. I confirmed my understanding that either one of them could decide to nix the video for any reason after they reviewed it. I wanted to reassure them about these key points.

The two parties were two doctors—neurologists—who

worked together for three years at a local teaching hospital. Both appeared to be in their mid- to late-thirties. The woman's demeanor conveyed a sense of confidence and calmness. The man seemed apprehensive, almost jittery. He kept his eyes focused on me and he scribbled nervously on a notepad that he brought to the room with him. The woman had a large purse with her, but she did not take anything from it. She sat straight up with her hands folded on the table, looking ready to say what she had prepared. The man looked concerned about what might unfold and seemed less ready to speak.

The issues involved a charge of possible sexual harassment. The woman had consulted with the sexual harassment ombudsperson at the hospital prior to seeking mediation. After describing to the ombudsperson what had happened with her co-worker, the ombudsperson told the female physician she had a case for charging harassment against her medical colleague. The choice was up to her. The female doctor considered the lawsuit option but decided instead to ask for a mediation, while not waiving her right to sue. The male physician agreed to participate in the mediation. Neither knew what would come of their conversation.

During their emotional session, the woman described a series of interactions and events that happened between her and the male doctor. She pointed to one specific instance of inappropriate and unwanted touching that she knew "crossed the line." But she explained that she wanted to mediate instead of pressing legal charges because she felt she had engaged in some sexual banter with her colleague that ultimately led to the harassment. While not blaming herself, she felt she had some accountability for where things ended up between them. She felt she had contributed to the "direction of the behavior." She wanted to be sure that the co-worker understood exactly where he stepped too far. She warned him that if he ever did anything like it again, she would definitely file legal charges against him.

The male doctor did not question the claims made by the female physician. It was obvious that he was afraid and worried that something he might say now would offend her and she would have a change of heart. He said he was sincerely sorry for the offense and did not realize at the time that she had an issue with his behavior. He wanted to be sure that she knew that he understood now what he had done, and he would never come close to that line again. He made this point several times during their conversation. He knew that his whole professional career was riding on the decision she made not to press charges and he was grateful to her for that decision. He certainly did not want to risk making the same mistake again.

There were several specific points of agreement that the woman asked to be written down as the official outcomes of the mediation. In this case, writing the points of agreement was requested because of the lack of trust she had in him. This decision seemed not to be increasing mistrust but establishing clear accountability. The agreement included the following. The man agreed to attend a two-day sexual harassment training. He also agreed to move his office, so they were farther apart at work. Any conversations that transpired between them needed to remain purely professional, no small talk or banter. She made it clear that any violation of these points would mean that she would file charges with the assistance of the hospital ombudsperson.

The mediation session lasted about 45 minutes. Both parties were given copies of the video. Sandy asked them to review the session over the next three days and to let her know if there were any concerns that would prohibit use of the tape from their point of view. If she did not hear from them, Sandy said she would assume they approved of the video.

Although I needed to review the tape myself, I felt good about the work I had done in the mediation, and I did not think my actions were adversely affected by the recording process. The case proved to be an excellent one for a sample mediation.

It was an emotional and intense workplace conflict that had clear legal implications. It was not too prolonged or overly complicated. Both parties had a sense coming into the mediation of what the issues and options were. Both parties thanked me at the end of the mediation and made positive comments on the feedback forms that Sandy gave them.

I decided to immediately drop the video off at Adam's office to see whether he thought the tape is a satisfactory example of our approach to practice. I was eager to hear whether he felt the "performances"—including my own—were good enough to be a useful pilot for the TV producer in Los Angeles.

CHAPTER TWENTY-ONE

The Audition

Adam looked at the videotaped mediation and called me right afterwards. He said, "Terrific job. It is a wonderful illustration of non-directive mediation, and it is an interesting case as well. The issues raised will make viewers think about what sexual harassment is and how it can develop between two people. A lot of subtle emotions were expressed, not the usual screaming matches that are on typical training role plays. You stayed with each of the parties and supported their voices but did not lead them. And you look great on the video, Kent."

Adam only had one suggestion. He said the video should have a catchy name. He suggested something like "Sexual Harassment: Through Her Eyes." Or "Sexual Harassment: Finding the Line." A snazzy title would create the impression that this is the first episode in a series of shows. I thanked him and told him that I would be setting up a time to meet with the TV producer, Sheldon Backland, within the next few days. I also told him that I would send the video and a copy of his book ahead of time to Backland so he has plenty of time to think about the ideas and the mediation practice before I arrive.

I called Backland's office and was able to arrange a meeting with the producer at two p.m. on Monday the twenty first of December. This was perfect timing because it would allow Gio and I to spend time around the holidays with Gio's sister Mia in Orange County. We hadn't been able to visit her and Gio's nieces and nephews in two years. I knew this visit would make Gio quite happy regardless of what happens with the television producer.

Gio was able to arrange time off from work, so we flew to southern California on Friday the eighteenth. Mia picked us up at LAX and drove us south to her home. She had recently moved from trendy West Hollywood to an over-55 gated community in Laguna Woods. The community is a small city with upwards of 18,000 seniors. It is a boomer's heaven (or hell, depending on your perspective) with several golf courses, pools, party houses, a theater and about 200 clubs to join, everything from horseback riding to a group that lobbies for the legalization of marijuana. On the first visit to Mia's place, she said to us: "This senior city keeps everybody busy, so they forget they are close to death."

Mia had been a stand-up comic and writer for shows in L.A. for years. So she was familiar with "the business," as she called it. She was excited about the prospects for a mediation TV show, especially after she saw the video of the sexual harassment case. She felt the dialogue between the two doctors was "riveting." She could see the connection to popular judge shows—the new spin on an existing genre. Her advice to me was to quickly get the copyright on not just the video, but the idea of the show overall. Otherwise, she warned, "It will be quickly stolen out from under you. That happens all the time out here. Despite the palm trees gently swaying in the wind everywhere, it's a dog-eat-dog world out here." I wished I had talked to her earlier because I did not pursue a copyright and Backland already had the video. I would have to trust the man but let him know that the copyright is pending. The whole thing is a gamble, I thought, so why worry about rights at this point?

Sunday evening Gio, Mia and I had a fun conversation over a homemade dinner Mia cooked of calamari and linguini. We talked about the "what-ifs" of a mediation show. If the production is done in L.A., how could I arrange to be involved? How much time would I have to spend on the west coast? Or could the show be taped in New York? Would I want a stage name? Gio jokingly suggested Clarke Kent. How would we get the ideas for cases? Would the parties be actors or "real people?" Might the parties be well known people—a mediating-with-the-stars twist? Did there need to be theme song for the show? Maybe I could get Sondheim to compose a tune. Would there be a narrator who would comment on the cases? We knew we were jumping the gun by talking about these speculative questions. Nonetheless, it was entertaining to think we were already signed on and to consider some of the decisions that would need to be made. As my mother used to say on family outings "getting there is half the fun." If the whole thing fell through, we still would have had the memorable fantasy.

I had little experience driving in L.A. traffic and don't like to drive much anywhere. But there were no inexpensive public transportation options. So I borrowed Mia's car and headed up "The 5" as they say in Southern California. The route to Backland's office was fairly easy but I was still apprehensive about possible delays, so I left a cushion of one hour just in case the traffic was worse than expected or I made a wrong turn. I figured it would give me time to feel the vibe of the city and think about what to say to Backland. I wanted my head to be clear. Along the drive I thought about how perfect the weather is almost every day here. So perfect that southern Californians come to believe that any fantasy is possible for them and that no one ever dies. Who could leave such perfect weather? I did notice, though, that even a slight increase in humidity sparks complaints from the locals. Weather is a source of irritation wherever one lives.

As I approached Backland's office building just off Santa Monica Blvd, I could not help but feel like the thousands of aspiring adventurers who come to L.A. each year hoping for a big break, a connection, or just a beginner's slot in the business. It is a place where every waiter looks like a leading man and most successful actors are hidden in the Malibu hills. These thoughts of dreamers and wild aspirations made me feel a little cheap and cheesy. But then I reminded myself that this effort was bigger than me. I was putting myself out there for a worthwhile cause that I firmly believed in, like making a pitch for money from corporate America for a worthwhile charity.

Backland's office building was a five-story mid-century modern structure covered in shiny blue glass with a shiny white marble entranceway. The receptionist at the door told me where I should park and gave me Backland's office number on the third floor. When I reached the third floor a friendly, well-dressed receptionist escorted me to Backland's office and offered me a seat. No one was there.

"He is in a meeting that is running a little late," she said. "Can I get you something to drink?"

"Some water would be great," I said. "No ice please." I was afraid that ice might upset my already turbulent stomach. She brought me vitamin mineral water. Very California I thought.

Backland's office had a definite Southern California feel to it, very bright and horizontal. His desk and credenza were light blond wood with sleek stainless-steel hardware. A small clear glass vase with six white tulips sat on one corner of the desk. I was seated on one of four white leather Ortrud lounge chairs placed in front of the desk. A glass top coffee table sat between the chairs. There were several large fern plants in front of the floor-to-ceiling windows and two modern floor lamps that looked as if they might be designed in Italy. There were several plush tan throw rugs on the light hardwood floor. Attractive casual chic. Nothing Wall Street about it.

What interested me the most was the wall of photos to the left of the desk. There were pictures of a man, who I assume was Backland, with a range of TV personalities including Phil Donahue, Arsenio Hall, Rosie O'Donnell, and Judge Kingly. Kingly is the judge with the TV divorce court show. There were six or seven other photos of Backland with people I did not recognize. Judging from the personality parade on his wall, he had a solid track record in the industry. I looked around for an Emmy statue but did not see one. Perhaps he kept it safe at home. No doubt, though, he was the real thing. Given his history of successful productions I wondered whether he would be hungry enough for a new and untested project. He must be close to the end of his career so why take new risks? Or was he the type who never quits because his work is his life?

The man I saw in the wall photos returned to his office after about 20 minutes. Backland was a tall slender man probably in his early sixties. His look was striking. His soft gray hair was pulled straight back in a short ponytail. His shirt was bright fuchsia with an Asian knot print on it. He had on light tan dress pants with a white woven rope belt and dark brown sandals. Seeing him in person confirmed instantly that I wasn't in Philadelphia anymore. I was also glad that Gio warned me not to wear a tie. That would have been way too East Coast preppy.

Backland greeted me cordially, "Hello Mr. Foxe. Welcome to L.A. May I call you Kent?"

"Sure. Is it best to call you Sheldon?" I asked.

"Most people call me Shelly. You certainly can use that name as well. I feel I know you somewhat having watched you on the mediation video you sent."

Backland talked slowly as if each sentence had a double meaning that I was supposed to catch. He kept fastidious eye contact. His bright green eyes made the contact somewhat unnerving. It was difficult to look away whether he or I was speaking. I soon felt that he was more intense than his casual clothing conveyed. There was somewhat of a mixed message to his persona. I wasn't uncomfortable but nor was I totally relaxed.

He took no time in getting down to business. "I have read most of the book and watched the video you so kindly sent me," he said. "Thank you for forwarding these artifacts ahead of time. It was helpful preparation for our meeting today. And I was attracted to the work."

"You are welcome and thank you for taking the time to review them," I said politely, hoping not to sound obsequious. I was somewhat taken aback by his use of the word artifacts to describe the book and video. Did he see the items as museum-worthy? Things dug out of an archeological site?

"I don't mean to get too personal, but I need to ask you something. Are you or Adam Maurie linked in any way to the Eastern philosophies or religions?" Backland asked.

"No, not in any personal sense. I've read some about Hinduism and Buddhism years ago in a world religions course I took. I have never heard Adam mention it either, certainly not with respect to mediation."

"Interesting. I did not see references in the book, but I was just wondering. I am a devotee of Eastern philosophy and some of its reflective practices such as meditation. I have been to Tibet, and I participate in the Shambhala community, mostly through attending their lengthy meditation retreats. I could not help but see natural links in your work to core beliefs of some of these traditions."

I waited a couple seconds to see if he was going to elaborate then I said, "There have been connections made by some people to other philosophical and spiritual traditions. But for sure the theory and practice, as described in Adam's book, is pure social science. Adam makes explicit ties to moral development theory. I am very interested in hearing more about the connections you have made to your beliefs."

I had a faint sense that Backland wanted to say more about what he saw in the tape and its underlying theory but was a little hesitant. I hoped that mentioning other traditions and social science was not heard as dismissive and did not discourage him from continuing to talk about what he saw in our work. His take was certainly interesting and might be controversial in some ways. He could see the intense interest on my face.

"Well, there are connections woven throughout these ideas and through the process you demonstrate so beautifully on the tape," he continued. "To start, the method supports people in their efforts to move from aggression to compassion. It seems to assume there is underlying goodness—expressed at times through compassion—in each person even though this goodness may be buried in anger, fear, frustration, closed-mindedness or other temporary debilitating states.

"Your method also assumes that it is healthy and productive to experience conflict with our full senses. Hearing someone's voice, sensing their intensity, seeing the subtlety of facial expressions all bring valuable insights about issues and differences. Our senses are powerful tools in life. They ultimately link our common humanity. When we are fully present in conflict, we pick up on subtle cues of worry and concern, uncertainty and tentativeness, lies and omissions, regrets and implied apologies. Personal communication prevents many of the misunderstandings and false assumptions that usually come with separation and distance. The senses are profoundly restorative, if only we relied on them more as a species.

"There are also links in your mediation work to assumptions about the value of living through chaos. Your methods do not stifle chaos by imposing structure and prohibitive rules. Chaos is a sign of change and flexibility. Your methods do not curtail the creative potential of turmoil that conflict creates. People can lose their fear of chaos and learn to see its value in your approach. This offers people a rare experience. And it shows courage on your part. Most people run from chaos before its benefits emerge."

"It actually is quite rare, especially in the way mediation is commonly practiced," I said. "As you probably saw in the video, we encourage mediators to be comfortable with conflict even when it escalates around them. Many mediators are trained to prohibit or squelch normal conflict behaviors such as the expression of deep emotions. This often stifles the parties' voices and undermines the possibility of understanding. I agree that you have to be able to be with the chaos that conflict creates."

"That is certain," Backland said. "In the video I have to say that I also saw incredible bravery. In the Shambhala tradition, bravery means doing the right thing with inner confidence. The woman in particular illustrated this virtue stunningly. She made a thoughtful, difficult decision to accept some degree of accountability and show some significant understanding. At the same time, she stood up for herself against bad behavior. She felt her decision was the right one and she had the confidence to act on it in the opportunity mediation gave her. This decision was ultimately built on a belief in her own, and the male doctor's human goodness. That is admirable, influential bravery."

As Backland spoke, I was prompted to think about conflicts I had seen in mediation and in my own life. In many of these conflicts human weakness prevailed. Inner confidence was missing for Bill and Rosa, James D'Antes, Daniel Simel, Celia Franks, Susskind and even Thomas Binder. When Backland paused, I asked him, "Do your principles acknowledge that some people are just weaker people, sometimes through no fault of their own? If so, how do stronger people deal with those who are weaker?"

"Great question," he said. "The stronger have to figure out how to be with the weaker. This means wrestling with difficult questions such as: What is the line between empathy and futility? How far do you go to help, to accommodate, to understand, or to accept behaviors that stem from weakness? When is it unfair to challenge weaker people to become stronger? An important assumption is that weakness is not often a permanent state. The weaker can become the stronger and the stronger the weaker. Realizing this is itself an act of compassion."

As he spoke, I could not help but think more about Bill and Rosa and the struggle Gio and I were going through in deciding how much involvement we should have in their lives. Backland's response to my question was gratifying and insightful. It made me less unsettled about the situation with them. Grappling with the right questions is itself a move toward greater strength even if nothing gets fully resolved. I had seen this in several of my mediations, but hearing Backland describe it made me appreciate its value much more.

I began to wonder how the topic of the TV pilot was going to come up in the heady discussion we were having about Eastern philosophy. I felt I should not be the one to bring it up. His comments so far were certainly encouraging. So much praise for what was put forth in both Adam's book and the mediation video he had reviewed. He obviously made powerful personal connections to the work.

"It is gratifying to see how you relate to this material," I said. "You bring a different sensibility but one that is true to the theoretical foundations and applied practices we advocate. Not many people would have your insightful perspective. If we raised these connections, we would be cast disparagingly in academia as 'new age charlatans.'" We need to allow others like yourself to draw the links that you are describing."

"You are right," he said. "There aren't many who can actually appreciate the unique value of what you are doing here. That is why it would be impossible to build a TV show based on this work. The genre of TV shows with third-party interveners like judges is built around charismatic and effusive gurus who purport to hold the wisdom that people need to fix their lives. The Dr. Phil and the Judge Judy types. Big, domineering personalities who dispense the answers to life's problems to people who are eager to thoughtlessly adopt them. Your work argues for the very opposite type of intervention. It assumes that when you give people the time and space to figure things out for themselves, they will do just that. They will draw on their own strength, goodness and humanity to find the way that will work best for them. They do enough to reaffirm a belief in the worthwhile, difficult struggles of humanity. But watching your video is akin to watching someone meditate—there are powerful changes and questioning going on inside people that are usually subtle and incremental. TV critics would say this is too "cool" a medium to be successful. The viewer would have to do too much work to engage meaningfully with this type of mediation show."

As Backland spoke, my heart sank. The quick drop left me speechless. I felt a sense of painful rejection. But simultaneously I knew Backland was right—totally right. I was like an actor who had been rejected for a part in a movie that he knew deep down was absolutely wrong for him. The lull in our conversation was filled by the compassion I could tell Backland had for me in the moment. I felt like I needed time right then to sort through my conflicting feelings. That was impossible in the middle of the conversation we were having. I had to say something no matter how emotionally garbled it might sound.

"What you say is true, but it is a sad commentary on viewers' lack of sophistication," I said hesitantly.

"It is not so much that there are no sophisticated audiences. There are. But just not for this genre of show. The sophisticated audiences are not tuning into Judge Judy. The genre dictates the audience. I was trying to think of a good comparison I could give you. Suppose someone told me that they had an idea for a new TV game show. Game shows are popular, and a new twist might be welcome. Then this person says the show would involve highly rated chess masters playing each other. Now, although chess is somewhat popular and it is certainly for a sophisticated audience, it would make for disastrous TV. Those who faithfully watch The Price is Right or Let's Make a Deal would never watch the chess show."

It was obvious Backland knew his business and he clearly understood why, from our perspective, the mediator could not be a charismatic expert and take center stage. That would defeat the whole point of a non-directive process. All the value he had astutely seen in our work would be lost if we or anyone did a mediation program of that sort. I felt disillusioned but strangely consoled by that knowledge. There was a sense of loss that Backland felt as much as I did. It was out of clarity and compassion that Backland told me about his personal interest in our work. In a way, his response was more supportive than I ever imagined. That alone was enough to make the cross-country trip to California worthwhile.

The rest of the conversation was mostly a blur. I asked him how he got interested in Eastern thought. He said that it was his personal search for meaning. He added that it was a way to turn from the terrible damage the media industry had done to society with depictions of violence and human insensitivity. I asked him about his meditative practices—how often he meditates, the length of the longest solitary retreat he'd been on, what meditating does for him. At points, I worried that he could see I was feigning interest. I did not want to be inattentive, but my mind kept wandering to the call I needed to make to Adam and what I would say to him.

When I got back to Mia's home in Laguna Hills, Gio and Mia were watching TV, drinking cinnamon eggnog, and nibbling on holiday cookies. I laughed to myself when I saw that they were halfway through the film *It's a Wonderful Life*. I could see how happy Gio was to be together with me and his closest family. I knew then that I would have a great visit, even though the warm California weather would defy the festive holiday spirit. I thought about the unique and beautiful house we had on the east coast, and I felt a little homesick for its northern European charm. It was designed as a house for snowy winter holidays.

I sat with them and watched the rest of the film. My mind kept drifting to thoughts of where I was headed in my own life. Was it as wonderful as it could be? How would I keep a satisfying balance and still create a worthwhile career? I did make one decision. I would let Gio know when we return to New Jersey that I will start ballroom dancing again, just for the pure enjoyment of it. Gio was right—I missed what moving to music does for my soul.

The next morning I called Adam and told him what happened with Backland. He was not surprised and said it was probably all for the best. He said if the show got started, we might lose artistic control and a Dr. Phil character could be cast as the mediator. If that happened, we would have created our own monster and defeated our purpose. I agreed. Adam loved hearing about the deep value Backland saw in the work. It was a thoughtful confirmation of what we were trying to create. I lamented that an opportunity to clear up what mediation is in the public's mind had evaporated. My vow was not going to be realized—at least not for now.

Adam and I wished each other a safe and memorable holiday season and said warm good-byes.

The next day Adam sent me a short email:

Thanks for the update on your meeting with Backland.

How's this for a Sondheim-esque lyric, capturing us at the moment?

Revel in the guru's reaffirming rejection,
Celebrate what he insightfully reveals.

269

Above all, avoid the tempting dejection,
Ahead are more promising deals.

Without hesitation, I wrote back:

Perfect. All we need now is the catchy Broadway melody.

ACKNOWLEDGEMENTS

My sincere thanks to Asata Radcliffe for her insightful editorial comments and suggestions. I am also deeply grateful to the friends, family, and colleagues who read drafts of chapters along the way and provided helpful feedback, including Baruch Bush, Kathleen Kemps, Don Simione, Dan Simon, Winnie Backlund, Larry Krafft, Meghan Taylor, Christian Hartwig, Thomas Hartwig, Gustavo Farina, Celia Abrams, Deborah Dennis, Randall Stutman and Jay Herman. Special thanks to Joe Smargisso for shaping the title and visualizing the book's themes. Thank you also to the many mediation colleagues I've worked with over the years who have helped build a valuable approach to mediation practice. Finally, this novel would not have been written if it were not for eight unexpected months of quarantine.

About Atmosphere Press

Atmosphere Press is an independent, full-service publisher for excellent books in all genres and for all audiences. Learn more about what we do at atmospherepress.com.

We encourage you to check out some of Atmosphere's latest releases, which are available at Amazon.com and via order from your local bookstore:

Out and Back: Essays on a Family in Motion, by Elizabeth Templeman

Just Be Honest, by Cindy Yates

You Crazy Vegan: Coming Out as a Vegan Intuitive, by Jessica Ang

Detour: Lose Your Way, Find Your Path, by S. Mariah Rose

To B&B or Not to B&B: Deromanticizing the Dream, by Sue Marko

Convergence: The Interconnection of Extraordinary Experiences, by Barbara Mango and Lynn Miller

Sacred Fool, by Nathan Dean Talamantez

My Place in the Spiral, by Rebecca Beardsall

My Eight Dads, by Mark Kirby

Dinner's Ready! Recipes for Working Moms, by Rebecca Cailor

Vespers' Lament: Essays Culture Critique, Future Suffering, and Christian Salvation, by Brian Howard Luce

Without Her: Memoir of a Family, by Patsy Creedy

Relief leaving
train station
Pg 100.
We are comfortable
with what we know.
- Differences with goal/expectation/outcome
value

Three day traing pg 140
more directive than
I think it could be
self reflective

Pg 190
- who you want to
be from here

Don't like he
talks to husband
Our Judgements Pg 239

ABOUT THE AUTHOR

Joseph P. Folger is Professor Emeritus at Temple University in Philadelphia, PA, where he taught courses in mediation and conflict management for thirty years. He is co-author (with Baruch Bush) of the award-winning volume **The Promise of Mediation** and is co-founder of the **Institute for the Study of Conflict Transformation** (www.transformativemediation.org). He also worked extensively as an executive coach and organizational consultant.

Manufactured by Amazon.ca
Bolton, ON

21579908R00164